Praise for the Novels of Kate White

Such a Perfect Wife

"What's not to love in Kate White's latest? . . . *Such a Perfect Wife* is deep and dark and twisty, and packed with a delicious array of questionable characters, each harboring their own secrets." —*Entertainment Weekly*

"Intricately plotted. . . . [An] intense page-turner that never lets up."

—*Library Journal*, starred review and "Pick of the Month"

"Intrepid—and stylish!—crime reporter Bailey Weggins finds herself on the front line of a murder investigation. . . . Fun and fast-paced. . . . Bailey is fearless, determined, and always fashionable. A grown-up Nancy Drew for grown-up girl detectives." —*Kirkus Reviews*

"Highly entertaining. . . . The ethical and tenacious Bailey soon earns the respect of the local police, who come to see her as an ally rather than an intruder. Readers will cheer her every step of the way." —*Publishers Weekly*

"An always-entertaining series." —*Booklist*

Even If It Kills Her

"A titillating novel of secrecy and suspense, *Even If It Kills Her* will have you hanging on every word." —*Bustle.com*

"A twisty mystery full of clues and red herrings that are hard to distinguish between. This makes for a very thrilling read.

The end is a surprise, and most readers will gasp at the unveiling of the real killer." —Bookreporter.com

"White builds suspense masterfully, and this seventh in the Bailey Weggins series has the makings of another hit. Bailey is a smart, sexy sleuth, and her exploits make for thoroughly entertaining reading." —*Booklist*

The Secrets You Keep

" A psychological thriller that doubles as a cautionary tale, *The Secrets You Keep* marks another success for a prolific author and casts an intelligent if grim eye on love—love that can warm, and love that can burn."

—*Richmond Times-Dispatch*

"True to form, Kate White's *The Secrets You Keep* kept me up way past my bedtime, anxiously turning the pages. Taut, tense, and utterly gripping, I could not go to sleep until I found out whodunit."

—Jessica Knoll, *New York Times* bestselling author of *Luckiest Girl Alive*

"Suspenseful, twisty, and sharply observed, Kate White's clever psychological thriller lures us into the life of vulnerable narrator Bryn whose marriage is not what she thought it was. The uncertainty develops as the stakes ramp up ever higher, and I was holding my breath as I turned the last few pages."

—Gilly Macmillan, *New York Times* bestselling author of *What She Knew*

The Wrong Man

"A juicy beach book: a thriller with a smart female main character." —*People*

"This is a must-have summer read and an enjoyable whodunit." —*Seattle Post-Intelligencer*

"Breezy. . . . An intriguing heroine who holds her own."
                                        —*Kirkus Reviews*

Eyes on You

"[A] delicious tale." —*New York Post*

"A smart, sexy sleuth with a growing fan base." —*Booklist*

"Sharp as a stiletto! White captures the cut-throat world of entertainment TV where the latest star should trust no one if she's to build her show . . . or save her very life."
        —Lisa Gardner, *New York Times* bestselling author

The Sixes

"You won't be able to put it down; just remember to reapply your sunscreen every so often."
                        —*Harper's Bazaar*, Labor Day
                                Weekend "Must Reads"

"This is the perfect book to take on a transatlantic flight to Europe. Trust me, I just did it. . . . A fast-paced plot that wraps itself up in time for you to race to the bathroom before the plane starts its descent." —*Vanity Fair*

"A coed's gone missing at leafy Lyle College, and visiting prof Phoebe Hall is asking too many questions. A nifty spine-tingler."   —*People*

"A terrifying psychological thriller that takes 'mean girls' to a whole *new* level of creepy."

—Harlan Coben, #1 *New York Times* bestselling author of *Live Wire*

Hush

"A real page-turner."   —*Today* show

"A sharp-edged thriller. . . . Sexy suspense."

—*New York Daily News*

"Kate White places her wily heroine in a real jam, then keeps her, as well as readers, asking 'Whodunit?' right up till the gripping finale."

—Sandra Brown, author of *Rainwater*

HAVE YOU **SEEN** ME?

ALSO BY KATE WHITE

Fiction

If Looks Could Kill

A Body to Die For

Till Death Do Us Part

Over Her Dead Body

Lethally Blond

Hush

The Sixes

Eyes on You

The Wrong Man

So Pretty It Hurts

The Secrets You Keep

Even If It Kills Her

Such a Perfect Wife

Nonfiction

Why Good Girls Don't Get Ahead but Gutsy Girls Do

I Shouldn't Be Telling You This: How to Ask for the Money, Snag the Promotion, and Create the Career You Deserve

The Gutsy Girl Handbook: Your Manifesto for Success

HAVE YOU SEEN ME?

A NOVEL OF SUSPENSE

KATE WHITE

HARPER

An Imprint of HarperCollins*Publishers*

HAVE YOU SEEN ME? Copyright © 2020 by Kate White. All rights reserved. Printed in the United States of America. No part of this book may be used or reproduced in any manner whatsoever without written permission except in the case of brief quotations embodied in critical articles and reviews. For information, address HarperCollins Publishers, 195 Broadway, New York, NY 10007.

HarperCollins books may be purchased for educational, business, or sales promotional use. For information, please email the Special Markets Department at SPsales@harpercollins.com.

FIRST EDITION

Designed by Jamie Kerner

Library of Congress Cataloging-in-Publication Data has been applied for.

ISBN 978-0-06-274747-1 (pbk.)
ISBN 978-0-06-297208-8 (Library edition)

20 21 22 23 24 LSC 10 9 8 7 6 5 4 3 2 1

HAVE YOU SEEN ME?

1

As soon as I step off the elevator, something seems weird to me, off-kilter or unaligned—like a friend forcing a smile when she's secretly livid with you.

Staring through the large glass doors at the end of the corridor, I realize that it's dark inside the office and that no one else is here yet. That must be what's throwing me off.

I pull my wrist through the sleeve of my trench coat and check my watch. It's 8:05. For the first time since I've been at the company, I've beaten everyone in.

My gaze runs up my sleeve, and I suddenly notice how wet I am. What had felt like a drizzle outside was clearly heavier rain than that, and my coat's soaked. Shoes, too. When I touch my head, I feel my hair plastered to my scalp.

And then, to make everything worse, I fumble in my pocket for my key card and discover it's not there. *Shit.* I've either lost it or left it at home. My assistant has never been a morning person—there's no chance of her showing up before nine. And the earliest the office manager, Caryn, will surface is probably eight thirty. I've got almost thirty minutes to kill.

I knead my forehead with my fingers, trying to decide what to do. I could trudge over to a café at Twenty-Second and Broadway. But I hate the thought of sitting there in my wet shoes, feeling the squishy leather pluck at my feet. And the trips there and back will do nothing for my appearance, which I'm sure is disheveled enough as it is.

Then, miraculously, I hear the elevator door slide open, and as I pivot, a young Asian guy in a black hooded sweatshirt steps off, carrying his phone in one hand and shaking out a collapsible umbrella with the other. It takes a second before he looks up from his screen and registers my presence. He must be brand-new at Greenbacks, because I've never seen him before.

"Is everything okay?" he asks. He's looking at me as if my mouth's started to foam. Hasn't he ever seen anyone undone by the weather before?

"I've been away and I must have left my key at home today," I say. "Would you mind letting me in?"

"Um, sure. You are . . . ?"

Does he really not know? "Ally. Ally Linden."

"Right," he says, nodding. But it clearly doesn't ring a bell. He's definitely new, probably on the tech side, a team I don't interact with all that often.

He snaps his key card from his wallet, swipes it over the black box, and swings open the door as soon as we hear the click. He motions for me to go first, and without having to look, he thrusts his arm to the right and taps a switch. The front section of the office floods with light, unveiling row after row of empty workstations.

"You all set?" he asks, turning back to me.

"Yes, thanks. You're . . . ?"

"Nick. Nick Fukuyama."

"Great. Thanks for your help."

He's halfway across the floor, tapping more light switches with a flick of his wrist, when I discover I'm also missing the key to my office, one of the few private ones. I moan in frustration. It's my first day back and I'm going to have a ton to do. I'll have to wait for Caryn to unlock my door with her master key once she arrives.

I traipse across the lobby area to the glass-walled conference room and nudge the door open with my hip. After shrugging out of my coat, I drape it on the back of a chair by the wall to dry. I take a seat at the table and kick off my soggy shoes. There's a pen holder on the table, stuffed tight with Dixon No. 2s—Damien Howe's favorite brand of pencil—and a stack of pads as well, bearing the Greenbacks logo. I can at least make notes, I decide. A plan for the day, for the week ahead.

It's hard to focus, though. I feel at loose ends, as if I haven't acclimated yet from my trip. Through the window, I can see that the rain's coming down really hard now, driven sideways by the wind so that it lashes the glass, with a sound at times like a train rumbling along the tracks. I notice that my throat feels slightly sore, and there's a faint, throbbing pain in my temples.

I ignore both and force my attention to the pad. I scribble the words "To Do" across the top of the page. And then a row of question marks. I sense an answer hovering, but the words refuse to form.

The muffled ding of the elevator bell pulls me from my

thoughts. *Please, let this be Caryn,* I pray, but when I look up, I see a woman, wearing a black baseball hat letting herself into the office. I can't make out her face, but I can tell from the height and the shape that it's not Caryn. I glance again at my watch. Eight twenty-two. Surely, it won't be much longer.

I try to refocus on my notes, but seconds later, another noise from the front teases away my attention. I raise my head and spot a shock of blond hair, the sight of which jolts me.

God, that hair. Thick, a little shaggy on the sides, and honey-gold in color. So wildly improbable here in gritty, grungy, hipster-bearded, black-is-the-new-black New York City. Once, riding the train with him to a meeting uptown, I watched as two women jerked their heads in his direction, their eyes widening, as if they'd suddenly found themselves in a subway car with a merman.

Damien Howe is on his phone, talking, nodding in agreement. Striking a deal, maybe. He seems oblivious to everything else, but it's probably not the case. As long as I've known him, he's always been intensely aware of his environment.

He halts at the wide counter to the right of the entrance, opposite the Pullman-style kitchen, and grabs a coffee capsule. Probably dark roast. He likes his coffee strong and never takes milk or sugar. It's surprising he doesn't keep an espresso machine in his office, because that's what he *really* prefers, especially the moment he rolls out of bed.

I watch as he waits the few seconds for the coffee to brew, seemingly lost in thought now that the call's finished. I've been so good since we split about *not* looking at him, stopping myself from searching, sonarlike, for his presence, refusing to think of the body beneath those clothes, the sea-salt smell of his skin that used to make me wonder if he *was* a merman.

Five months. That's all it lasted. We were ridiculously careful, betraying not even a hint of flirtation at work. But our coworkers had started to put two and two together. I sensed it before Damien did, conscious of their eyes swinging in slo-mo between us in meetings. Someone, somehow, detected a tell in Damien's interactions with me that gave us away, like Jason Bourne catching the reflection of an asset in the blade of a butter knife.

Aware that the truth was seeping out, we agreed to cool things between us for the time being, and I put on as good a face as I could. It never restarted. And for weeks, months really, it hurt like hell.

His coffee's done brewing. He secures a lid on the cup, adjusts the messenger bag that's strapped over his torso, and turns, clearly bound for his office. I lower my gaze, back to the notepad, but I sense his attention land on me. And soon, out of the corner of my eye, I see him striding in my direction. Oh, lovely. He's about to be treated to my best impression of a sewer rat.

There's a whoosh as the door opens, and instinctively I stuff both feet back into my shoes and sit up a bit straighter.

"Ally?" he says.

I glance up, feigning nonchalance. "Morning, Damien."

He looks serious, possibly even annoyed with me. Has a project of mine blown up while I was gone?

"What are you doing here?" he demands.

"I'm sorry. Do you need the room?" That possibility had just occurred to me.

"No, I'm asking why you're *here*. At Greenbacks."

"Today, you mean?" The pulsing in my head intensifies. "It's my first day back."

"What are you talking about?" He steps closer, his eyes burrowing into me. "You haven't worked here in years."

My head's practically pounding now.

"Damien," I say. "I-I-I *work* here. I—"

But even as the words sputter from my lips, I realize they're not true. I don't work here. I don't come to this place anymore. I press a hand to my head, urging alternate images to form in my mind, but I can't seem to remember where I *do* work.

My eyes fill with tears. *Don't cry*, I think. But a drop plops on the sleek black table.

"Ally, what's going on?" Damien asks, his voice softening. "Tell me."

"I don't know."

"Did you come here to see me?"

I shake my head. The answer's hopelessly out of reach. I start trembling, shaking, really. When I glance back at Damien, his expression reads as more concerned than cross.

"Let's go into my office, okay?" he says.

He leads me from the room, abandoning his coffee cup so he can both grasp my arm and open the door. The work area is still mostly empty, with just one woman settled in a cube outside Damien's office door, possibly the person I saw in the baseball hat. She raises her eyes from beneath a fringe of black hair, curiosity piqued.

He guides me to a chair inside his office and then shoves the door closed. Instead of sitting at his desk, he drags the other visitor chair over next to me.

"Okay, talk to me," he says, taking a seat. His voice, so cool before, is almost tender now. "You must have come here for a reason. To speak to someone?"

I search the room with my eyes, hoping a clue will miraculously leap into view, but there's nothing.

"I'm sorry," I say with a shake of my head, "but I'm not sure how I ended up here. I can't remember."

"It's okay, don't worry. We can call someone to help you. Where's your phone?"

"Um, in my purse." He lowers his gaze to my lap and sees I'm not in possession of one.

"It's probably in the conference room. Stay here, and I'll get it."

When he's gone, I think as hard as I can, squeezing my head in my hands as if it were dough, but I still can't picture where I work. Or what I do. Or where I should be at this moment.

It's only a few seconds before Damien comes hurrying back. I see the woman with the black hair raise her eyes again, managing to monitor his actions without moving her head even an inch.

"It's not in there," Damien says, shutting the office door behind him. He remains standing this time. "Could you have left it someplace?"

"I—I don't know." My anxiety spikes. If I don't have my purse, I don't have my phone. Or my wallet, either.

"Where did you come from just now? From home?"

I stare up at him, not comprehending at first, my heart beginning to hammer.

And then it hits me that I have no sense of that, either—where I was before I arrived or where my home is. There's a thick, dark curtain between this moment and everything that came before it.

Damien says something else, but I can barely hear him. The outer rings of my vision shrink so that he now looks tiny, like he's at the end of a peephole. A wave of nausea swells inside me.

I sense myself start to slump in the chair and before I can straighten up, I keel over onto the floor.

A loud hum fills my head, and I hear beeping, too.

Then a woman's voice, talking into a phone or radio. "The patient is currently conscious, but not alert," she says. "Twelve-lead ECG is unremarkable." There are other snippets: "BP:120/80 . . . pulse 100. Blood sugar is 120. . . . No HX or seizures, unknown medications."

I force my eyes open to see that I'm in an ambulance on a gurney with my coat and shirt open and little white discs stuck to my chest. I don't hear a siren, but the lights must be flashing, because I can see their red reflection dancing on the inside walls of the vehicle.

It comes back in a rush. Damien's office. Not remembering. The dizziness. Blacking out.

Panic bubbles up inside me and then geysers, shooting to the very end of my fingers and toes. I twist my head to the left as far as I'm able to. A dark-haired woman sits next to me on a jump seat, dressed in black pants and a white shirt. Her eyes flick between several monitors on the inside wall of the ambulance.

She catches me looking at her and smiles.

"How you feeling, hon? Any better?"

"A little," I tell her, but really, I don't have a clue, not having a baseline to judge it against. "Can you tell me what happened to me?"

"You passed out, and your colleague was having trouble fully reviving you. I did a quick test for hypoglycemia and it came up negative. Do you have any history of that?"

I have a vague memory of my finger being pricked with a needle, back in Damien's office. I was on the floor, my arms and legs too limp to move.

"Um, not that I'm aware of."

"Any history of fainting?"

"No. I mean, I don't think so."

"It's possible you're just dehydrated. Your vitals are normal, at least."

I lift my arm and notice that there's an IV needle inserted into my vein.

"It's just saline, to get you hydrated," she says. "Be careful not to dislodge it."

"Okay," I say, grateful to have someone telling me what to do.

"The person who was with you said you were having trouble with your recall this morning. Can you tell me your name?"

"Ally. Ally Linden."

"And how old are you, Ally?"

"Thirty-four." I feel a flood of relief that the number spilled from my lips without me even having to think about it.

"Good. Can you tell me where you live—the actual address?"

"I—" This time I fail miserably. I have no idea what my address is. I rake through my mind, desperate for images—of me turning a key, entering an apartment. Nothing.

"That's okay, just try to stay calm for now," the paramedic says, her voice gentle.

"Why can't I remember?" I plead. "Is something wrong with my head?"

"Don't worry, we'll get you to the hospital and they'll figure it all out. And the colleague who helped you said his office would let the hospital know how to reach your husband."

The bag of saline jostles as we hit a pothole and I realize I'm shaking, softly at first and then so hard my legs are bouncing.

I don't remember being married. And I don't have a single clue as to who my husband might be.

4

If I think too hard about where I am right now, I almost lose it. I have to fight the urge to jump off the bed and take off like a bat out of hell.

I'm in the ER, but not the regular part, where you go for a kidney stone or broken collarbone. I'm in a private room in this section completely removed from the fray. It's the *psych* unit. The place for patients who are manic or paranoid or hallucinating out of their minds or dangerous to themselves or others. God, how have I ended up here?

This isn't where I started the process, though. As soon as the ambulance arrived at the hospital, I was wheeled into the main emergency room. They drew blood and had me give a urine sample, clearly checking for drugs. They also examined my vision, reflexes, and coordination to rule out the possibility of a concussion.

Please let it be as simple as that, I'd prayed. Though there was no obvious bruising, I did have a throbbing headache. As I lay on a bed in a curtained-off area, I tried to summon a muscle memory of my skull smacking against a pointy edge of a cabinet or coffee table. But a coffee table *where*? I still couldn't recall a thing about my current life beyond my name and age.

In the end there was nothing to suggest a concussion.

Over time, nurses and physician's assistants came and went, whisking the faded curtain back and forth with a snap, and I waited, enveloped by sounds of beeping and pinging and gurneys rolling by, my panic ballooning with each passing minute.

"The paramedic said that the hospital was trying to reach someone on my behalf," I told a nurse at one point. It was too distressing to even say the word *husband* out loud. "Do you know if they did?"

"Let me check," she replied, but I never saw her again.

And then after three endless hours, I was told I was being moved for a psychiatric evaluation. *Stay totally calm*, I warned myself. *Do not appear frantic or unhinged.* I was sure if I did, it would become like one of those movie scenes in which someone starts screaming over and over that she's *not* insane, which only guarantees that everyone believes she is.

I wondered if the psych section would be on a secret floor or hard to access, but the orderly simply wheeled me through a set of automatic doors at the far end of the regular ER, and there I was, like in one of those dreams in which you discover a series of unknown rooms in the house you've lived in for years.

I'm alone for now, in a private room, dressed in the paper scrubs they gave me. If I didn't know better—and couldn't glimpse the two uniformed guards out in the center area— I'd think I was in the *VIP* wing of the hospital—freshly painted, uncluttered, and very quiet, since there aren't any beeping machines or monitors here.

There must be plenty of days, though, when it *isn't* hush-hush, when patients are shouting, demanding to be let out.

Just thinking about it makes my breathing shallow. I inhale for four seconds, hold it for four, exhale for four and then do it all over again. Somehow the person I am knows how to take deep relaxing breaths, but doesn't have a clue who she is.

I'm exhaling again when a woman enters, smiling kindly and carrying a clipboard. She's fiftysomething, I guess, with a youngish vibe. Her shoulder-length gray hair is flipped a little on the ends, and she's wearing knee-high brown suede boots beneath her wrap dress.

"Ally, good morning," she says. "I'm Evelyn Capron, one of the clinicians here. How are you feeling now?"

The answer: Scared shitless. Worried sick. Frantic about being married to someone I can't even picture.

"Concerned, of course," I say, as evenly as I can master. "I'm not sure why I've lost my memory."

Evelyn nods, her expression sympathetic. "Dr. Agarwal is going to be in to speak to you very shortly. In the meantime, I need to ask a few questions, just as background."

"Okay." But how can I possibly answer? For me, there *is* no background. Only today.

"Ally, are you feeling any inclination to harm yourself?"

Her question jolts me. I know it must be a routine question in the psych ward, but I can't possibly fit the profile of a suicidal patient. Can I?

"No."

"Do you feel any desire to harm someone else?"

This question seems even more far-fetched than the first. I'm not even aware of who the people in my life *are*, let alone who I'd want to harm.

"No, no one."

She has me fill out admission papers and then says she's going to give me two printed screening tests. They're attached to the clipboard, which she hands me. I rest it on my lap, on top of the bedsheet, and scan through questions and multiple-choice answers like, "I was very worried or scared about a lot of things in my life . . . never; a few times; sometimes; often; constantly."

"But how do I answer these?"

"What do you mean, Ally?"

"I only know what my life is like this morning. I don't know anything from before now."

"Of course, then, just with regard to this morning."

I lower my gaze to the paper and for a moment my attention drifts to the sheet covering my legs. An image blooms in my mind. I'm sitting on a big white sofa with a laptop resting on my thighs. It's a sofa in my apartment, I feel sure.

"I'm a writer," I announce to Evelyn, my eyes pricking with tears. "I work out of my apartment sometimes."

"That's good, Ally," she says.

A split second later, another image trips over the first. I'm standing at a window on a high floor, coffee mug in hand, staring at Manhattan stretched out before me. It's a stunning view, lots of sky and silvery buildings, and I'm smiling. I turn to say something to someone sitting behind me. A man.

"I live by Lincoln Center," I blurt out this time. "In—in the West Sixties."

"Very good. Anything else?"

My brain is trying to claw its way out from a landslide.

"No, nothing else," I say, feeling desperate again.

"Try to relax. Let things come on their own."

And then, as if by magic, more images appear, slowly at first and then in rapid succession, flooding my mind. With my words tumbling over one another, I share each new detail with Evelyn. She scribbles them down quickly—is she fearful they might vanish again? Soon, it's no longer a collection of fragments but something that seems whole, like a tapestry. *Me.*

I'm a personal finance journalist, I tell her. I write a monthly column, give talks, host a weekly podcast. I'm working on a book called . . . it's tentatively called *25 Money Rules You Should Always Ignore.* I spend part of the week in a communal work space, though I used to hold a key position at Greenbacks, the company I showed up at this morning. I grew up in Millerstown, New Jersey. My mother's dead but my father, a retired pediatrician, is still alive. I have two half brothers, Quinn and Roger.

And I'm married to *Hugh.* Hugh Buckley. Loving husband, lawyer, runner, Civil War history buff, Monopoly champion, Boston born and raised, and Ivy League graduate—though there's nothing entitled-seeming about him. Our wedding was three years ago, and we spent our honeymoon in the Seychelles.

My god, Hugh. Where *is* he?

"Do you know if they've made contact with my husband yet?" I say to Evelyn.

"I know they've been trying, but let me check again now."

As soon as she departs, the tears that have been welling in my eyes spill over, wetting the paper scrubs. I have my life back.

Evelyn returns five minutes later. "We've reached your husband's office," she reports, "but he's been out on business most of the morning, and they haven't been able to get through to him yet."

I squint, trying to remember what Hugh said about what he had planned for today. But I'm drawing a blank. In fact, I still don't remember anything about the hours before showing up at Greenbacks—getting dressed, or saying good-bye to Hugh, or traveling downtown. And I still don't have any clue why I went there.

What I need to do, I suddenly realize, is to split and sort this out with my own doctor and therapist, people I'm familiar with. Maybe I should even have further tests.

"Since you can't reach my husband, it seems like the best idea is for me to head home on my own now," I volunteer. "I don't have keys, but our concierge can let me into the apartment."

Evelyn's eyes widen slightly.

"I know you're eager to be home, Ally, but it's essential for you to have someone accompany you. And it's also important that you be examined by Dr. Agarwal. Let me see how long it will be before he can speak to you."

So that's the bottom line: there's no way they're giving me back my clothes and letting me out of here unless I'm accompanied.

"Okay," I say pleasantly, realizing it's in my best interest to act compliant.

Evelyn smiles and promises to be back soon, but it's Dr. Agarwal who shows up instead. He's carrying a clipboard of his own, thick with pages. He's in his mid- to late forties and has wavy black hair and deep brown eyes.

"Ben Agarwal," he says, shaking my hand. "So sorry for the delay, Ms. Linden. I'm sure this has been a harrowing day for you."

"Ally, please. And yes, it *was* scary earlier, but fortunately I'm much better now."

"Has anything like this ever happened to you before?"

"No, never. Not even close."

"Ms. Capron said that things have been coming back to you. What have you begun to remember?"

"Pretty much everything."

"I'm glad to hear that. Can you tell me your mother's maiden name?"

"Hemmings."

"And can you tell me what year it is and who the US president is?"

I rattle off the answers and throw in a few extra newsy facts as backup.

He smiles and thumbs through a couple of pages on the clipboard.

"You said pretty much everything came back. What's still missing?"

"Just what happened very early this morning, really. I don't recall getting up or leaving my apartment—or why I ended up at an office I haven't worked at in five years."

"Where would you ordinarily go first thing in the morning?"

"Generally to WorkSpace on West Fifty-Fifth Street. It's a coworking setup where I have a small office. But lately I've been working at home a lot. I'm under deadline for a book I'm writing, and it's quieter there."

"What about last night? What do you recall about the evening?"

I look off, trying to summon the details.

"That part's a little fuzzy actually," I admit. "I know my husband and I had dinner at home. I'm sure he'll be able to fill in the gaps when he arrives—though they seem to be having trouble finding him."

"I have good news on that front. His office was able to reach him at his appointment a few minutes ago, and he's headed here now from Connecticut."

My sense of relief is diluted by frustration. Hugh must be at least an hour away, and so it's up to me to take as much control of the situation as possible.

"I know I don't have any obvious signs of a head injury," I say. "But it seems that something along those lines must have happened to me. It was raining this morning—maybe I slipped and fell on the street."

Agarwal purses his lips briefly, and I can tell he's not buying it.

"A severe concussion can cause amnesia, but it usually involves forgetting events just prior to the injury—anywhere from a few minutes beforehand to a few days. In your case, you were missing big chunks of your identity. It seems what you actually experienced was what we call a dissociative state."

"Dissociative?" I say, feeling myself frown in confusion. "What does that mean exactly?"

"In layman's terms, it's an involuntary escape from reality. It's generally characterized by a disconnection between thoughts, identity, and memory—meaning you have difficulty recalling important information about who you are and events in your life."

He's reeled this off calmly enough, like he's telling me I've slipped a disc or popped a blood vessel, but his words make my breath catch. How could something like this have happened to *me*?

"But that makes no sense," I tell him. "I've never felt disconnected from my thoughts in any way." Before I can chicken out, I ask him the terrifying question that's been at the front of my mind. "Could—could it happen again?"

"Unfortunately, yes. A person can experience multiple episodes throughout his or her life. That's why it's key to determine the trigger."

"Can something *physical* trigger it?" *Please*, I think, *don't let me have a brain tumor.*

"Generally, not. The symptoms usually first develop as a response to trauma. It might be physical abuse or sexual abuse, or in certain cases, a military combat injury. It's the brain's way of keeping painful memories under control."

My heart skips. I've never been abused or been to war, thankfully, so does that mean something traumatic has happened to me recently? Today, even?

"There's nothing like that in my life. What—what if I were mugged on my way to work this morning?" I say, as the thought suddenly pops into my mind. "And—that would explain my purse being missing."

"Do you think having your purse snatched would have been highly traumatic for you?"

"Well," I respond, managing a smile. "I'm constantly advising people to be smart with their money and not let go of it stupidly—so that probably *would* have upset me."

This provokes a chuckle, but his expression quickly turns serious again.

"Tell me again about last night," he says. "Even if it's a little fuzzy."

"Uh, like I said, we ate at home. We'd ordered in. And we watched something on TV. A pretty typical weeknight evening these days."

"What about earlier in the day? Do you recall anything upsetting or stressful? Something related to your job—or personal life?"

"I've been a little stressed about finishing the book I mentioned, but not anything I haven't experienced before."

Agarwal says nothing in response but instead studies me quietly, his kind eyes glistening. I can tell he's waiting for me to elaborate. And then I realize he's probably wondering if the trauma has to do with my husband, that he might be physically or emotionally abusive. But Hugh's a great guy—and he's never been abusive in any way.

"There *is* one thing that's been on my mind," I say. There's no harm in mentioning it, I decide. "When my husband and I got engaged, we were on the same page about wanting kids one day, but lately I've . . . I've had second thoughts. I'm not totally sure anymore, and it's been, well . . . it's been a source of a little friction. But we're hardly at any kind of crisis point."

And we're *not*.

"Where do things stand at the moment?" Agarwal asks.

"We agreed a few weeks ago to table the discussion for a while. With the pressure off, I feel it'll be easier for me to make a rational decision. And I've started seeing a therapist, someone to talk it over with.

"So it's stressful but hardly traumatic," I add, shrugging. "It hardly seems like something that could make me disconnect from my identity."

Agarwal nods, as if weighing my comment.

"The traumatic event doesn't have to have happened recently," he says. "It could be an episode from your past that's rising to the surface again for some reason."

I look off again, thinking. Suddenly my lips part as my brain pries something away, like I'm opening an orange or tangerine and the thin white membrane is tearing apart. No, this can't really be what it's all about, can it?

I glance back at Agarwal, and the alertness in his eyes intensifies. He knows he's touched a nerve.

"Is there something that's been troubling you lately, Ally?" he continues. "Something from your past?"

"Nothing I can think of," I lie. "At least not off the top of my head."

5

Agarwal's expression gives nothing away this time, but I can sense anticipation morphing quickly into resignation below the surface. Though he seems caring and competent, this isn't something I intend to discuss with him.

He studies me for another minute before speaking. "The therapist you're seeing. How many sessions have you had so far?"

"Uh, I've seen her five or six times."

"Do you know if your therapist does cognitive behavioral therapy? That's what is most often recommended in these cases."

"Um, yes, I remember seeing that in her bio."

"If I have your permission, I'd like to speak with her in the next day or so and review what's happened."

"Sure." That seemed to make sense. "Her name is Elaine Erling. I don't have her number with me, obviously, but my husband can provide it or you can find it online. She's got an office in the city and also one in Westchester County—in Larchmont."

"When is your next appointment?"

"Wednesday. But I'll try to get in to see her before then. Tomorrow if possible."

Hopefully Erling can squeeze me in, and with luck she'll be working out of her Manhattan office. I've been to the Larchmont office just once—when I had a scheduling conflict—and a trip there is not something I could pull off under these circumstances.

"Yes, it's important to see her as soon as possible. Now, why don't you try to rest a little before your husband arrives."

After he departs, I realize how bone-achingly tired I am, something I've been too wired and vigilant to notice until now. I finally allow myself to sink fully into the bed. Hugh is coming and he'll take me home. I don't have to fret anymore. Within seconds I'm drifting off to sleep.

When my eyes finally flutter open, I discover Evelyn standing along the side of my bed. Her fingers rest on my arm and she's gently stirring me awake.

"Look who I've brought," she says.

Hugh steps from behind her, his face pinched with worry.

"Hey, sweetheart," he says.

I project myself forward and we embrace, hugging tightly. His silky tie, the soft, rich cotton of his shirt, the feel of his fingers softly raking my hair—it all seems so *real*. My body pulses with relief. This whole horrible day—maybe it's nothing more than a momentary blip in my life.

"I'm so glad you're finally here," I tell him.

"I'm sorry it took forever. Traffic from Connecticut was a mess, and there was one annoying delay after another."

I glance at Evelyn. "I hope this means I can be released now."

"Why don't we have Dr. Agarwal weigh in on the timing?" she says. "He'll be back shortly, I'm sure."

"Oh god, Hugh. I'm so embarrassed about this," I say as soon as she steps out of the room.

"Don't be silly. But can you fill me in? They wouldn't tell me anything on the phone, only that you were being held in the ER for observation. I've been going out of my mind."

You and me both, I almost say, but he's probably not in the right mood for gallows humor. I explain about showing up at Greenbacks this morning, purseless and phoneless, passing out, remembering nothing, and then, almost all at once, everything flooding back. Despite how calmly he appears to take it, I can read the concern in his light brown eyes.

"Why Greenbacks?" he asks when I'm finished. I guess I shouldn't be surprised that's his first question. He knows about my years there. And he knows, too, about my prior relationship with Damien.

"I have no idea. Maybe I was so disoriented, I lost track of where I actually work now."

"Could you have had a concussion?"

"They don't think so, but—"

I'm spared from recounting my psychiatric assessment by the return of Dr. Agarwal, who offers Hugh a recap of what he shared with me earlier. I have to hand it to my husband: as freaked out as he must be listening to Agarwal, especially when he brings up the fact that reoccurrences are common, Hugh appears to take it all in with perfect equanimity.

"How can I be of help to my wife?" he asks when Agarwal finishes.

"Just be as supportive as possible. Ally should do her

absolute best to avoid stress. It's possible her memory from this morning will return in time."

Hugh is quiet for a moment. "Understood," he says finally.

We soon discover that the only obstacle blocking my departure now is paperwork, and because several staffers don't seem to know where the release forms are at the moment, it feels like I might never be discharged. Hugh springs into action, not in an aggressive, alpha-male way, but in that subtle lawyer style of his, sorting through the confusion, finding a person to take charge, and flashing me a conspiratorial grin when the designated hero finally appears, papers in hand.

I wonder again how distressed he really is. We've navigated our share of tough times in our four years together—his younger sister's serious car accident, which thankfully she fully recovered from; my father's heart attack this past summer; the stressful periods when Hugh's smack in the middle of a big case and working nights and weekends with very little time for me. But this is a whole other ball of wax.

Once my clothes and watch have been returned to me and I'm dressed, Hugh squeezes my hand.

"You all set?" he asks.

"Yup."

"You don't have a coat?"

I glance down at my blouse and pants, wrinkled from being balled into a plastic bag, and my black kitten heels, still damp from the rain. I remember a coat—my black trench.

"Maybe it was left behind in the ambulance."

"Why don't I follow up on that later—let's get you home now."

Outside I see that the rain has stopped, though it's left behind a bruised, swollen October sky. In the cab Hugh pulls me toward him and leaves his arm draped around me. My right cheek rests on the soft worsted wool of his suit. My friend Gabby once joked that Hugh probably showered in his suits, but I *like* them, especially seeing them lined up in his closet. To me they're a reminder of how hard he's worked, never taking anything for granted.

I'm sure he has a billion more questions but is saving them till we're home and I'm feeling better. It's a relief to not *have* to talk and yet at the same time I feel wired again, my limbs jittery.

Finally, we're inside our building lobby, hurrying past the doorman and concierge—who probably note my disheveled appearance but would never betray their surprise—and riding the twenty-seven floors to our apartment.

"Would you like something to drink?" Hugh asks as we pass from the foyer into the great room, which serves as a combination living, dining, and kitchen area.

"A glass of sparkling water, if you don't mind," I tell him, taking in the clean open space as if I'm seeing it for the first time: the white couch and armchairs, the glass-topped dining table, the floor-to-ceiling windows with the city views spilling out below and beyond.

"What about something more nourishing? Like some soup?"

"Honey," I say smiling, hoping to lighten the mood a little. "I'm sure we don't have any soup. Unless you count the three old cubes of chicken bouillon that I brought along as part of my wedding dowry."

He chuckles. "Right. How about takeout then? We can order from Pavone's."

"Um, sure, sounds good." I'm not hungry, but I need to be sitting across from Hugh at our dining table, a regular nightly ritual for us.

As Hugh pours me a glass of Pellegrino water, I wander the length of the room.

"What's the matter, Ally?" he asks, furrowing his brow.

"My purse. I was praying it might be here—along with my keys and my phone. Can you call my number?"

"Yeah, but I don't think it's here. I would have heard your phone ringing before." After handing me the glass, he slides his phone from his pants pocket and taps the screen.

I hold my breath, but there's only silence.

"I still have my old iPhone, so I can use it with a new SIM card—but darn, all our credit cards. They have to be canceled."

"Don't worry, I'll handle it. And you can use our spare key. I'll have another one made for us."

"I hate to dump this all on you."

"I don't mind, truly. I just want you to relax, take it easy tonight."

I realize how achy I still am. "I think what I want most of all before dinner is a shower."

"Of course. Can you handle it alone?"

"I think so. I don't feel faint anymore, really."

"I might hang in the bedroom while you're showering."

"Hugh, I appreciate the thought, but it's really not necessary."

He steps forward and encircles me with his arms. "You'll

have to forgive me if I glom on to you over the next few days. I want to be sure you're okay."

"I like the idea of you glomming on to me, but I'll be fine showering."

"Okay, I'll order dinner and cancel the cards. How about chicken piccata? And a salad?"

"Sounds good."

Leaving Hugh behind, I traipse down the long corridor to the master bedroom. After draining the water glass, I peel off my blouse, bra, pants, and underwear and stuff them all into the hamper, though I'm tempted to chuck them in the waste basket. There's a sour, sweaty smell emanating from them, and they have a clammy feel, too, as if I've been in them for days.

After grabbing my robe, I search all around the space, and also in the alcove off the bedroom, which I use as a home office when I don't go to WorkSpace. There's no sign of my purse anywhere, but my laptop is here, in the middle of my desk—exactly where I always keep it when I'm home. I breathe a sigh of relief that I hadn't had it with me today, because surely it would be missing now, too.

I open the laptop and click on "find my phone," hoping for a miracle. But a miracle doesn't happen. The response is *phone not found*. It was either turned off or ran out of battery in the general vicinity of my apartment building.

Next, I check the day's calendar to see what light it can shed. The hours from 8:30 to 11:00 are blocked off with the notation "work on book," and at 11:30, there's a note to myself to "call Jackie," a reference to my book agent. Obviously, that call never happened.

I'm not usually an early morning person, and I can't

figure out why in the world I'd gotten up and left the house by 7:15, which is when I must have departed to have arrived at Greenbacks by 8:05. Had I planned something I hadn't noted on the calendar?

I rest my hands on the desk, one on each side of the computer, and try to picture myself here. Hugh generally leaves in the morning before I do—he's recently been made a junior partner at his law firm and likes to be in his office most days by 7:30—and after he's gone I like to take my coffee into the alcove. I scan through the *Wall Street Journal* online and review my schedule. But my efforts to recall this morning are futile. It feels as if I'm trying to light a match that's been soaked in water.

I trudge to the bathroom, start the shower, and close my eyes as the warm water gushes over me. I soap my hair twice with shampoo, kneading my scalp with my fingers.

Once I'm finished, I dry off and settle onto the stool in the bathroom, finally sensing my body relax a little. I've always loved this room. It's entirely white and spalike, with shelves holding impossibly thick bath towels, one of which I've swaddled myself in. At the end of a tough day, I'll often light the room with candles and soak in the tub, feeling my tension melt away. Letting go of the silly need to do everything perfectly. Yet somehow, for a few hours this morning, I managed to forget that this room, this entire *apartment*, even existed.

What if it happens *again*? Me not knowing where I live or who my husband is or who *I* really am? I grip the edges of the stool, terrified at the thought.

I rise quickly from the stool and return to the alcove, where I type out an email to Dr. Erling.

Can you possibly squeeze me in for an extra appointment before Wednesday? Tomorrow would be best.
Something really scary happened to me and I need to
see you urgently.

A few minutes later, dressed in a long-sleeved tee and
sweats, I find Hugh standing at the granite-topped island
that separates the kitchen area from the rest of the great
room, opening a bottle of Italian red wine. His tie's off now,
as well as his jacket, both draped over the back of one of the
barstools along the island.

"I thought I'd have a glass of wine, but you probably
shouldn't, right? At least not tonight."

"Right, I'd better not. Water is fine."

"Let's sit for a bit, okay?" he adds, pouring me another
glass of sparkling water. "Dinner should be here soon."

He's dimmed the overhead lights, I notice, and switched
on a few table lamps so that the lighting is soft and soothing.
The city is sparkling outside the windows now. This is the
kind of apartment I fantasized about during my early days
in New York, and though we were able to buy it in large
part because of Hugh's generous salary, I contributed a nice
chunk to the down payment thanks to the savings I'd duti-
fully squirreled away. I've always practiced what I preach as a
personal finance reporter.

We settle onto the couch a foot or so apart. There's something slightly awkward about our interaction, I notice. This
can't be easy for him.

"You must have been really worried when the hospital
called you," I say.

"Forget about me. I was just concerned about *you* . . . and not being able to get there fast enough. There was a brief moment when all I could think was, 'How do I hire a freaking chopper?'"

I smile. "I don't think that hospital has a helipad on the roof, though." I take a long sip of water, realizing how thirsty I am. "They said they couldn't reach you for a while."

"Yeah, I'd gone to Westport to meet with that potential client—Ben Sachs—and two of his associates."

"That's what I guessed."

"Unbeknownst to me, he'd decided to turn the office meeting we'd set up into brunch on his boat, and needless to say, the cell service sucked. Apparently, Melinda was trying to reach me for hours without any luck, so she ended up sending someone to the marina to wait for me."

"Well, I'm just glad she finally got through." I let my eyes roam the great room, hoping that clues will present themselves. "Hugh, I really need you to help me fill in a few blanks, okay? According to my calendar, I'd blocked off time this morning to work on my book, so why would I have left here so early? Did I mention anything to you about an appointment or last-minute meeting today?"

His expression clouds. "I can't help you with this morning."

"What do you mean?" I ask, puzzled.

"I didn't see you."

"You mean I left even earlier than you did?"

"No, Ally, you weren't here at all. You've been gone for two whole days."

hear his words, but they stall out in my brain.

"Hugh, I don't understand," I say. "What are you talking about?"

"I haven't set eyes on you since Tuesday morning."

The full-blown panic I experienced this morning had slowly subsided, but it now it rears its head again like a jungle cat catching the scent of prey on the wind.

"But . . . we ordered in." I think of the vague memory of the evening I'd shared with Dr. Agarwal. "We watched TV."

"That was *Monday* night." Hugh's expression is pained. "You were in bed when I left the next morning at around— I'd say, seven—and I assumed you were asleep. That was the last time I saw you before I came to pick you up at the hospital."

My heart races as I grasp the truth. I've been so focused on making sense of today that I didn't give much thought to the days immediately prior. But Tuesday and Wednesday, I now realize, are a total blank. Where the hell *was* I?

"Why didn't you explain this to Dr. Agarwal?"

"I wanted to get you out of there, and it seemed that the less said at the moment, the better."

"But . . . weren't you worried about where I was?" I say, almost pleading. Why hadn't Hugh called the police?

"Yes, of course I was, but not because I thought you were in any danger." He takes a breath, exhales. "We . . . we had a big argument before bed Monday night. I thought you'd gone to stay with a friend for a couple of nights. Gabby, maybe."

It's not that odd that his mind went to her. Gabby's the first important friend I made in New York—we ended up sharing an apartment after we met through mutual friends—and though we're wildly different, we've been close for more than a decade. But the idea of my taking off seems unfathomable.

"Hugh, that's crazy. How could you think I would just move out for a few days?"

He swipes a hand over his scalp, raking his fingers through his short brown hair. "You said you needed space, that you wanted time alone to think, and so I took you at your word. I tried calling you, of course—a bunch of times. But you never called me back."

I push myself up from the sofa, stumbling slightly on the edge of the rug.

"Ally, please sit down," he insists.

But I can't, and instead pace in front of the coffee table, trying to grapple with what he's just revealed.

"So what was the fight about?" I ask. That's the million-dollar question, after all.

He rises from the couch himself and heads to the island, where he pours another glass of wine.

"It was my fault," he says, avoiding my gaze momentarily. "It was a discussion I was hoping to keep positive, but it ended up spiraling in the wrong direction."

"A discussion about *what*?"

"Kids. I pressed you again."

"Well, how bad did it get?"

"We weren't screaming, if that's what you mean."

No, we wouldn't have screamed. We're both controlled and averse to messiness, and that's how I prefer it.

"But it did get a little heated," he adds. "And you seemed really upset."

Mostly I've tried to be understanding of Hugh's position. I mean, let's face it, I pulled a bait and switch on the guy, leading him to believe when we married that I was enthusiastic about parenthood but then developing cold feet. That said, the sudden pressure from him was unexpected. It was as if "have a kid" was the next box he wanted to tick off after "make partner" and "buy a dream apartment." But as I'd told Dr. Agarwal, Hugh had promised to table the issue for a while. I must have been really pissed when he raised it again the other night.

And yet, how could a fight on well-trodden terrain be enough to make me disassociate, lose track of my identity?

"Do you think I *was* at Gabby's all this time?" That would be some kind of relief—meaning (1) at least I was safe and (2) she'll have a few answers for me.

"No. I called her Wednesday morning, hoping to make contact with you, and it was clear you hadn't gone there."

"Did you ask her directly?"

He shakes his head. "I didn't want to let on what had

happened in case you *weren't* there. So I told her I needed a few ideas for your birthday, and she ended up giving me a bunch of suggestions. It was clear from her tone that you weren't at her place, and that she probably had no clue about our argument."

I throw up my hands, more confused than ever. "If I wasn't with Gabby, where *was* I?"

"At another friend's, I guess."

It's hard to imagine who that could be. My other two closest friends aren't in New York at the moment: Diane recently accepted a job in Chicago, and John is freelance writing from Dallas while his partner handles a two-month project there.

"Maybe I stayed in a hotel. Do you know if I took a bag?"

"I assumed you did, but I haven't taken a look in your closet. But I don't think you were at a hotel. I checked the credit card statement on Wednesday afternoon. Like I said, I wasn't worried at that point, but of course I wanted to know where you were. The only charge was for around fifteen dollars for food on Wednesday. It must have been for lunch."

"Where was it?"

"A place called Eastside Eats. I googled it and it's on Fifty-First Street between Third and Lex."

I can't imagine what I would be doing in Midtown East. I'm rarely in that part of the city.

"According to the website," Hugh adds, "it looks like it's your standard-issue gourmet café."

That tells me nothing other than the fact that at some point while I was missing, I went hunting for a cup of coffee and maybe my usual tuna salad and sprouts on multigrain.

"What about my bank card? Did I ever take cash from an ATM?"

"Nope."

I glance around the room, hoping again for a prompt, for a hint of any kind.

"Was the fight in here?"

He shakes his head. "It started in the den, right after we turned off the TV."

"What did we watch?"

"A documentary. About the financial meltdown in 2008."

"Okay," I say, as images from that day pop up in my memory, "I *do* remember Monday." I spent a chunk of the day at WorkSpace with my assistant/researcher, Nicole. Then Hugh and I had dinner and watched the documentary. "But nothing after that."

Nothing. I grab my head in my hands. "This is crazy."

"Ally, as Dr. Agarwal said, it's important not to stress yourself out."

"I'd be much less stressed if I could figure out where I was all this time. . . . I wonder if I managed to show up for my appointment with Dr. Erling on Wednesday."

"If you missed it, Erling will clearly understand. You're going to get ahold of her, right?"

"I already left her a message. God, she has to help me remember."

"Is it really the end of the world if you don't end up remembering everything? The key thing is that it doesn't happen again, and that means getting the best medical help."

It *does* feel catastrophic to me; there's a sense of fear

creeping up my back, spreading over me. Fear about the missing days and what happened to me during that time. I grip my head again, as if the pressure could somehow force the memories to the surface.

"I also think you should see a neurologist for a second opinion," Hugh adds. "Maybe you did sustain a concussion."

"Yes, that makes sense, I guess," I say, but I'm still thinking about Tuesday and Wednesday. "Shit, what about my podcast on Tuesday? What if I didn't show for it?"

"You're okay on that front. You'd told me before this that you'd banked one last Tuesday and weren't recording this week."

That's right. I remember that now.

"Ally, why don't we table this until tomorrow?" Hugh steps toward me and pulls me against his chest. "This can't be doing you any good tonight."

He's right, I realize. I'm exhausted and feeling weirdly fragile. By rehashing this, I'm doing the opposite of what Agarwal suggested. The last thing I want is to find myself back in the psych unit.

Five seconds later the intercom rings with the concierge announcing our food is here, and while we wait for the knock on our door, I set the table, grateful for a menial task to occupy my mind.

During the meal I ask Hugh about the boat ride with the potential client. He doesn't like the guy, he admits, and is thinking of foisting him onto another lawyer in the firm. The conversation seems stilted at times, as if we're two strangers attending a convention and eating lunch side by side in the hotel ballroom.

Shortly after ten o'clock, we dress for bed. A peek at the top shelf of my closet indicates that my overnight bag is still there, and it appears as though my clothes are all accounted for. I think of the foul-smelling skirt and blouse I'd stuffed in the hamper earlier. Clearly, I *had* been wearing them for days.

Once I crawl beneath the covers, Hugh reaches out and spoons me, and I relax a little into his strong, smooth arms. Before long, his breathing goes deep, indicating he's drifted off. I'm bone-tired, but every inch of me resists sleep. I'm afraid that when I wake up this might all be gone again.

After close to an hour of lying in bed wide-eyed and wired, I unwrap Hugh's arms, slip out of bed, and grab my laptop and calendar from the alcove. Quietly I pad down the hall to the living room. I know I should be giving my brain a rest, but there must be answers waiting for me if I'm willing to dig.

Using our portable phone—which despite the endless robocalls, I've kept for years as a backup—I start with a call to Gabby, whose cell-phone number I know by heart. It's after eleven, but she's a night owl. She's also a good fibber when she has to be, and I'm praying that she knows more than she let on to Hugh. The call goes to voice mail. I leave a message saying I need to speak to her ASAP, and asking her to call our apartment phone because my iPhone is missing in action.

Next I open my laptop and google "dissociative state." It's defined just as Dr. Agarwal described. "Dissociative disorders," I read, "are typically experienced as startling, autonomous intrusions into the person's usual way of responding or functioning. Due to their unexpected and largely inexplicable nature, they tend to be quite unsettling."

The understatement of the year.

As I continue to read, I learn they're sometimes referred to as "fugue" states, but the medical profession has moved away from using that term.

And then there's this: "The major characteristic for all dissociative phenomena involves a detachment from reality, rather than a loss of reality, as in psychosis."

Thank god for small favors, but none of this is telling me what I really want to know.

I open a new window and call up the website for Eastside Eats. I definitely don't remember being there. I stare hard at the home-page photos. Did I sit at one of those wooden tables, consume a croissant or sandwich? It's distressing to think I don't recall a second of it.

I move on to my calendar next, starting with Tuesday. Like today, most of the morning was blocked off for writing. I reach for my laptop again and click on the "book" folder only to discover that it was last saved on Monday. So that's not what I was doing Tuesday morning.

Tuesday afternoon on the calendar is mostly blank since, as Hugh had pointed out, I didn't need to be in the podcast studio that day. At 3:30 I'd scheduled a phone interview with a new source for my book, a woman named Glenda Payne, but I have no idea whether I ended up calling her.

Wednesday morning is also blocked off for work on the book, followed by my appointment with Erling at one P.M. After that is a notation to "shop for new coat." I had saved that activity for after Columbus Day, when winter coat prices always start to drop.

Next, I scroll through emails received and sent, starting

with Tuesday morning. Though I have no recollection of doing so, I composed several messages between 9:00 and 9:17 A.M. One was to my editor regarding the proposed catalog copy for my book. I sound perfectly coherent, as if nothing was awry. "The copy is great in general, but the phrase we want in this context is 'money market fund,' not 'money market account,'" I'd told the editor. "They're not interchangeable." Hardly the sound of a woman who's becoming unhinged.

Another email was to Nicole about a flight for an upcoming speech, nothing unusual there. She replied that she was on it and also reminded me she was headed out of town that day to attend her sister's wedding and wouldn't be back at WorkSpace until next week.

Interestingly, this batch of emails was sent from my phone rather than my laptop, which suggests I might have been on the move during that period.

From 9:17 A.M. onward, there were no outgoing emails, and every one *to* me since then—and there are plenty— has gone unanswered. To my chagrin, I see a message from Glenda Payne asking if we ended up with our wires crossed about the time. Lovely. And also one Wednesday evening from Dr. Erling, wondering why I didn't make the appointment and asking if everything is okay.

So I was a no-show, which means Erling won't be able to offer any clues.

I see there's also a "just checking in" email from my father, who's been spending the fall in San Diego with my half brother Quinn and his family, gaining his strength back after his heart attack in July. God, it's been three days since I had any contact with my dad, when we usually talk every day or every other. I quickly reply saying hi, love you, sorry I've been so busy but will write more later.

Finally, I glance through emails from the week before, wondering if anything I see will shed light on why I showed up at Greenbacks, but there's nothing. Just for the hell of it, I search for my last email exchange with Damien. It turns out it was roughly five years ago, the week I left the company.

I chew on my thumb for a minute and then jump up. I grab a pad and pencil from the island counter, and return to the couch, where I begin scribbling down a timeline. I know I can be really anal, but it helps me to put things in writing.

MONDAY
　　evening: dinner, TV, argument

TUESDAY
　　7:00: still in bed
　　9:00–9:17: sent emails

WEDNESDAY
　　Possibly lunchtime: bought food at Eastside Eats

THURSDAY
　　8:05: arrived at Greenbacks

This offers next to nothing about where I was those days, especially after dark. What did I do for food? And where did I *sleep*? Somehow, no matter what it takes, I'm going to have to fill in the blanks.

But ultimately, I need answers to more than the "where?" and "when?" questions. I need to know *why* I lost my sense of self. Was it really because of a fight with Hugh regarding kids?

Or was it instead—as Agarwal prompted me to wonder—because of a trauma from the past? The only thing that fits the bill is something that happened to me when I was nine years old. But that can't be it, can it? Would a dreadful afternoon from so long ago really have made the wheels come off for me?

7

When I wake the next morning, I still feel exhausted and frayed at the edges. Hugh's side of the bed is empty, though I detect the aroma of sautéing onions drifting from the living area. He's making breakfast. Perched on the edge of the mattress, I quickly comb through my memory, praying that somehow the missing days have emerged as I slept, but they haven't.

At least I've woken up in my own bed.

After dressing, I find Hugh at the stovetop, standing over a sizzling skillet with a Williams Sonoma dish towel tucked into his khakis. He smiles but I detect a wariness in his eyes.

"Hey, how you feeling?" he asks.

"Okay, I guess. Rested." Though that's a stretch. I didn't crawl into bed again until after midnight.

"I thought you could use one of my pepper and onion omelets."

"Fantastic . . . Why aren't you dressed for work?"

"I figured I'd hang around here for the day. There's nothing on my schedule that can't be rearranged."

I'd love his company, but he's in the middle of a big case

at work, and I hate to take him from it. "Hugh, I promise I'll be fine, and if you're here, it'll only make me feel more like a patient."

He looks relieved. "Are you sure?"

"Yes, please."

"Okay, but I'd really appreciate it if you stayed in today and just tried to relax."

I nod, knowing I shouldn't push myself.

"By the way," he adds. "I've emailed a few people for neurologist recommendations, without saying what the issue is. I hope to have a name by later today. Any word from Dr. Erling?"

"Not yet, but I'm sure I'll hear from her as soon she checks her email."

"Let me know when you do. By the way, do you plan to tell your family what happened?"

"Roger, yes, but definitely not my dad. It would be too stressful for him."

"How about my parents? Should I say anything to them?"

"Let's not for now, Hugh. I'm counting on this sorting itself out, and I don't want to worry them unnecessarily."

There's a bit more to it than that. I like Hugh's parents, who have been generally lovely to me. But they're fairly high on the uptight scale, and I'm sure this news would wig them out.

Hugh and I eat breakfast at the table, watching the nearly cloudless sky brighten. At several junctures we seem oddly at a loss for words. Is he on pins and needles, I wonder, terrified I'll unravel again?

After changing into a suit, Hugh tells me good-bye, promising to stop by an AT&T store this morning and outfit my old phone with a new SIM card so I can start making calls.

I pour myself another cup of coffee and, using my laptop, respond to the most urgent emails in my in-box, including the one from Glenda Payne, the interview subject I dropped the ball on. I apologize profusely and ask her if we can reschedule. I also shoot a response to Sasha Hyatt, a former beauty editor who's convinced she can transform herself into a personal finance guru and has been foisted on me as an intern by an executive with the company that's sponsoring my podcast. She's written me three times since Tuesday, wondering if I received the research she'd emailed me for the next show. I tell her yes, I have it, but I've been under the weather and will need to follow up later.

Just as I'm finishing my coffee, the portable phone by the couch rings. When I lift the receiver, I see Gabby's name on the screen and the sight of it triggers a rush of relief.

"Hot date?" I answer. "Or did you go to bed ridiculously early?"

"What? Wait, did you forget?"

My blood seems to freeze. "Forget what?"

"That I'm in London?"

"Oh gosh, sorry," I say, suddenly recalling that she'd planned to leave this week on a trip for the jewelry business she runs. And it means that she probably won't be able to offer me any clues.

"Is everything okay?"

"Uh—not exactly. But it can wait until you return."

"No way. I'm just hanging out in the hotel until my next appointment. What's going on?"

I spill it all then—about the fight with Hugh, how he assumed that I was at her place, my amnesia, my long, distressing day in the ER.

"Ally, this is so scary," she exclaims. "Hugh *did* call me, right before I left on Wednesday, but I never sensed anything was wrong. I'm supposed to fly back Monday, but let me call my assistant and see if she can get me out of here earlier."

"No, please, don't even think about it. You can answer a few questions for me, though."

"Of course, fire away."

"When was the last time we spoke?"

"Let's see—it must have been Monday, late in the afternoon."

That's one thing I do remember now that she mentions it.

"Did I give you any hint I was coming undone?"

"No, you sounded fine. The only thing that seems odd in hindsight is that you promised to call me before I left for London, but I never heard from you. I just figured you were busy and forgot."

My pulse quickens. "Have I been forgetful lately?"

She sighs. "To be honest, a little."

"About important stuff?"

"Nothing like that. Maybe distracted is a better word. Like last weekend, you said you were going to swing by my apartment at three but you showed at three thirty."

I picture her sitting at her wooden table, her long red hair fanned out around her shoulders. We chatted about a thriller we'd both read, a new guy she's seeing, her search for a better publicist for her rapidly expanding business.

"I'm sorry I screwed that up. Why didn't you say anything?"

"It wasn't a big deal. I know the baby stuff has been eating at you. Do you think all the stress caused this?"

"I'm not sure, but now I'm even *more* stressed, and I will be until I figure out where I was."

In my mind's eye I can see the wheels turning in my friend's mind. "You know what I would do if I were you?" she says. "Hire a private detective."

Gabby's an out-of-the-box thinker—it's what makes her jewelry designs unique and riveting—so I'm not surprised she's going there. But her suggestion feels like a move I'm not ready to make yet.

"Maybe."

"Why maybe?"

"It would be an awfully big step. Besides, I'm hoping my therapist can help me regain my memory, and then I won't need a detective on the case . . . but anyway, I should let you go."

"Okay, but promise you'll call me day or night if you need *anything*. And why don't I plan to drop by right after I get back on Monday? My flight lands around four."

"You'll be exhausted."

"Don't worry about it. I need to be with you."

As soon as we hang up, I check my email to see if Dr. Erling has responded, but there's no word from her. Then I google "private detective agencies NYC," simply to see what surfaces. The number of possibilities seems overwhelming and after perusing the first dozen or so, I shut my laptop with a sigh.

The house phone rings again, startling me. I assume it's a robocall, but to my shock, I find myself staring at the main number for Greenbacks. *Damien*? When I answer, however, a woman's voice asks for Ally Linden.

"This is she."

"I'm Damien Howe's assistant. I have your trench coat—you left it in the conference room—and I wanted to arrange to send it over to you. We're lucky we still had an old home number for you."

I'm grateful to hear it. The coat wasn't pricey, but I liked it. Besides, I can take comfort in the fact that unlike my memory, it hasn't been sucked into a black hole and lost forever. Maybe today won't be as much of a hot mess as yesterday.

After I provide the address, she tells me the messenger should be there in a few hours. Something about her tone and uptalk suggests she's young, and I wonder if she's the woman I'd seen in the cubicle outside Damien's office yesterday. Is he sitting in his office with the door open, eavesdropping on the call?

"Oh, and Damien wanted me to ask how you were feeling," she adds. "He called the hospital, but they weren't allowed to give out any information."

I cringe as I flash back on the face-plant I did in his office and being hauled out on a stretcher, my hair slicked back with rainwater. I must have looked like a marooned seal.

"Please tell him I'm doing fine today, and that I appreciate his concern."

Of course, I think, after we've signed off, *he didn't call to inquire himself. Does the idea of us speaking to each other unsettle him as much as it does me?*

When I open my laptop again, I see to my relief that Dr. Erling's responded, asking if I'm free to talk and giving me her number. I call her New York office immediately.

"Ally, please tell me what's happened." The sound of her deep, steady voice provides instant comfort.

"Everything's such a mess. I spent most of yesterday in a psych ward."

"Yes, I spoke to Dr. Agarwal only a few moments ago," she says.

I quickly recap from my perspective, offering details she wouldn't have heard from Agarwal, like how long I was actually gone.

"I know I never made the appointment Wednesday," I add. "We didn't speak at all, did we?"

"We did, actually—but Tuesday morning. I called you around nine and asked if there was any chance you could switch this week's appointment to my Larchmont office, and you said you could. But you never showed up the next day."

"Did I sound okay when we talked?"

"Yes, but you mentioned you were upset about something to do with Hugh and eager to see me."

It's not much, but I have a couple more clues now: I had a conversation with Erling, which I can add to my timeline, and the fight with Hugh was clearly on my mind.

"I know how jammed your schedule is, but is there any way you can see me today?"

"Yes, of course. This is important. I had a cancellation at two thirty. Can you make that?"

I tell her that works perfectly and promise to see her in a few hours. As soon as we sign off, I schedule an Uber so I won't have to be out on the street hunting down a cab.

I feel my shoulders relax a little. What I told Agarwal was true. I've valued my sessions with Erling, and though I don't yet feel closer to understanding the origins of my ambivalence around having children, I've sensed I'll get there with her guidance.

Now, I need her more than ever—to help me unlock the door to my memory and make sure I don't unspool again.

I have zero appetite, but around noon I serve myself a few spoonfuls of Greek yogurt. Hugh calls—for the second time—to check on me and explains that he's having my old iPhone messengered back to the apartment, complete with the SIM card.

Out of nowhere, fatigue ambushes me, and I lean back onto the couch, permitting my eyes to close. I can't fall asleep, though. I need to leave soon for Dr. Erling's.

The intercom buzzer jars me out of my stupor. The concierge announces I have a delivery from Greenbacks. Once again, the mere sound of the name kicks my pulse into higher gear.

The person who arrives at the door several minutes later isn't a messenger but a bearded twentysomething guy who explains he's a company intern—someone I'm sure who's in awe of Damien and studying his every move. He hands me a large green shopping bag, his expression curious. The same stench that I noticed emanating from my clothes yesterday is now wafting from the bag, and the guy's probably curious as to why.

After he's gone, I dump the coat onto the foyer floor. There's a chance, I suddenly realize, that the now fetid trench might hold clues to my whereabouts. I check the right pocket first. There's nothing in there but a fistful of bills—three tens and seven ones. Okay, interesting: I'd managed to transfer cash from my wallet to my pocket before losing my purse. Maybe I'd used the cash to buy more food.

Before I can try the other pocket, I notice it's bulging, as if something thick has been stuffed in there. I reach in and tug out a large wad of white tissues.

Not white anymore, though. They're almost entirely covered with dried brown splotches, and crusty in places, as if they were used to help clean up a serious spill. I stare, summoning a memory that never comes. And then, finally, I decipher what I'm seeing.

The tissues are caked with dried blood.

8

SESSION WITH DR. ELAINE ERLING

arrive at Dr. Erling's building a full ten minutes ahead of schedule, feeling relieved to be there. I'm eager to pour everything out without the urge to edit myself the way I had with Dr. Agarwal.

But when the elevator reaches her floor, I'm surprised to find that my breathing is shallow, and there's a hard pit in my stomach.

Am I scared? I wonder. Fearful of what I might learn if Dr. Erling helps me unravel the mystery of the missing days? Or am I still uneasy from my discovery of the bloody tissues, which I've stuffed in a Ziploc bag in my dresser drawer, in case . . . in case, I'm not sure what?

Outside Erling's office, I press the bell, and hear the faint click of the door unlocking. I push it open and step into the foyer, a space featuring two straight-backed chairs, a small table with copies of *Time* and *The Atlantic*, and, on the floor, the de rigeur white noise machine. Despite its whir, I'm able to detect the low murmur of voices coming from the other side of the inside door. I'm early, and Erling must be finishing up with the patient ahead of me.

Though it's going to be impossible to relax, I take a seat and grab a magazine. I flip aimlessly through the pages, my eyes never resting on a single word.

The inner door quietly swings open. Out of courtesy to the other patient, I keep my eyes lowered, though I can tell from the shoes that it's a man. He departs, and I wait a few minutes more until Dr. Erling opens the door again. Finally, it's my turn.

She greets me warmly and beckons me in. From her appearance and the research I've done online, I've surmised she's in her mid- to late forties. She's an attractive woman, with shoulder-length auburn hair and deep brown eyes, though a sharp nose detracts from her being classically beautiful.

I settle myself into the same spot I've sat in on my other visits—a wide, nubby gray armchair directly across from hers. Erling waits for me to get comfortable before she takes her seat. She's wearing a navy pencil skirt today, paired with a satiny ivory-colored blouse, and as she crosses one leg over the other, I notice her classy, pointy-toe navy pumps.

"Ally, I'm eager to hear more about your experience," she says, "but please tell me first how you're feeling at the moment."

"Right this second, things feel fairly normal," I tell her honestly. "But I'm really anxious—about losing my memory— and beyond that, I'm worried it might happen again."

"Have you ever experienced anything like this before?"

"Never," I say without hesitating. "And I can't make sense of why it's happened *now*. I don't mean to brag, but I'm a pretty together person. I'm comfortable with who I am and can't imagine why I'd want to detach from this identity. And there weren't any warning signs, at least that I noticed. My best friend told me I've been a little distracted lately, but that's the only thing I can think of."

"And do you feel fully present now? In the moment?"

"Right now, yes."

"Do you have any sense that you're standing outside your body? Watching yourself from a distance?"

"No, nothing like that." I make a mental note of what she's said, though, realizing that such a sensation must be a red flag. "Other than being totally drained, I feel like myself. But I have no clue where I was or what I was doing for two whole days. And I'm freaking out about it."

"That's a totally normal reaction, Ally." She leans forward a little, her expression sympathetic. "Not remembering what happened to you is very unsettling. But we're going to do a bit of detective work here and see if we can start piecing things together."

I nod gratefully, as tears well in my eyes.

"Tell me about the last thing you remember from this week," she says.

I ease into my chair a little and take a deep breath, as if mentally rolling up my sleeves. I tell her about working Monday afternoon and later eating take-out food with Hugh but admit I have no recollection of the fight, even the start of it. I also share what Hugh revealed about my call to him and the charge on my credit card for food, and wrap up with my disastrous morning at Greenbacks.

Though Erling generally doesn't take many notes during a session, she jots a few down today. During the brief moments her eyes leave mine, I scan the office. It's attractive, decorated in pleasant shades of blue and gray, but I actually prefer her Larchmont office—with its cinnamon-colored couch and cream-colored walls and curtains. Maybe that space feels more inviting because it's part of her home, a room that I suspect also serves as her study.

"What type of tests did they perform in the ER?" she asks, glancing up again.

"Blood and urine, which turned up nothing. A few cognitive tests. They didn't do any kind of head x-ray because they said I had no signs of a concussion. Though it's weird—this morning I found tissues with dried blood in my coat pocket."

"But you didn't have any cuts or bruises?"

"No, so I wonder if I might have had a nosebleed. Maybe from getting hit in the face somehow? I used to get those when I was playing sports in school—when someone whacked me by mistake with a hockey stick or an elbow. And . . . sometimes they used to happen all on their own. When I was upset—or stressed out."

Erling silently holds my gaze, as if waiting for me to elaborate.

"Part of me wishes I *was* bumped in the nose," I tell her. "If my amnesia occurred because of a physical trauma, it would make it so much easier to understand. I can't believe this is all because of the argument with Hugh."

"Tell me what it's been like when you and Hugh fought in the past."

"We've always been civilized, though Hugh claimed I was pretty angry this time."

"During our last session, you said that Hugh promised to give you some breathing room, that you could put the baby discussion on hold for a while."

"I know, so the fact that he brought it up again must have made me feel really under the gun. And that's exactly when the memory loss began."

Erling cocks her head. "With a dissociative state," she says, "memory loss doesn't necessarily begin at the exact moment of a trauma. It can actually encompass a period of time prior to a traumatic event."

I take a second to digest the information.

"So the fight might *not* have been the trigger?"

"Maybe not. Or it could have been one of a series of triggers. So we need to consider other possible sources of stress or trauma. I'd like to hear about the place you went to yesterday morning, the company you used to work for. What does it mean to you?"

Sigh. I knew we'd get here sooner or later.

I give her a brief overview of Greenbacks: it's a website offering a ton of posts on personal finance topics, but there are other services, too, like individual money management handled totally online. I explain I worked there for more than four years, first as an editor, then as chief content officer—and that overall, I really enjoyed it. My coworkers were smart and interesting, and I found the work exciting. But since I'd always had a desire to make a name as a personal finance expert, I started working on my own about five years ago.

"I really don't have any idea why I went back there," I add, knowing that's what she's really wondering. "The friends I made have moved on, too . . . but there's one thing I should mention. When I worked at Greenbacks, I was involved romantically with the founder and CEO, Damien Howe."

"This man was married?" she says. Her expression still gives nothing away, though I swear her eyes widen almost imperceptibly.

"Definitely not. We were both single at the time. But he was my boss—and we kept it a secret from the other employees."

"How do you feel about the relationship in retrospect?"

"Well, I never felt taken advantage of, if that's what you mean. I was in my late twenties, already in a big job there, and he wasn't all that much older, so it wasn't some kind of crazy power imbalance. I was in love with him. I was. And I think he was in love with *me*. But once it became clear that some of my colleagues were on to us, I decided we should cool it for a while . . . for both our sakes. And he agreed . . . but then we never got back together."

She waits, and when I don't fill the silence, she asks how I felt about it ending.

"There were no repercussions," I say. "This was never a hashtagmetoo thing. But I was confused—and hurt, too. Like I said, I thought we were only on hiatus. I figured I'd find a job elsewhere or accelerate my plan to go freelance, and then we could start seeing each other again. But he seemed to, I don't know, lose interest."

The room suddenly seems so quiet. Her office is only on the seventh floor of the building, but there isn't even a hint of the traffic below.

"Can you describe your feelings for Damien now?" she asks.

"I swear I don't have any. I can't even tell you the last time I thought about him."

Her right eyebrow shoots up, fast as a knee tapped with a reflex hammer. She's not hiding her reaction this time.

"You look surprised," I say.

"I am. It's common for a person to hold on to some feelings for someone he or she was in love with once. It's perfectly normal, even if you're happily married now. It's even normal to check up on a former partner, particularly on the internet."

I find myself shrugging. "Okay, I *have* thought about him at times, and I used to google him now and again. But it's honestly been ages since I did that. I have no clue whatsoever why I would go to Greenbacks. And I definitely don't think I'm holding any residual stress related to Damien or the company."

Erling taps a finger to her lips. She's wearing a rose-colored lipstick that I've been too preoccupied to notice until now.

"In our earlier sessions, we'd been discussing the experience you had when you were nine. How do you think that may be playing into what's happened this week?"

"Oh god," I say, pressing my hands to my face. I knew we would get *here*, too. What I failed to tell the doctor yesterday was that my decision to see Erling wasn't based only on my family-planning discussions. I've been worried that my ambivalence is related to this—this *thing* that happened to me years ago, and I knew I needed to talk it through with a professional. From the moment Dr. Agarwal used the phrase "trauma from the past," I've been nagged by the idea that something that happened twenty-five years ago might also play a role in my current nightmare.

I lower my hands. "Do you think talking about it with you churned everything up and made me detach from myself?"

"What do *you* think, Ally?" That's something she often does, throw my question back at me.

"I don't know. *Maybe.* Like I told you before, I certainly don't feel haunted by it every day. My parents were so supportive—staying home from work in the days after, even sending me to a therapist. But parts of that day are still confusing to me. Everybody seemed to be talking in hushed tones, and I wasn't always sure what was going on."

"Have you been thinking a lot about that event?"

"Yes," I say and realize that I'm wringing my hands. "You—you said during another session that it might help for me to see if my brother Roger remembers anything about the episode. In light of everything this week, I think I need to do that."

"I'm not sure this is the right moment for that. But I think we need to return to the topic during the next session, when we have more time to focus on it."

"Okay." I glance at my watch and discover to my shock that the session is almost over. "But I still haven't remembered anything."

"It's going to take time, Ally." She crosses one leg over the other. "I'm curious. What were you doing when most of your memory returned at the hospital?"

"Filling out some forms. It sounds kind of crazy, but when I glanced down at the white sheet on the bed, I suddenly had an image of our living room—we have a white sofa and white walls. And then things all came back in a tumble."

"That's important to note. It often helps jog a memory

when you stop pushing your brain so hard. Give it a chance to work on its own. Like I said, it can take time for these memories to surface."

I nod, realizing she's making perfect sense.

"And I think it's best for you to take things very easy this weekend. With a dissociative state, the body has separated from the mind, so use your mind to stay as much in touch with your body as possible. Savor the food you eat. Do some yoga every day, really letting yourself engage with the positions. And I often recommend that patients keep cinnamon Altoids with them."

"*Altoids?*"

"Yes, if you really concentrate on the flavor, it can help you be aware of your body and physical sensations. If you start to feel stressed or detached in any way, practice the breathing technique we talked about a few weeks ago, and of course, don't hesitate to call me."

"And I'll see you next Wednesday—at our usual time?"

"In light of your situation, Ally, I'd like to see you twice a week for now. Does that work for you?" I nod, and she grabs her calendar. "I have an opening at three on Monday, here in the city."

"That's fine," I say, relieved to think I'll be coming more frequently. "Thank you."

"And if it's doable on your end, let's move your regular appointment to Thursdays so the sessions are evenly spaced."

"That works, too."

As Erling accompanies me to the door, I steal a glance at my watch, part of me certain that fifty minutes *couldn't* have passed. But they have. I'm on my own again.

Standing in the corridor, I order an Uber and then, while waiting for the elevator, mentally catalog the takeaways from the session, a little habit I initiated after my first visit with Erling:

Not pushing myself may make it easier for the memories to return.

The fugue state might not be related to the fight with Hugh.

It could, however, be related to what happened in Millerstown. To me. And to Jaycee Long—the little girl I found murdered in the woods so many years ago.

9

As the Uber driver zigzags west and north toward the Central Park–Seventy-Ninth Street transverse, I realize I feel even more wired than I did before the session. Jittery, unable to stop gnawing on my thumb. Or keep a zillion questions from ricocheting in my head.

My agitation, I realize, is due in part to my returning home empty-handed. On some level I'd allowed myself to believe that the session today would be a magic bullet, kick-starting my memory. But as Erling stressed, it might take time for memories to be recovered. Did she mean days? I wonder. Or *weeks*? I can't stand the thought of being in the dark for so long.

There's something else eating at me, too. The memory of Jaycee Long refuses to loosen its grip on me.

It's not as if I didn't obtain all the help I needed at the time. I had six months' worth of weekly sessions with a child psychologist, an intent listener who for some reason always wore a shawl pinned around the shoulders of her blazer.

And it wasn't as if the bad thing had *really* happened to me. I was simply a bystander, a nine-year-old who took a shortcut through the woods on her way home from school, kicking at leaves until her foot came into contact with something it shouldn't have.

The body of a two-year-old toddler whose skull had been fractured.

I swear that for the past couple of decades, I haven't really thought much about Jaycee. It was only recently that memories of finding her bubbled up in my mind, making me wonder if that early episode was somehow squelching my desire to be a mother.

Since Erling wants to circle back to the topic in our next session, it's clear to me that she's also wondering if the experience triggered my fugue state.

My pulse is racing, and I command my mind to go elsewhere. I have to follow Erling's instructions, do my best to keep stress at bay. That also means giving my brain a chance to recuperate and arrive at the truth at its own pace.

Hugh calls when I'm ten minutes into the ride. "How did it go?"

"Okay, I guess. We weren't able to trigger any memories, but she gave me a few exercises for stress."

"Nothing at all?"

"Nothing."

"By the way, I ended up with a good recommendation for a neurologist at NewYork-Presbyterian. I made an appointment for midday next Wednesday. I wish it was sooner, but that's the earliest they could squeeze you in."

I know Hugh's banking on this appointment, probably rooting for a physical origin, but as the hours pass, I'm growing more certain that a neurologist won't turn up a thing.

"I appreciate you doing that," I say. "What about tonight? Will you be home for dinner?"

"Definitely—and on the early side. And I'll grab food on the way."

"Great, thanks." Navigating a crowded grocery store is exactly the kind of thing I should avoid.

Before dropping my phone into my purse, I do a fast scroll through my in-box. Needless to say, the pileup of emails is growing larger, but most of them can be ignored for the time being. There's one I do need to deal with—from my podcast intern, Sasha. She says she hopes I'm feeling better, but mostly she's pressing to meet with me before the next studio session in order to review her research. Will you be going to WorkSpace today? she asks, because if so, I'll drop by there.

I email back to say I'm working from home, but we can review the research over the phone at around five, which seems easy enough. Her irritating reply, less than sixty seconds later: I have to be on the Upper West Side around that time. Why don't I drop by your place?

Begrudgingly, I tell her that's fine. She and Derek Kane seem to be really tight, and I don't want her to tell her buddy that I've been hard to pin down. I wonder, not for the first time, if she and Kane are in a relationship—and that's why he pushed so hard to have me take on someone with next to zero background in financial reporting.

I look up to see we're nearing my building. I end up asking the driver to drop me at the deli a half block away, where I pick up a tin of cinnamon Altoids and immediately pop one in my mouth.

Back in my apartment, I dig out my yoga mat from the

back of the closet and engage in twenty minutes' worth of poses in the great room, concentrating fully on each position and doing my best not to let my mind wander. I feel energized when I'm finished, and an espresso also helps. *I'm going to get through this crisis*, I tell myself. *I am.*

Inspired, I grab my laptop, answer a batch of emails, and then open the chapter of my book that I worked on last. I'm not that far behind, but it's definitely time to hustle.

But focusing turns out to be more difficult than I anticipated. Every sentence I manage to type is six words long and totally pedestrian.

Plus, the questions are back, slowly lapping against my brain at first and then flooding it. Where was I for two whole days? Why did I flee my home? Was it really because of the fight with Hugh, or does that terrible day from my childhood still haunt me in some way?

My gaze falls on my old iPhone, lying on the desk. I know Erling said this isn't the right moment to be talking to Roger about the past, but I'm close to my half brother and I need to bring him up to speed about what's happened anyway. There's even a chance, I realize, that I made contact with him when I was gone. I grab the phone and tap his name. The call goes to voice mail, but I know I'll hear from him soon enough. Rog is like that.

Our father, Ben, had been married to Roger's mother for nearly twenty years when she died unexpectedly of sepsis. Two years later, he met my mother, Lilly, and they married six months later. According to my mom, Roger and his younger brother, Quinn, fourteen and twelve at the time, were lovely, easygoing boys, who maturely accepted their father's desire to remarry and embraced her presence—and mine, too, when I brazenly popped up a year later. I adore them both, but it's Roger who's always seemed more enchanted by my existence and eager to engage. He was especially caring when my own mother died of cancer seven years ago.

My mother whom I miss and think of every day. My mother who, if she were alive, would surely be able to help me find a path out of this nightmare.

My phone rings and, yup, it's Roger.

"Hey, Button," he says, using a nickname my father once bestowed on me for being so buttoned-up about schoolwork. "Nice to hear your voice."

"Nice to hear yours, too. How is the lord of the manor today?" Roger lives in an impeccably restored manor house along the banks of the Delaware River, a few minutes away from Millerstown, the town where we grew up.

"In fairly good form for a middle-aged man. Is everything okay?"

There's an urgency to the last question. *Had* I made contact with him on Tuesday or Wednesday?

"What makes you say that?"

"Something in your voice. And Dad mentioned he hadn't heard from you in a few days. You're usually so Johnny-on-the-spot with your calls."

"I had an issue this week, but I emailed him late last night."

"What's going on?"

"Something weird. But I don't want Dad to know."

"Talk to me."

I blurt it all out, except for the part about the fight with

Hugh. As close as I am to Roger, I like keeping my marriage private.

"Ally, how awful for you. Do you feel you're getting the best medical care?"

"I have a good therapist, and I'm going to see a neurologist for a second opinion. But I didn't call you this week, did I?"

"No, we haven't talked since last weekend. Gosh, I feel terrible. Tell me what I can do."

"I mostly wanted to fill you in, but maybe we could get together soon, too."

"Absolutely. You could come out for the day, have lunch here."

Of course, any social engagement would surely have to be run by Roger's wife, Marion, who seems to prefer having Roger all for herself.

"That's sweet, but you don't have to go to any trouble. I just want to see you—and also, to ask you some questions."

I blurt out the last part without even seeing it coming—and against Erling's advice.

"Are you wondering if there's any family history with this sort of thing?"

"No one's mentioned that as a factor. But lately I've been thinking a lot about what happened when I was nine, finding Jaycee Long. Dissociative states are sometimes caused by past trauma, and I'm wondering if that experience could have been a trigger."

There's a long pause, and I can picture him doing his usual little scratch on the side of his head.

"I'm not sure how much I can help, but I'll try," he finally says. "Though wouldn't Dad be a better person to ask?"

"Probably, but if I start asking questions, I'm sure he'll get suspicious, and I don't want to upset him."

"Good point. Well, I'm happy to talk, and actually, you may not need to drive all the way out. Marion surprised me with tickets for the New York Philharmonic Sunday afternoon and then we're going to some friends' apartment for dinner. We could grab a drink after the concert—maybe around five? Marion can shop or head to our friends' place early."

That *is* more convenient for me, but I can't help but be bugged by the mention of the concert. Regardless of how many times I've invited him and Marion here for a Sunday brunch or suggested we grab a play and dinner in the city, he usually passes, bemoaning the fact that he's become a bit of a homebody since his early retirement from a hedge fund. And now Marion's organized a day in Manhattan without even factoring in me and Hugh. But really, I shouldn't be taken aback. From the moment Roger married her a few years ago, she's been boxing me out in lots of little ways that my brother doesn't even seem to notice.

"Are you sure? I don't want to throw off your plans."

"No, I'm dying to see you, Button. I want to be there for you."

"Thanks, Rog. That means a lot."

After agreeing to firm up our plans in the next day or so, we sign off. I get up to boil water for tea. Daylight has faded, and lights are blinking on in the endless high-rises visible from the apartment. Living here, with this breathtaking view of Manhattan at night, I'm always struck by how the building lights always seem dabbed on here and there at random, like the backdrop of a Broadway show.

I sip my tea and reflect on the conversation with Roger. I'm glad I asked for his help, and I'm grateful for the chance to see him even sooner than I'd hoped. But something makes my stomach knot, something beyond the fact that he'd planned to be in Manhattan and hadn't told me. That Marion had surprised him with tickets? And then I realize I've completely forgotten Roger's birthday. It was ten, no eleven, days ago.

Shit. It's like Gabby said—I've been distracted, forgetful. Was it because of having so much on my mind lately, or a precursor to my memory loss?

I shoot him a quick email apologizing and order him a cookbook that I'd eyed for him months ago. Roger's always been a bit of a bon vivant, someone who loves fine decor, the best wines he can get his hands on, and gourmet cooking.

Absentmindedly I glance at my phone and to my shock, notice it's almost five. Sasha is due momentarily. I set my laptop on the dining table and open it to the research notes she'd emailed for the podcast. Two minutes later the concierge rings to say my guest has arrived, and I use the time Sasha's on the elevator to swap my boots for ballet flats.

"Are you sure you're up to this?" she says as soon as I swing open the front door of the apartment. "I more or less invited myself."

"No, it's fine. Come in." She's carrying a wrapped bouquet of flowers and a tiny shopping bag. "Let me take your coat."

"First, these are for you." She hands me both packages. "I thought the flowers could cheer you up. And I've brought chicken soup, too. I know this deli makes the absolute best in the city."

"Sasha, you shouldn't have." On the surface it seems like a lovely gesture, but to me it's excessive. And from what I've learned about Sasha so far, she often has a secret agenda. I know to keep my guard up with her.

"Oh please, my pleasure," she gushes. "It's so hard to be sick, especially when your plate is as full as yours is."

For a second, I wonder if she's gotten wind of what happened to me. People I know in the field might have heard via the rumor mill of my bizarre visit at Greenbacks, learned it was me who was rolled out on a stretcher. But her expression doesn't seem to be alluding to it.

She shrugs off the strap of a quilted tote bag and slips out of her coat, revealing a striking drop-waist dress, black on top, with a row of black and white knife pleats on the lower half. It looks great with her blond bob. And it's sleeveless, emphasizing her perfectly buffed arms.

An awkward moment follows in which I can't take her coat because I'm holding her offerings. She ends up hanging up the coat herself and then follows me into the great room, where I set the soup on the counter and tear the paper off the bouquet. The flowers are a stunning orange, a type of rose I've never seen.

"These are amazing," I tell her as I pull a glass vase from one of the cabinets.

"I remember you saying your apartment was all white, so I thought you'd enjoy a pop of color on a gloomy day."

After I fill a vase with water and arrange the flowers, I carry it to the dining table, where I've gestured for Sasha to take a seat.

"Your place is absolutely *gorgeous*," she declares, scanning the room. "How long have you lived here?"

"About three years. We bought it right after Hugh and I were married."

"How did you two meet, anyway?"

"At a dinner party thrown by a mutual friend. Can I get you an espresso? Or a glass of chardonnay?"

There's a beat before she answers, and I sense she's considering saying wine, a chance to make the meeting more social, but fortunately she opts for the espresso instead. I'm not in the mood for chitchat. While I'm preparing our drinks, I talk over my shoulder, switching topics to the podcast.

By the time I set the two cups on the table, she's spread out a sheaf of papers and begins to brief me. As planned, Sasha's preinterviewed the main guest, Jamie Parkin, a female Wall Street veteran who's written a book on developing everyday fearlessness, and drafted questions for me to ask. She's also included a boatload of backup research on subjects such as grit and confidence in the workplace.

There's way more than I need here. I'm a major fan of research—you have to be, with financial topics—but too many statistics can suck the freshness and spontaneity out of an interview. Though I'm briefly tempted to tell Sasha this, I bite my tongue. Being research-crazy is probably good for her at this stage, and the bottom line is that I need projects to occupy her time.

"Let's focus for a few minutes on the last part of the

podcast," I tell her. As a favor, I'm allowing her to partici-
pate in the final segment of the show, a ten-minute "chat"
with me that I usually do with my producer, Casey. It's my
chance to riff on a current financial news headline or trend
and offer insights as to how it might affect listeners.

"I've already made a list of things that are in the air right
now, though that could change this week."

"Actually, I'd like to try a different tack this week," I tell
her. "Since the interview is going to be mainly about career
strategies, and not as much personal finance, I thought you
and I could chat about the financial mistakes people make
early on in their careers."

"You mean like buying a toasted white chocolate mocha
on the way to work instead of making coffee at home or in
the office kitchenette?"

"That's been overdone lately, so let's talk about factors
that have a much bigger impact. Credit card debt. Not opening an IRA. That's always a big mistake."

"If that's what you want." I detect a hint of sullenness in
her tone. She was clearly banking on me going with one of
her ideas.

"Yes, I think that will be best in the mix. . . . Unfortunately,
we're going to have to wrap up now." She's been here far longer
than I planned, and the conversation has started to drain me.
"I need to take care of a few other things before dinner."

"Of course," she says crisply, beginning to gather her
belongings—the stack of papers, manila folders, a fancy rollerball pen. "Thanks for taking the time today."

"And thank *you*. For the soup—and the flowers." I tug
my phone from my sweater pocket to check if Hugh's texted.

"Oh good, you found it," she says.

"Excuse me?"

"Your phone."

"Um, no, this is a spare." I don't recall mentioning my phone was MIA. "How did you know it was missing?"

"Because you called on Tuesday to say you lost it."

freeze. I spoke to *Sasha* on Tuesday? Does this mean she knows something about my whereabouts that day? For a moment I sit tongue-tied at the table, not sure how to play this.

"Don't you remember?" she asks.

"The two of us speaking?" I say finally, trying to fake awareness.

"No, you called the reception desk at WorkSpace. I guess you wanted to let Nicole know you'd lost your phone, but she'd already left for vacation so you talked to Carson. He told me when I dropped by later that day."

I pick up the notepad I've been using and tap it lightly on the table a couple of times, a feeble attempt at nonchalance.

"Did he mention where I was calling from?"

"No, he didn't," she says, clearly wondering why I'm in the dark.

"That was the day I started coming down with something, and the afternoon is a bit of a blur."

She furrows her brow. "Maybe you should get checked out."

"Oh, that doesn't seem necessary. I'm totally on the mend now."

I feel desperate to learn more, but my gut tells me Sasha's shared the extent of what she knows, and besides, it wouldn't be smart to pique her interest any further.

I rise and collect the espresso cups from the table and carry them to the counter. Sasha slips the last of her papers into her nylon Prada tote and rises from the table.

I lead her back to the foyer and retrieve her coat from the closet, and while I'm waiting for her to slip into it, I hear Hugh's key turn in the lock. Sasha glances quickly toward the door, looking startled. Before I have time to say, "It's my husband," Hugh steps through the doorway, reeking of rotisserie chicken and loaded down with a briefcase and two plastic grocery bags. He seems taken aback by the sight of the two of us standing there.

"Hugh, hi," I say. "This is Sasha Hyatt, the intern who's been working with me on the podcasts."

"Oh, right," he says, dropping the briefcase at his feet so he can shake her hand. "Nice to meet you."

Sasha spares him the head-to-toe assessment I've seen her give other men on a couple of occasions, but he's definitely gained her attention. She evaluates Hugh's face as if it's a designer handbag she's deciding whether to buy.

"Actually," she says after a moment, "I think we've already met."

Hugh narrows his eyes. "I'm sorry, but I'm drawing a blank."

"Now *I'm* drawing a blank," she admits. "But somewhere. I never forget a face."

He shrugs neutrally. "Someone told me the other day that I look like the guy in the new Volvo commercial. Maybe that's what you're thinking of. Will you excuse me?"

"Of course," she says as Hugh hurries with his bags and briefcase into the great room. Sasha appears mildly vexed, as if she senses my husband has charm to spare and she's been cheated of her share.

"See you Tuesday at the studio," I tell her, opening the door. "And thanks again for the goodies."

"You're welcome. Feel better."

As soon as I ease the door shut, it seems as if this weird tension has been siphoned from the space along with her.

"Feel *better*?" Hugh says when I join him at the island. He's unloading his purchases onto the counter.

"Yes, much," I say, sliding onto one of the barstools.

"Glad to hear that, of course, but what I meant was why was *Sasha* saying that? You didn't tell her what happened, did you?"

"God, no. But I had to explain being out of touch for a couple of days, so I said I'd been sick. *Have* you met her someplace?"

"No—at least not that I have any memory of. It almost seemed she was trying to be provocative."

"Yeah, well, I'm beginning to sense that's her MO."

I notice his attention suddenly snagged by the bouquet on the table.

"What was she doing here, anyway?" he asks. "I thought you were going to take it easy today."

"She was desperate to review some research with me before next week and basically invited herself over."

"*That's* annoying." He glances down at the food on the

counter. "I'm going to set all this up, but give me a minute to change, will you?"

"Sure. What can I do?"

"Nothing, just relax."

But as soon as he heads down the hall to the bedroom, I call the front desk at WorkSpace. Carson's shift must be ending around now, and I'm relieved when he picks up. I identify myself and ask if he remembers talking to me on Tuesday about my lost phone.

"Yes, did you find it?" he says.

"Unfortunately, not. Can I ask you a couple of questions, though? I was ill at the time and kind of discombobulated when we spoke."

"I figured. You sounded pretty frazzled."

Because I was beginning to separate from who I was?

"By any chance, do you remember the time of the call?"

"Uh, it must have been after lunch. Maybe around three, three-thirty?"

"And did I say where I was calling from?"

"No, but it sounded like you were on the street. You said you'd lost your phone somewhere and borrowed a stranger's to make the call."

"Right, right, a passerby was nice enough to loan me theirs," I say, winging it. "I wish I had the number so I could send a thank-you text."

"Unfortunately, I can't help you with that. It would be tough to go back through caller ID."

Damn it, I think. "Understood."

"Anything else I can be of assistance with?"

He sounds eager to be done, but I can't let him go yet.

"Nothing specific, no. I . . . I just hope I wasn't a bother. I didn't go on and on about what was wrong, did I?"

"No, you were fine. And no worries, we've all been there. Did you figure out the deal with the doctor?"

My heart jerks.

"Doctor? I told you I needed one?"

"It sounded like you had an appointment with someone, but you weren't sure of the exact time—I guess because you'd lost your phone. You were hoping Nicole would know, but she wasn't here. I think you mentioned a Dr. Early or something."

"Right, right," I say.

Okay, I've got another piece of the puzzle. It seems as if I was especially eager, maybe even desperate, to meet with Erling, but due to whatever mental distress I was experiencing, I must have lost track of when my next appointment was, even though Dr. Erling said she talked to me at nine that day. As I'm processing this detail, Carson is interrupted by someone with a question, and I realize I need to let him go. I thank him for his help and sign off.

Just as I set the phone down, Hugh saunters back into the great room, dressed in jeans and his heather green V-neck sweater. After shoving up the sleeves, he pops the plastic lid off the rotisserie chicken, whose juicy, herby scent, usually so inviting, turns my stomach.

"Something up?" he asks, grabbing a pair of poultry scissors.

"Sort of. That was Carson, one of the managers at

WorkSpace, and he's just filled me in about one detail from Tuesday."

"Really?"

"I apparently called the front desk that afternoon, sounding frazzled. I told him I'd lost my phone and had borrowed one from a stranger. I must have used it to look up the main number at WorkSpace before calling there."

"Wow," Hugh says, pausing. "What about your purse? Was that missing then, too?"

"Doesn't sound like it."

"So you may have ended up separated from your purse and phone at two different times."

"Right. And there's something else."

Hugh's started to carve the chicken, but he pauses again, the scissors in midair. "Tell me."

"According to Carson, I was trying to contact Nicole to see if I'd mentioned the time of my appointment with Erling."

"So you were already having memory issues?"

"*Or* I was just really desperate to see her and didn't have my phone to double-check my schedule."

"Do you think you were anxious to meet with her because of our argument?"

"Possibly. But I'm starting to wonder if something really upsetting happened to me on Tuesday, midday, which would explain those bloody tissues I told you about. Maybe I lost my phone when this—this incident occurred, or right afterwards, possibly because I was rattled. And then I started to come unglued and was anxious to see Erling."

Hugh nods his head lightly, pondering my words. He's

done cutting the chicken and pries off the lids from a couple of salads he's bought.

"Okay, but if the dissociative state actually kicked in on Tuesday afternoon," he says, "why don't you recall anything from late Monday night or Tuesday morning?"

"From what I've learned, memory loss in this kind of situation can include a period of time before the traumatic event you experienced. I guess in the same way someone with a concussion might not remember events immediately leading up to the injury."

"What do you think could have happened to you, Ally?"

"Maybe I was mugged?"

"But if you still had your purse later that day . . ."

"I could have struggled with the person but managed to save my purse. And gotten a nosebleed in the process."

He smiles ruefully. "I don't know whether your new theory makes me grateful or even more concerned."

"What do you mean?"

"It scares me to think of you in a bad situation in the city somewhere, but I'm also relieved to know I might not have done anything to instigate this hell you've been going through."

"You've been worried you *caused* this? Hugh, you can't think like that. Even if the fight did make me unravel, I was part of it, too."

"You're giving me a pass on the famous 'it-takes-two-to-tango' grounds?"

I lean across the counter and lace my fingers through his.

"Absolutely," I say. Feeling his hand in mine, I realize how little skin-to-skin contact we've had since yesterday. I want more than anything to be in sync with him again. Maybe this is a start.

During dinner I try to savor the food, as Erling suggested, but the chicken is dry, as if it's spent too many hours churning in one of those supermarket roasting furnaces, and the salads—coleslaw and macaroni, both dripping in mayo—are almost indistinguishable from each other. A glass of wine might help, but I've decided to swear off alcohol for at least another day.

"We've done nothing so far tonight but talk about me," I say, setting my fork down. "What's happening with the Brewster case?"

This is the case Hugh's currently in the thick of, and it's a pivotal one for him. It was probably tough for him to focus on it when I was missing.

"Unfortunately, there's not great news to report."

"Wait, what?" A swell of panic forms. Am I forgetting something *else*? "I thought it was going well."

"Seemed that way, but we had an ugly surprise this morning. It turns out a member of the company's senior team sent an email several months ago to several colleagues about possible improprieties related to the case. This is going to blow up in their faces—and ours."

"Oh, Hugh, I'm sorry." I empathize totally but at the same time I'm relieved this is a new development, not one I should have recalled. "I can't believe you have to deal with that and all *this* at the same time."

"Look, it's their own fault for not divulging earlier. But

I'm going to have to revise my strategy and pray there's a way to curtail the potential damage."

"If you need to work this weekend, don't hesitate on my account. Plus, I'm meeting Roger for a drink Sunday afternoon."

We end up crawling under the covers at around ten, iPads in our laps. Hugh, I notice, is halfway through a biography of Ulysses S. Grant. Do I remember that? Yes, yes. We talked about going uptown one day to see the Grant Memorial.

I open a novel I'd started reading over the weekend and try to connect with it again, but my eyes slide across the screen, unable to gain traction. After only a few minutes, Hugh snaps off his bedside light and flips onto his side, facing away from me. Though my libido currently seems to be on the lowest flame possible, I consider reaching over and running my hand along his thigh. We have sex several nights most weeks, and it might be good for me right now, fostering not only a connection with Hugh, but a sense of being fully present. Before I can make a move, though, I hear him begin to snore lightly.

I turn off my own light and lie wide-eyed in the darkness. Despite my exhaustion, sleep once more eludes me. After throwing off the covers on my side of the bed, I move down the hall to the great room. Lying on the coffee table is the pad I scribbled my timeline onto late last night. I grab a pencil and add in what I've learned today.

MONDAY
   evening: dinner, TV, argument

TUESDAY
  7:00: still in bed
  9:00-ish: took call from Dr. Erling
  9:00–9:17: sent emails
  Before 3:00: lost phone
  3:00–3:30-ish: called WorkSpace

WEDNESDAY
  Possibly lunchtime: bought food at Eastside Eats

THURSDAY
  8:05: arrived at Greenbacks

I stretch my legs out across the coffee table. Today's revelations aren't much but they're *something*. It's been hard to believe that a fight with Hugh over familiar ground could have derailed me so completely, and what I've found out today suggests that hunch is right.

I've also had a hard time wrapping my head around the idea of my fugue state being related to my discovery in the woods long ago. Yes, I'd been revisiting it in my mind lately, and it's definitely stirred up both memories and questions, but why would it knock my wheels off so many years later? It *can't* be that, can it? Regardless, I'm still eager to discuss the details with Roger.

What I'm left with is the *x factor*. A possibly traumatic event midday on Tuesday, one that I have no recollection of for the time being.

My thoughts stray back to today's session with Erling,

who wouldn't be pleased to know I was ruminating this way. I struggle up from the couch, intent on trying to fall asleep. Before returning to the bedroom, I grab my phone from the kitchen counter and plug it into the charger nearby. As I'm turning away, it pings with a text. Shocked, I see that the message is from Damien Howe:

Can we meet? I need to see you.

11

When I wake the next day shortly before eight, I immediately regret my second-night-in-a-row late-night session on the couch. My stomach is queasy and my head hurts.

At least I'm here at home again. And I'm fully aware of who I am.

When I traipse into the great room, I discover Hugh already hard at work, coffee mug by his side and files and briefs strewn across the dining table.

"Morning," he says, looking up with a smile. "How are you feeling?"

"Pretty good."

"Is it going to be a problem if I hog the table today?"

"Not at all. It's really nice to have you here."

He glances back at his yellow legal pad, covered with carefully jotted notes, but then quickly looks up at me again.

"And you're sure you're okay?"

"Yes, definitely." There's no point in whining about my headache when I have only myself to blame. And I'm certainly not going to admit to nausea. There's a chance that's due to fatigue as well, but it could actually be tied to the dull pulse of guilt I'm feeling from my response to Damien last night. Hugh's aware that Damien was more than a fling in my eyes, and he'd be annoyed—justifiably—to learn we were in contact, especially after the bizarre mystery of me turning up at Greenbacks. But I *have* to meet with Damien. I need to know if he has any clue why I arrived at his company out of the blue with my coat dripping wet and my brain on idle.

Okay, I'd texted back. When?

How about Tuesday? he'd said. Six o'clock?

Six o'clock always suggests cocktails to me, rather than, let's say, coffee, and there's no way I'm going down that road. I countered with Can you do five instead? and he'd agreed, saying he'd get back to me with a location.

There's another reason for five o'clock. This way I'll be home by around six, greatly limiting my chance of bumping into Hugh on his way into the building and thus having to deceive him about where I'm coming from.

Okay, so I won't have to lie, but still, it will be a sin of omission—because when Hugh asks about my day, I won't mention anything about the meeting. This isn't really how we do things as a couple. We're not in the habit of . . . I was about to tell myself we're not in the habit of keeping secrets from each other but that's untrue now, isn't it? My whereabouts from Tuesday to Thursday morning before 8:05 are a total secret to both of us.

After a breakfast of plain toast and tea, I grab my laptop and peruse a few headlines, but my attention soon flags. I toy with the idea of hitting the gym—it's been a week since I've worked out—but eventually decide against it. I'm scared,

I realize, about heading outside on my own. So I spend the next hours velcroed to the sofa, chiding myself for being such a sloth. At one point I slip into the bedroom to phone my dad, and though there's comfort in hearing his voice, it's painful that I can't tell him what's happened.

I'm relieved when finally, late in the day, Hugh suggests we take a walk in Central Park. As we emerge from the building, the air is crisp, and it's the first time since I left the hospital that I'm actually aware of the season. The trees in the park haven't peaked in color yet, but there's an autumn scent along the paths that triggers a slew of recollections for me—buying pumpkins as a girl at a farm stand near our home in Millerstown, watching a college boyfriend tear across a rugby field, driving through New England on a "girls' trip" with my mother the year before she died. If those memories are all there in my mind, tucked safely away, surely the ones from the missing days must be, too. I have to find a way to unearth them.

Hugh and I walk arm in arm through the park and end up eating dinner at a Japanese restaurant we both like. I feel more connected to the world suddenly—to the kick of the wasabi paste, the smell of the soy sauce, the image of Hugh using his chopsticks so adeptly. *Good*, I think, *Dr. Erling would be pleased. Certainly, this is the definition of present.*

"Any luck devising a new strategy for your case?" I ask Hugh.

He grimaces, plucking a piece of tuna roll. "I've managed to come up with a plan B, but if we win this, it's going to be a miracle."

"Please, Hugh, if you need to spend time in the office tomorrow, don't hesitate on my account."

He shakes his head. "I think I'm fine working from home, but I'll have to hunker down for the rest of the weekend."

Back at the apartment, I find a Scandinavian crime drama on Netflix, watch an episode and a half, and then dress for bed. I want sex tonight, I realize, as I massage lotion onto my arms and breasts. My loins aren't exactly on fire, but I yearn for that kind of contact with Hugh, for us being back in sync sexually. But when I peek my head into the great room, I discover that Hugh's still ensconced at the table, his brow furrowed in concentration and his fingers drumming lightly on the legal pad. I drift off to sleep alone.

Sunday morning proceeds pretty much like Saturday. Hugh does, however, squeeze in forty-five minutes for a run in the park along with his buddy Tyler, and I use the time to wander the apartment with a cup of tea, finding my bearings. I feel stronger, I realize, more *centered*.

Midday I text Roger and say there's no need for him to swing by later and pick me up as planned; I'll simply meet him at the bistro we've decided on. Later, when it's time to leave, Hugh urges me to let him play escort, but I tell him I want to try it on my own.

And it turns out I'm fine. As soon as I exit the building, in fact, the twinge of nervousness passes. It's crisp out again today, and sunny, too, one of those October afternoons promising that anything is possible. As I stride the few blocks uptown, I pass several familiar faces from the neighborhood, and a few neighbors nod hello. A little boy in a stroller smiles and gives me a joyful wave.

I suddenly feel like *me* again, I realize. A city girl with places to go and people to see. *This crazy episode is only a blip in my life*, I tell myself. I'm going to figure out what the hell caused the fugue state and then guarantee it never occurs again.

My mood sours, however, as I approach the entrance to the bistro and catch a glimpse, through the window, of Marion seated next to my brother, each with a wineglass. I can't believe it. I pause and consider my next step. I certainly can't ask her to leave; that would upset Roger too much. Instead, I'll have a quick drink and beat a retreat.

For half a minute I study them through the window. Marion's back is to me and she's shifted her position slightly, so I see only a sliver of my brother now. She's doing all the talking. I can tell because she has a way of bobbing or cocking her head to punctuate every thought, opinion, conviction, and critique.

I've never understood the allure she holds for my brother. I adored his first wife, Kaitlin. She was fun and irreverent—at least in the early days—but over time, years of infertility took a toll on her demeanor and their marriage. Roger had earned millions by that point, and he made sure Kaitlin was compensated generously in the divorce. When he retired early and moved back near Millerstown, he told me he wanted a quieter, easier life, one filled with hiking, kayaking, polishing his culinary skills, and occasional trips into the city for an influx of culture. He eventually bumped into Marion, a former high school classmate, and married her soon after.

I've always suspected that what he appreciates about the relationship is the lack of turmoil and angst, compared to the final years with Kaitlin. Marion has no children from her previous marriage and claimed to Roger she never wanted any. Plus, every inch of her seems to relish playing lady of the manor and keeping their life together humming pleasantly along. It just doesn't include me and Hugh much of the time.

I step away from my position on the sidewalk and push open the door.

"Hey, Ally, there you are," Roger says, leaping to his feet. He embraces me in a bear hug, and Marion rises, too, brushing my cheek with her lipstick-thick lips. She's wearing a crisp long-sleeved white blouse, open at the neck to reveal a gold and diamond pendant necklace. Her dark blond hair's cut short but with a stylish flip in the back.

"It's nice to see you," I say, doing my best not to seem vexed. "Please sit."

"I'm not staying, dear," Marion tells me. "I know you need time alone with Roger. But I couldn't pass up the chance to at least say hello."

That's funny because it seems that lately she's been more than happy to pass up any opportunity for that.

"Thank you for understanding."

She clasps my hands, squeezing my fingers so hard the knuckles pinch against each other. "We've *missed* you," she says. "And Hugh, too."

"Likewise."

Now she narrows her eyes, staring right into mine with a concerned but knowing look. I can smell her fragrance, a mix, it seems, of roses and jasmine. "You're always in our thoughts, dear. And we just want the best for you."

I'm not sure what her game is today. I'm almost certain Roger's stayed mum about our phone conversation, so this might be a simple power play, her way of pretending she's in the loop. Or maybe she's rummaging for info. Marion has a truffle hog's need to sniff and unearth.

"I appreciate that, Marion. And thanks for stopping by. I'll talk to Roger about the four of us getting together later in the fall."

"Unfortunately, as you know, it's not going to be for Thanksgiving this year. With your dad away and not doing the big meal, my younger brother Adam insisted we come to his place. Do you and Hugh have a back-up? I could always ask . . ."

"We're going to see Hugh's parents in Boston."

"Perfect." She graces me with another lip brush before she departs; Roger is treated to a squeeze of the arm.

"I hope you didn't mind," Roger says once we're both seated. "She thought it would be rude not to stop by."

"You didn't tell her what was going on, did you?"

"No, no, of course not. Though she's aware something's up because I've been preoccupied ever since you called. I'm so worried about you, Button."

"I'm actually feeling a little better today—and seeing you is already helping."

It's true. Being in Roger's steady, dependable presence anchors me, as it has since I was young—whether he was teaching me how to make scrambled eggs, explaining the stories behind the constellations, or sticking his head beneath my bed to prove there weren't any monsters lurking there.

At the same time, I'm a little surprised. The last time I saw Roger, two months ago when our father left for San Diego, his light brown hair along the side of his head was tipped with pewter, but he's almost entirely gray now. There was a time when, despite our age gap, we looked unmistakably like siblings—we both have full lips and hazel-colored eyes set slightly far apart. But it's hard to imagine anyone thinking that today.

"So give me an update," he says after the waitress has taken my order for a sparkling water. "Have you pieced together any more details?"

"Unfortunately, not. Those two days are a total dead zone."

"And they don't know what caused it?"

"Not so far. Though as I mentioned on the phone, there's a small possibility it was related to the whole Jaycee Long business."

"I know that was a terrible experience for you. But why would it play havoc with you *now*, after so many years?"

"Maybe I never fully processed things. And it's actually been on my mind quite a lot lately. Because—gosh, Rog, I haven't wanted to burden you with this, but Hugh and I have been having issues lately over whether or not to start a family. He definitely wants kids, and I originally thought I did, too, but I'm now balking."

"Ally, I'm so sorry." He reaches across the table and briefly clasps my hand. "Trust me, it's never a burden to have you share whatever is going on with you."

"Thanks—and I'm sure Hugh and I will work it out," I say. Though as the words spill from my mouth, I wonder how confident I really am that they're true.

"Anyway, I was hoping that speaking to you would help me fill in a few blanks about Jaycee Long."

"Blanks?" His face darkens with even more concern. "Are you saying there are parts you don't remember about that period either?"

"No, it's not that. Blanks is the wrong word. It's more that certain things still seem shrouded in mystery. Mom and Dad whispering. The *police* whispering. People in town staring at me once the word was out."

"Do you remember much about that day? Finding her?"

I smile grimly. "Pretty much. I'd hung around too long after school that afternoon instead of going straight home like I was supposed to, so I took a shortcut through the woods. Another no-no. While I was walking, I stumbled over this pile of leaves—and she was there. Practically underfoot."

My voice cracks. I take another deep breath and slowly exhale. "At first I didn't even realize what I was looking at."

"That must have been so awful, Ally."

"Tell me what *you* remember, will you?"

"I remember how shaken you seemed. And how sad I felt for you. . . . Dad must have called and I decided to come home."

The waitress interrupts before I can say anything, setting my water on the table.

"But weren't you already there for some reason?" I ask. "I remember sitting with you in the family room that Friday night when the police talked to Dad and Mom in the kitchen."

He pulls back in his chair. "God, you're right. I was going to travel that summer before grad school, and I came home for a few weeks in the spring."

"I take it Dad filled you in on everything then?"

"He did, though some of it's fuzzy now. I remember the

girl was only two and that she'd died from a blow to her head. I also know Dad and your mom were pretty distraught."

"I was worried they were mad at me. For taking the shortcut, for hanging at school."

"I don't think they had any room left over to be mad. For starters, they were incredibly concerned about the impact the experience would have on you, and I remember your mom working so hard to find you a good therapist. You know, I wonder if it would be of any use for you to talk to the psychologist you saw back then. See if she has any insight."

"Louise Hadley was her name. But she was at least in her late forties. She might not even be alive."

"Let me ask around and see what I can find out."

"I'd appreciate that. What did you mean by 'for starters,' though?"

"What?"

"You said that *for starters* they were worried how finding the body would affect me. What else?"

"Oh, they weren't happy about all the time you had to spend with the cops. They were afraid that being questioned was as tough for you as finding the body."

"It *was* tough. The first time was bad enough—when they came to the house and I had to go to the woods with them and point out where she was. But then a day or two later I had to talk to them all over again."

"Ah, right. They didn't take you to the police station, did they?"

"No, the second interview—and I think there was a third, too—was in a room at some kind of municipal center." It's still all there in my mind's eye. The yellow walls. The small chair

I sat in. The huge pit in my stomach. "I guess it was where they took kids so it would be easier for them to talk. But it was unnerving. I didn't understand why they kept asking me the same questions over and over again."

"They had an agenda."

I feel a prick of anxiety. "What do you mean?"

"Are you sure you want to get into this?"

"Of course."

Roger sighs. "One guy—I don't even remember his name—told Dad and Lilly they thought you were being evasive."

"Evasive? What?"

"I'm sure he was a total jerk."

"If I seemed evasive, it was because I was shell-shocked," I say, disturbed by his revelation. I can feel my pulse quickening. "And I was worried that *they'd* be upset about the shortcut part, too. That maybe I'd gone someplace I wasn't allowed to."

Roger turns his attention to a small bowl of homemade potato chips he must have ordered with his wine. "You want one?" he asks. "They're totally decadent but worth it."

"No thanks," I say. His sudden shift in focus confuses me. "Is there something you're not saying?"

He sighs, clearly conflicted. "Yes, there's a bit more, though I hate to lay it on you like this. They told Dad they thought you were holding something back."

My heart's jackhammering at this point, propelled by a weird mix of indignation and alarm.

"But what could I have been holding back?" I ask. "It's not like I saw someone put her—" A thought explodes in my head like a firecracker. "Wait, are you saying they thought I had something to do with her death?"

"God no, I can't imagine that. Okay, maybe for five seconds they did. But you were *nine*. And there wasn't a shred of evidence to support it."

Roger reaches across the table and clasps my hand again. "Ally, listen to me. You can't let this get under your skin. Cops are trained to be suspicious of *everyone*. And it became obvious pretty quickly that the mother and that sketchy boyfriend of hers—Frank Wargo—must have done it."

"Why weren't they ever arrested?" I ask. I had looked up the story in the local paper several years later and seen both their pictures. Wargo and the gaunt, straggly-haired mother, Audrey Long.

"From what Dad told me, they had these convoluted alibis that turned out to be hard to puncture. As I recall, the girl had been missing for a couple of days, but the mother hadn't reported it until the same day you found her. She said that she thought the girl was with the boyfriend, who sometimes took care of her when the mother worked, but it turned out Wargo wasn't even in town. Or something like that."

"Do you think they're both still in the area?"

"I heard once that she is, but I don't think anyone's seen hide nor hair of him. He might still have family there, though. He was a few years behind me in school and I vaguely remember him."

"Were there any other suspects?"

"Not that I was aware of. Let me see what I can find out on that, too. The Millerstown chief of police occasionally joins a weekly guys' breakfast I go to at the diner. I'll give him a ring and ask for a bit of background. See if there were any developments."

"It would be good to know."

I reach for my coffee cup and notice my hand is trembling slightly.

"Ally, look, please don't think about this another second," Roger says. "I didn't mean to upset you."

"It's okay. I think it helped to talk about it. And I'm glad you told me about the cops being suspicious. Maybe on some level I always sensed that, and it added to my stress."

"Okay, but give me your word you won't dwell on it. None of that matters now."

"I swear."

Roger insists on walking me back to my building, promises to call me soon, and asks me to pick a weekend to come out to his place with Hugh. We hug tightly before parting. I try to draw comfort from the embrace, but I'm too fraught now to feel anything. Something seems to gnaw at me. What happened to that city girl from an hour ago, the one who was sure she had the world by the tail?

Once I'm in the apartment I find Hugh where I left him, hard at work at the dining table. He seems relieved to see me back safely, but he's also preoccupied, and after I promise to fill him in later, he buries his nose in his papers again.

I kick off my shoes and head to the den. I consider watching a movie to distract myself, but after I've settled onto the love seat, I don't bother turning on the TV or even a lamp. I simply sit in the waning light, thinking.

For the first time in a long time, I allow myself to travel

fully back to the April afternoon when I found Jaycee. The woods were so hushed, I remember, and the ground slightly spongy from a recent storm. There were piles of dead and decaying leaves left on the ground from the previous fall, and I trampled through them happily, not caring about my shoes.

Jaycee was hidden under one of those piles. I *felt* rather than saw her at first, nearly tripping over something. Curious, I glanced downward. My gaze fell on a sliver of white that didn't seem to belong. I kicked a section of leaves out of the way, and the wind did the rest, suddenly revealing her pale white face, eyes open. I lurched back in shock.

It's only a doll, I told myself. I quickly kicked the leaves back into place, thinking I shouldn't have disturbed them. And then I ran, so fast that even now, sitting in the fading light, I can still recall how much my lungs burned.

Leaning back against the cushions, I lift up my legs and tuck my feet underneath me. The room is as quiet as the woods were that day. I close my eyes, and after a moment a thought worms its way into my brain, something I'd buried deep in my memory and forgotten until just now.

I told a lie back then about finding the body. I lied to my parents, and to the police. I even lied to the therapist who wanted so much to help me.

12

SESSION WITH DR. ERLING

By the time my Monday appointment with Erling rolls around, I'm desperate to see her and unload. I'm also eager to continue the "detective work," hoping this time it produces results.

"So," she says as soon as I'm seated. "Tell me how you're doing, Ally." She laces her fingers together in her lap. There's no wedding band on her left hand so I've always assumed she's not married.

I give her a brief recap of my morning—that I managed to do a smidgen of work on my next column and even ventured outside for a while, having coffee and reading the newspaper at the neighborhood Le Pain Quotidien. But then I quickly take her back to my meeting with Roger.

"I know you said I should give my brain a rest," I say, "but I had a drink with my brother yesterday and ended up asking him to clear up some of the mystery about that case years ago. It was a bit upsetting—I mean, you obviously knew that it would be—but it was also good to understand more about what happened."

"How was it upsetting, Ally?"

"Roger said the police told my parents they thought I was being *evasive*. I suppose in hindsight I should have realized that something was off, because after the police talked to me at the house, they did a couple more interviews at this other location. Roger said they might have actually considered me a *suspect*."

There's a few seconds' pause before she speaks.

"That you'd been involved in the little girl's death?" she says.

"Yes. . . . The idea of it makes me sick—that they thought I could have hurt her. There was a story in the news once about two kids luring a toddler away from his mother in a shopping mall and then killing him, and I suppose it was natural for the cops to wonder."

"Can you think of any reason you might have seemed evasive to them?"

I take a deep breath, steeling myself to say this out loud for the first time.

"Because I *was*. Oh god, I can't believe what I'm about to tell you. I misled everyone back then."

"What was it you weren't truthful about?"

"The *timing* of everything. The day I came across the body. When I told my parents about finding Jaycee, I said it happened that afternoon, on a Friday. But I really discovered her two days before, on Wednesday. . . . And I only remembered that I'd lied when I came home from seeing Roger yesterday. Something was eating at me on the walk back, and finally, I found myself staring at this piece of truth that I'd stuffed away all these years."

It's a relief to finally spit it out, but it hasn't stopped the awful churning in my stomach.

"Why do you think you waited to tell anyone what you'd found?" Erling asks.

I take a minute to consider before answering. It's been a question I've been asking myself over and over since last night.

"I was worried my mom would be upset with me for taking the shortcut. I sometimes walked in those woods with her, but I was never supposed to go in there alone. Plus, I kept trying to convince myself I hadn't found anything bad, that maybe I had only seen an abandoned doll. But I couldn't get the image of her out of my mind, and I finally snuck back on Friday and looked from a distance. The mound was still there so I went home and told my mom."

"About Jaycee, but not about the time lapse."

"Right. I let her believe I'd just taken the shortcut and found the body. I must have decided not to make things worse for myself by saying I'd been sitting on the truth for two days. . . . And I allowed myself to forget the real story."

"How does it feel to bring it to the surface after all this time?"

I throw up my hands and at the same time feel my eyes prick with tears.

"I'm glad I remembered. I am. It seems important. But at the same time, I feel—*ashamed*. That lie was unfair not only to my parents but to the police, too."

"It makes sense that as a child you didn't want to disappoint your parents and told a lie to protect yourself. Lots of children do that, and it's nothing to be ashamed about."

Her tone is filled with assurance, and I nod in appreciation.

"By the way, I've already taken steps to update the police," I say. "I called Roger last night after I remembered, and he's going to talk to the police chief, whom he knows. I doubt that it will make any difference all these years later, but still, I want to get it off my chest."

"That seems like a very reasonable next step."

"Do you think it's possible that discussing the murder in the sessions with you finally made the memory surface? And that the guilt and shame I've felt about lying were the reason I . . . I lost myself?"

"What do *you* think?"

"Maybe. And it could also be one of the things making me confused about the idea of having kids with Hugh."

She holds it a beat.

"Why did you say with Hugh?"

"What?" I'm not following.

"You said, 'the idea of having kids with Hugh.' Do you feel conflicted about having children in general—or specifically with Hugh?"

"God, I'm sure that was simply a manner of speaking," I say, taken aback. "I love Hugh. I do. I want things to return to normal."

"I'm interested in hearing how things went with him this past weekend."

A sigh escapes my lips involuntarily. I dread articulating

what I'm feeling and possibly validating what she seems to be hinting at.

"Things are awkward between us at moments. Hugh's been attentive, but sometimes I sense we're like two strangers walking toward each other on the street and trying to anticipate which way the other is going to move so we don't collide, but we keep getting it wrong."

I elaborate: the weird silences at times during meals; the almost total lack of physical contact; Hugh's preoccupation with his case; the fact that last night he wolfed down Chinese takeout for dinner and immediately resumed working again.

"Can you set aside time tonight to sit together and talk for a while?" she asks. "Hugh might be even more concerned about you than he's expressing and needs help opening up."

"Yes, I can probably make that happen. And you're right, I know he's been concerned. It turns out he was really freaked out believing that our fight triggered my fugue state, though I told him I have doubts about that."

She cocks her head.

"Because?"

"The little information I *do* have suggests it began later the next day. For one thing, I sent out these totally coherent emails Tuesday morning."

"Disconnecting from reality can sometimes be a gradual process. You might have felt like yourself Tuesday morning, but as the day wore on, you became more distressed about the fight."

"But what about the tissues, then?"

"Tissues?" She glances down at her notes.

"The ones I found in my coat pocket—with dried blood?"

"Right, yes, we talked about that."

"What I'm thinking," I say, "is that the tissues are related to whatever incident caused me to dissociate. Something really stressful might have happened to me on Tuesday, and the stress ended up causing a nosebleed."

Her lips part ever so slightly, and I wait for a comment. But instead she sits quietly, studying me with her deep brown eyes.

"I get your desire for immediate answers, Ally," she says finally. "I also see why you wanted to speak to your brother. But it's really essential for you to keep your stress level down and allow your brain to recover at its own pace. Let the detective work take place here in our sessions. That's the best way to regain your footing completely and avoid triggering a relapse."

"Okay, I understand," I say, slightly chastened. "And do you think if I stop trying so hard, I *will* remember one day?"

"That's definitely possible, yes. But not always the case. It's important to recognize that memories can become so seriously fractured that they're not retrievable. We're out of time, but we can discuss this more when I see you Thursday."

I glance quickly at my watch, thinking she must be mistaken. But we *are* out of time.

And I feel almost worse than when I arrived.

13

As soon as I return to the apartment, I head to the fridge, hesitate, and then finally pour myself a glass of pinot grigio from a bottle that Hugh's already opened. I feel edgy as hell, and I know a few little yoga poses aren't going to make a difference.

I was really counting on today's session with Erling to move me forward, but it seems to have left me in even greater turmoil. I notice that the back of my top is drenched in sweat.

It's going to take a while to feel grounded again, I remind myself. Memories will take time to surface, too. And covering certain topics—my relationship with Hugh, my lie years ago—is bound to churn me up. I have to be patient with the process.

Maybe coming clean with the police this week will ease this new wave of anxiety. When I called Roger last night, the dinner party with friends was clearly still going on—I could hear wine-buzzy, winding-down chatter in the background—but he said of course he could talk. I expected him to be surprised by my admission, but he sounded more than that. His words caught a couple of times in his throat.

"I see," he'd said. "Well, you must have been very frightened back then. Would you like me to share this information
when I speak to the chief?"

"Yes, please."

"Will do. I probably should get back to the table, but I'll
give him a call tomorrow—and let you know as soon as I
have any news."

I guess I'd been hoping for him to say my actions back
then were completely understandable, and he did urge me
not to worry before he hung up, but I sensed that the revelation troubled him. Does he think less of me, that I'm a
little liar? Does he suspect there's more to the story than
I've let on?

My brother's reaction made me reluctant to update Hugh
last night. I *will* tell him, but not immediately, not when he
has so much on his mind.

Which means *two* sins of omission, of course. This and
the coffee with Damien tomorrow. Thank god Gabby's on
her way over now—I need the comfort of her presence.

Wineglass in hand, I head back to the bedroom, kick
off my shoes, and change into lounge-y pants and a sweater.
Then, for a while, I wander aimlessly around the apartment,
like someone who can't recall where she left her keys or set
down a glass. I realize that on some level, I *am* searching,
looking for the missing days. I know Erling keeps urging me
to relax, but if I knew where I'd been and what I'd been
doing, maybe I could make better sense of everything else.

Her last comment from the session echoes in my head:
that I might *never* remember. No, I can't accept that yet.

Finally, Gabby texts me to say she's five minutes away,

and then only seconds later, it seems, the buzzer to the apartment door is sounding and she's striding in, all five feet eleven inches of her. She's swaddled in a beige, drape-y shawl-collared coat, and her long red hair is tied in a high ponytail.

"Wait," I exclaim, spotting the aluminum roller bag she's hauling behind her. "Did you come straight from the airport?"

"Yup," she says, embracing me. "I couldn't wait. Omigod, I'm so relieved to see you."

"Same here." The mere sight of her has already begun to soothe my ragged nerves.

Leaving her bag behind in the foyer, she trails me into the great room.

"Are you up for wine?" I ask. "I've got a bottle already open."

"Just a splash. I don't want to crash too early or I'll wake up at two A.M. and never get back to sleep. Tell me what I've missed."

I've been keeping Gabby up to date by email, though I haven't told her yet about my recovered memory. I'm nearly certain she won't judge me harshly when I do, but I feel like I need to share it with Hugh first.

"Not much. I managed to do a little work today. Saw my therapist. Baby steps, really."

As Gabby settles onto the couch, I grab the wine bottle and an extra glass and plop down next to her. She shrugs off her coat and unwinds the scarf that's been wrapped around her neck. She's wearing jeans and a tight black jersey top, along with some of her jewelry—an amulet around her neck and eight or nine bangles and ribbon bracelets, each one unique but fabulous in combination. Gabby has an enviably stylish but nonchalant way of dressing that I've never been able to master. I'm useless at nonchalant.

"So just so I'm clear," she says after I've filled her wineglass, "the strategy is, basically, take it easy, see the therapist a couple of times a week, and get a second opinion from a neurologist."

"Yup, and suck away on Altoids to stay in the moment. I still can't believe this has happened. I don't *do* unraveling."

Gabby smiles. "That's for sure. Do you like this therapist? I mean, you went to her originally for a whole different reason."

"I do like her, and this latest stuff is in her wheelhouse. She's worked regularly with people who've experienced trauma."

"And she's been helpful?"

"It's been good to vent, but the process is going to take time. And she told me today that my memories might actually be too 'fractured' to retrieve, which is driving me crazy."

"I've already given you my opinion on that front. Hire a private detective. Once he's figured out where you went, it might trigger you to remember what you were doing."

"You probably think I'm going to hire someone superhot who calls himself a private dick, and that you could date him after he's done with my case. But I haven't spotted any Chris Hemsworth types in the mix."

She raises a ginger eyebrow. "You've started looking?"

"Just a basic Google search, that's all. It looks like there's a wide range of options. At one end are the really big agencies, which help companies deal with major risks and security issues. And then there are some small, local operations, often made up of ex-cops or ex-military guys."

"Try one of them."

I let out a long sigh. "Yeah, maybe I should. Plus, it's not simply a matter of wanting to know where I was those days. I keep wondering if something happened to me last Tuesday, something bad."

"While you were in this so-called fugue state?"

"Either in it or immediately beforehand, and *that's* what made me disconnect. Not the argument with Hugh."

Absentmindedly, Gabby uses her right foot to wiggle off the black suede ankle bootie on her left foot and then performs the same maneuver on the opposite side.

"Here's a thought," she says, once her legs are tucked beneath her on the couch. "What if you were freaked out by a bad thing that happened to someone *else*?"

"You mean like seeing a person being attacked?"

"Right. Or being hit by a car or, god—jumping from a building. *Something*. There was this woman I knew ages ago, a big-shot lawyer who dated my cousin Bradley. I bumped into her a couple of years ago and she told me she'd left her fancy law firm to get an MFA in *poetry*. And when I asked her why, she said that on one single day in Manhattan, she came across three different scenes with cops standing around a dead body under a white sheet. Three dead bodies all in one *day*! And it threw her so much she ended up changing her life entirely. That kind of stuff can fuck with your head."

"Your theory would explain the tissues I found in my pocket," I say, rolling the concept around in my head. "If someone near me was injured, I might have tried to stop the flow of blood."

"Exactly."

I circle the rim of my empty wineglass with a finger. Leave it to Gabby to see the matter from a fresh perspective.

"Okay, that's definitely worth mulling over," I say. "Now, if you're so damn good at this, tell me why I ended up at Greenbacks Thursday morning."

She takes a long drink of wine, then shakes her head. "Not sure on that one. Why do *you* think you did?"

"You sound like my therapist! I have no clue—but I'm hoping Damien might. I'm meeting him for coffee tomorrow."

"Danger, Will Robinson. Danger."

She knows how nuts I was over Damien, and how crushed I was when it ended.

"You think I'll try to tear his pants off the minute I set eyes on him."

"You said it, not me."

"I simply want to find out if he has an inkling of why I went to his company."

That's not a hundred percent accurate, I realize as soon as I say it. Yes, I'm eager to learn what I can from Damien, but I'm starting to think it's more complicated than that. I want to make sure that his most recent image of me isn't of a totally unglued woman. And, as much as I hate to admit it, I'm curious as to what his life is like now.

"But you already said you checked your email and you two haven't had any recent contact. What can he provide that's more than a wild guess?"

"At the moment I'll take anything I can get my hands on, including wild guesses."

I reach for the bottle of wine and raise it off the coffee table, flashing Gabby a look that asks if she wants more.

"Un poco."

I don't add any to my own glass. I'd love more wine, but my better instincts override the urge. Instead I jump up, grab a bottle of Perrier from the fridge, and carry it to the table along with two glasses. While I pour us each a few glugs of water, Gabby yanks the tie from her ponytail and shakes out her hair so that it fans out around from her head like a wildfire.

"I admit, part of me wants to set eyes on Damien again," I say, back on the couch. "The old touching-a-bruise thing. But if it wasn't for the chance of getting information from him, I wouldn't have responded to his text."

"Have you told Hugh?"

I glance away. "No, but not because I'm trying to deceive him. I'm just having a hard time slipping back into a groove with Hugh again, and I don't want to make it worse."

"What do you mean?"

"When we're together, it feels like we're on one of those awkward third dates—you know, the kind when, despite the fact that everything seemed great on dates one and two, you can't recapture the rhythm."

"Have you slept together already?"

"What?" Her question catches me off guard. Is she asking if I've had sex with Hugh since this happened? The answer, of course, is no.

"I'm asking about this imaginary third date you're on. Have you already fucked?"

"Gabby, it was just a dumb analogy."

"I'm trying to determine what made those first two dates so good. Maybe you need to figure out whatever it was."

"Okay, I see what you mean. Of course, there's still the kid issue. I bet he's terrified about bringing it up again."

"Well, he's going to have to chill on the topic for now."

Gabby untucks her legs and reaches for her boots.

"You're leaving?" I moan.

"I hate to bail, but if I don't beat it home soon, I'm afraid I'll pass out on your couch."

"But I haven't even asked about you yet. About London . . ."

"I'll call you tomorrow and fill you in," she says, stuffing her feet back into her boots. "And let's have dinner soon—whenever you're up to it."

"What's happening with that new guy you're seeing—Jake? Any potential there?"

She shrugs. "Reply hazy. Ask again later."

We rise and I thank Gabby profusely for coming by. After seeing her to the door and hugging her good-bye, I retreat back to the couch and further contemplate her theory: that I might have *observed* a traumatic event. That I was a witness rather than a victim.

I should have come up with that myself. I've always been intrigued with behavioral finance, the study of the influence of psychology on investors, including selective inattention, how we don't always notice what's going on around us and instead see only what we *expect* or want to see. I've been so focused on myself, on trying to figure out what happened to *me*, that I've failed to imagine a different scenario.

I quickly grab the pad on the coffee table and add a note about Gabby's theory to the timeline I've drafted.

After traipsing down to the bedroom alcove, I open my laptop and do another online search for detective agencies, narrowing it to smaller operations, most of which promise a range of services—like determining the whereabouts of a loved one, digging for possible dirt on a new boyfriend met via the internet, verifying a potential employee's references, or proving whether or not your spouse is shagging someone else. All the agencies promise discretion, a guarantee that no one will have to know you've hired an investigator.

There's one agency I keep coming back to: Mulroney and Williams Private Investigations. Two mid-fortysomething-looking partners, one a former New York City police detective, the other a former Navy SEAL. *Ha, surf and turf,* I think. Their bios highlight their long records and commendations, which I have absolutely no way of completely verifying—unless, of course, I hire them to do it.

A tab on their website says Missing Persons and I click there next—because that's what this is really about, right? I'm looking for a missing person: me during those two days.

The resulting page spells out their approach: they interview, gather physical evidence, do surveillance, in certain instances using wiretaps and global positioning devices. I love the final line: "Sometimes just having a professional outsider ask questions and look in different places is the key." God, that's what I need. Not the wiretaps or a GPD (too late for that!), but rather someone asking questions and looking in different places. And coming up with the truth.

Returning to the home page, I find a contact form, requesting a few personal details as well as information about the case. I type in a brief summary of the situation, bite my lip, and then hit send. It's not as if I've actually hired them. I'm simply making inquiries.

I return to the living area and clear the coffee table. The sun has set, and the city is beginning to sparkle. My mind circles back to another theory of Gabby's, about the way back into my usual groove with Hugh. Dr. Erling seemed to be encouraging that as well.

After setting the wineglasses in the dishwasher, I swing open the door to the pantry cupboard and scan its contents. Hugh is due home at seven—I told him there was no rush since Gabby was stopping by—and it would be really nice, I realize, to have dinner waiting, a homemade dish since we've been subsisting on takeout. The larder's close to bare, but I spot two cans of green olives and a box of penne.

What I'll make, I decide, is a simple meal my mother discovered on a trip with my dad to France a couple of years before she died. Pasta with a sauce made of mashed olives, extra virgin olive oil, a dash of cream, and grated parmesan. I check the fridge and see we have a small carton of cream that, miraculously, has not yet expired. And there's even a baguette in the freezer.

The plan energizes me, makes me feel a little giddy. I run the olives through the blender and set a large pot of water to boil on the stove top. I pull cloth napkins from the drawer along with matching place mats. And, yup, candles.

I switch on the pin lights in the ceiling above the dining area. As I set the first place mat, my gaze registers on the center of the table and I jerk in surprise. The orange roses that Sasha brought are no longer sitting in their vase here.

Hugh was working at the table much of yesterday, and perhaps he moved the vase out of his way. We ate takeout on the couch last night, which means I wouldn't have necessarily noticed they'd been displaced.

I swirl around, letting my gaze sweep across the great room, from the kitchen island, to the small chest near one of the armchairs, to a console table against the wall.

But the flowers aren't anywhere. I've clearly done something with them—and don't remember it at all.

14

With my breath caught in my throat, I tear down the hallway to the back of the apartment, checking the den, the bedroom, my work alcove, even the bathroom. No sign of the roses anywhere.

Returning to the living area, I search once more with just my eyes. It's as if they were never here, that I've simply conjured them up in my imagination. I circle to the far side of the island and pop the lid off the trash bin. And there they are, shoved deep inside, their thorny stems snapped in half so they'll fit in the bin.

My heart's hammering. I must have tossed them out last night, after dinner, because there are a few pieces of uneaten spring rolls scattered beneath. Pivoting, I fling open the door to the pantry closet, and sure enough, there's the vase. Washed. Sitting in its usual spot.

I plop onto one of the barstools, pressing a hand to my forehead. *Think*, I command myself. Maybe I threw the flowers away with my brain on autopilot, planning for the next day, thinking ahead to the podcast on Tuesday. But I don't have even the faintest memory of removing them from the vase, or trying to avoid the thorns, or rinsing out the vase afterward.

I snatch a fresh pad of paper from a drawer and scribble down every activity I can recall from last night and today: Chinese takeout with Hugh after my meeting with Roger; a bath, bed, breakfast this morning; working at Le Pain; the appointment with Dr. Erling; Gabby. What am I missing?

I breathe in for a count of four, hold it, release. And then repeat. The breathing technique ends up helping a tiny bit. So does resuming my focus on dinner. I turn the boiling water down to a simmer, scrape the olive paste from the blender into a ceramic bowl, heat a half cup of cream, then pop the baguette into the oven to warm. Creating this respectable meal from the little I had on hand is as close to a loaves-and-fishes-style miracle as I've ever pulled off in the kitchen, but I'm still too unsettled to truly relish the moment.

Should I call Erling and tell her about the flowers? I wonder.

I'm lighting the candles on the table when I hear Hugh's key in the lock a little after seven.

"What's this?" he asks, eyeing the table.

"I thought you could use a home-cooked meal for a change."

"That's sweet, but you shouldn't have gone to all the trouble."

"Honey, trust me. It's that olive pasta dish my mother learned to make in France. Easy-peasy."

"Uh, okay. Give me ten or so, will you?"

He heads to the bedroom, and by the time he returns, changed out of his suit, I've drained the penne and stirred it with the sauce. I'm still rattled but determined to make the evening with Hugh as pleasant as possible. After setting the serving bowl on the table, I pluck the bread from the oven and finally take my seat.

"I was craving pasta without even knowing it," Hugh says, heaping penne into my bowl and then his.

I smile, pleased that he seems more engaged than when he first walked in. "Any progress on the Brewster case?"

"I reviewed the strategy with one of the senior partners today, and he seems satisfied that it's the best we can do. Hopefully we can minimize the damage."

"How could the client be so stupid? Didn't they realize that emails last forever?"

"If people were smart, they'd never put *anything* in an email . . . but anyway, how was Gabby?"

"Good. It was a relief to finally talk to her face-to-face about everything."

He nods, snapping off the end of the baguette. I sense he's wondering how much Gabby knows about the issue in our marriage. I take care not to criticize Hugh to Gabby, but the kids' matter has been weighing on me so heavily in the last weeks, I felt I had to share it.

"Gabby thinks I should hire a private detective," I add.

He looks alarmed. "You mean to figure out where you were?"

"Right. I checked out places online today and even sent a query to one."

"They can be really pricey, Ally."

"But it would hardly be a frivolous expense," I say, surprised at his knee-jerk reaction. Doesn't he want answers as much as I do?

"No, I understand. I'm just not sure what one of these guys would be able to tell you."

"Many of them specialize in missing persons."

"I know. Our firm often uses private investigators on cases, and thanks to technology, they can turn up a lot these days. But one of the key ways they find missing people is surveillance. How would that work with you? There's nothing to surveil because you're home now."

I shrug, half chagrined, half annoyed at his response.

"There doesn't seem to be any harm in checking it out," I say.

"You just have to be prepared for the fact that there might not be much they can do—though they wouldn't necessarily tell you that up front."

"I get it, Hugh, and I'm not going to give money to some con artist. But I have to figure out where I was. It's driving me nuts."

"Of course—I understand. But I also think it's important to focus on the present, how you're doing *now*. I'm eager to hear what the neurologist will say on Wednesday."

"Speaking of not getting one's hopes up, I hope you're not banking too much on that. They were pretty clear at the hospital that my situation wasn't the result of a neurological event."

"At least we'll be crossing all our *t*'s." He rests his fork on the rim of the pasta bowl and studies me. There's something weirdly cool and distant in his gaze. But then he lays a hand over mine. "How are you feeling about doing the podcast tomorrow?"

"Pretty good, I guess."

"Would there be any merit in postponing it a week?"

It's not a bad question, especially in light of what's happened with the flowers. Maybe I should lie low for a few more days and not push my luck. And yet I can't stand the idea of bailing.

"It's such short notice at this point, Hugh. It wouldn't be fair."

"But will it be too stressful? I thought you were being encouraged to take it easy."

"I'll be fine. I mean, it's not like it's super stressful for me anymore."

"You don't sound a hundred percent convinced."

I glance down, aimlessly stabbing pieces of penne.

"Something happened tonight," I say. "Not anything big, but it's scaring me a little."

"What do you mean?"

"You remember Sasha, the woman who came by Friday night and brought those roses? Well, at some point last night or this morning, I managed to stuff them in the garbage and wash the vase without any memory of doing so."

"Ally . . ."

"It's like I was in some kind of *mini*-fugue state. I'm wondering if I should call Dr.—"

"Ally, hold on. You haven't forgotten anything. I tossed the flowers out."

I've been massaging my brow with one hand, my gaze

still lowered, and as Hugh's words sink in, I lift my head and stare at him.

"*You* tossed them out?" I say, simultaneously relieved and baffled. "If they were in your way, why not just move them? I'm sure they weren't cheap."

He shrugs. "The petals had started to drop. Gosh, I'm sorry to throw you off that way."

"You tossed them out because the petals were dropping?"

This makes no sense. Hugh does his share around the house—he helps clear the table and load and unload the dishwasher, handles his own laundry, makes the bed on days he's not up ahead of me. But I've always accepted that he's fairly clueless when it comes to "decor" stuff; that is, he would never zero in on things like pillows that require fluffing, cloth napkins that have seen better days, *or* flowers that need tossing. This gesture doesn't fit with the man I know. I half expect him to cup the skin at the base of his chin with both hands and tear upward, revealing he's a stranger wearing a latex mask of my husband's face.

"That wasn't the main reason," he admits. "I was trying to concentrate, and the smell was driving me crazy. It never occurred to me you would wonder."

"No problem," I say after a moment. I allow a sense of relief to take hold, embracing the realization that another sliver of my life hasn't been snatched away. "And it's good to hear, of course."

"Again, sorry."

"Do you want more pasta?"

"I do, but I better not. I've still got a few hours of work ahead of me."

"Why don't you let me handle the dishes, then."

"That would be great. Chip and I agreed to go over a bunch of notes on the phone, so I'll work in the den tonight."

As Hugh heads down the hall, I clear the table, noticing that he hasn't actually finished the pasta in his bowl. Does the dish not hold the same allure for him as it does for me? Or is the stress from the Brewster case playing havoc with his appetite? Or maybe the real stress is about me. About *us*. About the topic Hugh doesn't dare circle back to because of the impact it might have on me.

I scrape the bowls, place them and the glasses in the dishwasher, and wipe the table off with a thick yellow sponge. My brain feels as if it's foraging, rooting beneath brambles for something, but I'm not sure what. Almost instinctively, I don a pair of rubber dishwashing gloves and open the trash bin again. After hoisting out a few handfuls of congealed pasta and dropping them in the sink, I reach the roses. Sasha would be thrilled to know that even submerged in garbage, their color pops brilliantly.

I don't have to raise them to my nose to confirm in my mind that there's very little aroma. I unwrapped them after all. And besides, I know from a "Best (and Worst) Valentine Splurges for Your Money" blog post I wrote last year that as the flower industry tinkered with the genetics of roses to make them last longer, they bred out the fragrance along the way.

Gingerly, I remove a few stems and examine the blossoms. They're a little droopy from lack of water but they're hardly past their prime.

Then why did my husband stuff them in the trash bin?

My stomach twists. So much for getting back into a groove with Hugh. He's a puzzle to me at the moment. But I can't freak myself out now thinking about it. I toss the garbage back into the bin and head down the hall toward the bedroom. Though the door to the den is closed, I can hear the drone of Hugh's voice, clearly reading material into the phone.

For the next hour I sit at the desk in the alcove, reviewing notes for the podcast tomorrow, including the research Sasha prepared. Finished, I email some final thoughts to my producer, Casey. After stealing a few minutes to make a cup of chamomile tea, I catch up on financial news—the *Wall Street Journal, Financial Times, Yahoo Finance, Fortune's Broadsheet* for women—so I don't come across tomorrow like someone who's been in a coma for the past week.

I'm just about to shut my laptop when I see an email alert pop up onto the screen. It's a response from the private detective agency I contacted.

Yes, Kurt Mulroney, one of the two partners, has written, this is absolutely the type of case we handle. We've done more of these than you would expect. If you'd like to discuss further, you can call me at the number below tomorrow or even tonight. I know you're eager to have this situation resolved.

More of these than you would expect. Perhaps I should take comfort in the fact that there's apparently a subset of people roaming the metropolitan area in fugue states. Hey, there might even be a support group with meetings I could attend. Blank Slates Anonymous. Obviously, it couldn't work exactly like other support groups, where you talk about the wicked bender or food binge you've recently engaged in. Because you don't *remember* anything.

I'll call him in the morning, I decide. Even though Hugh was dismissive of the idea, I see no harm in learning more about the process and finding out what this guy would charge. I jot down the number on a purple Post-it and stick it to the base of my desk lamp.

But then without even thinking, I grab my phone and tap in the number. I don't want to wait until tomorrow.

"Mulroney," he answers. He has a deep voice, tinged with what sounds like a Bronx accent.

"It's Ally Linden calling. Thank you for getting back to me so quickly."

"My pleasure. We'd love to be able to assist you."

"Is this really something you specialize in?"

"I wouldn't call it a specialty—we do a wide variety of work—but we've handled similar cases."

"How have you managed them?"

"What I generally like to do first with a prospective client is meet for a free consultation and discuss our procedure in person. I'll take you through everything—and there's no obligation whatsoever on your part."

I hesitate. He sounds professional enough, though he's surely practiced at the kind of patter that encourages people to bite.

"You were a detective with the NYPD?"

"That's right. Seventeen years. Gold shield."

"I suppose that kind of training helps in your current line of work."

"Yes and no," he says with a chuckle. "It trained me to be a great detective, that's for sure. But on the other hand, cops get in the habit of rolling in loud and visible, and this line of work generally calls for a low profile."

I like the way he put it.

"Would we meet in your office?" I ask.

"Like a lot of P.I.s, I work out of my home, since so much work is done via computer these days. For meetings I usually suggest a coffee shop. What area would you be coming from?"

"The West Sixties, near Lincoln Center."

"I live pretty close—on West Ninety-Seventh Street. There's a diner I like on the corner of Ninety-Ninth and Broadway or I could come down your way. Whichever works best for you."

I prefer the idea of meeting on his turf, to gain a better sense of him.

"Why don't we meet at your diner? Does ten A.M. tomorrow work?

"Absolutely."

Mulroney provides the address for the imaginatively named Broadway Diner, a place I've surely passed but can't place in my mind. He explains that he's five eleven, with dark hair trimmed very short, and that he'll be wearing a black blazer.

"Thanks," I tell him. "I'm five seven, by the way, with long light brown hair and hazel eyes."

My guess is that he already knows this. He's probably googled me, has learned what I do for work and who I'm married to, has maybe even figured out my exact address. But hey, that's what he does for a living.

After signing off, I lean back in my desk chair and exhale. I'm glad I took this step. Even if there's no obligation,
I suspect I'm going to end up hiring him—and he'll dig up
answers for me.

Still, I can feel my pulse racing a little. Because there's
fear seeping out from beneath my relief.

What if Gabby's theory is wrong? What if in the two
days I was gone, I didn't witness another person being hurt?
What if nothing bad happened to me, either?

What if instead I did things that were incredibly foolish?
Or wrong, even? Things I'll totally regret once I learn what
they are?

15

When I show up at the diner the next morning, I find that it's a retro-feeling, old-style diner with red vinyl booths, thick white coffee mugs, and about four hundred items on the menu. I guess it's appropriate enough. Somehow, I can't quite picture sitting down with a private eye at a hipster café where they serve avocado toast topped with cumin salt and chia seeds.

Though it's ten o'clock, the diner is still half full of people finishing breakfast, and the air is ripe with the smells of pancakes, syrup, and bacon. I glance around and don't see anyone resembling Mulroney's photo. After hanging my coat on the hook attached to the end of a booth, I slide across the cushion and take a few deep breaths. This all seems so surreal to me, like I'm playing a part in a movie from the 1940s.

I never even had the chance to tell Hugh I was coming here. When I'd wandered down to the den later last night, I found him asleep on the love seat, his long legs draped over the arm.

"Uh, sorry," he said, as I'd nudged him awake. He

glanced bleary eyed at his watch. "Christ, I knew I shouldn't have lain down."

"Why don't you come to bed, honey," I urged.

"Yeah, maybe I'd better. I'll have to get a really early start tomorrow."

And he did, leaving before I was awake. A note from him on the island counter promised he'd be home early tonight.

As I'm trying to grab the waiter's attention, a man moves from the rear of the diner and sidles up to the booth I'm sitting in.

"Ms. Linden?" he asks quietly. I catch the heavy scent of a leathery aftershave.

"Yes?" I've never set eyes on him before.

"Kurt Mulroney," he says, thrusting out a hand. He's at least fifteen pounds heavier than he appears in the photos on the agency website, and his hair's been shaved off rather than trimmed short.

"Oh, I'm sorry, I didn't see you."

"No problem. Why don't we move to my booth?" He kicks his chin up toward the back of the room. "We'll have more privacy there."

"Sure," I say, grabbing my jacket and following him to the back booth, where we sit across from each other.

"Let's get you something to drink first," he tells me. "Coffee?"

"Yes, thanks." He catches the waitress's eye and with a couple of hand signals conveys that I'll have what he's having. I take him in for a minute. He's clean-shaven—no beard or mustache—and he's got a thin, white hockey-stick-shaped scar slicing through one eyebrow. His black blazer is nicely tailored but snug, as if purchased before the weight gain.

"Ms. Linden, why don't you start by telling me a bit more about your situation," Mulroney says.

I flesh out what I've already shared, not bothering with the fact that my dissociative state might have been triggered by a fight with my spouse and/or long-dormant stress from discovering the body of a child and then misleading the police and my parents. Which, granted, is a helluva lot to skip but not essential for him to hear.

He listens intently, a thick index finger placed sideways across his lips. Though it may be for show, I can see what looks like concern in his watery blue-green eyes.

"That's got to be incredibly upsetting," he says when I finish. "Do you mind my asking if you're continuing to receive medical help?"

"Yes, I'm all set on that front. But there's no guarantee my memory will come back, and that's why I need help figuring out where I went—and what I did. And if something might have happened to me."

"I can understand that. And I know we can be of assistance."

"You've had other cases like this, you said?"

"To be perfectly frank, we've never worked with this *exact* situation, but similar ones. You've probably read stories about elderly people with dementia wandering away from their homes—or autistic kids doing the same. They can't either remember or describe where they went, but the families want to know, even once their loved ones have returned safely."

"But why would it matter once they're back?"

"With autistic kids, parents want to make certain no one lured them away and abused them. In the case of one of the elderly ladies we investigated, it was actually the nursing home that hired us. I'm sure the liability aspect worried them."

"Can you tell me a little more about your process?"

"Sure." He takes a swig of his coffee and sets the mug down with a thunk. "It really comes down to a combo of shoe-leather investigation and modern technology. We'll seek to gain access to as much security camera footage as possible and use that to track the person's whereabouts during the period in question. A lot of people don't realize this, but if you live in New York, you're almost constantly being videotaped."

"I know many companies have security cameras, but aren't there still plenty of streets in New York without them?"

"We don't have the kind of coverage London does, but it's really expanded in recent years, with cameras on both commercial and residential buildings."

So there were eyes on me when I was missing, and a digital record of my whereabouts. The thought is creepy but at the same time reassuring—because it might be easier than I anticipated to find the truth.

"But how do you get access to the footage?"

"Security guards tend to be very respectful of my experience as a cop, and my partner's as a Navy SEAL." He raps his knuckles lightly on the table a couple of times. "And we don't only rely on video, of course. We talk to people. Ask questions."

Instinctively I flick my hand up, palm forward. "My doorman may know something about the day I left—which direction I was headed in, for instance—but I wouldn't want you speaking to him. I don't want most people in my life clued in about what's going on."

"Fine. And I'll probably start at the end point anyway. This place Greenbacks you mentioned. What kind of building is it in?"

Hearing the company name reminds me of my meeting with Damien later today, and my heart does a nervous skip.

"A smallish one, but they have a manned security desk."

"Excellent."

"But how would it help to see footage of me showing up in the lobby?"

Mulroney cocks his head. "It's not about you in the lobby. It's about what direction you entered the building from. Once we've figured it out—and I say 'we' because if you retain me, my partner might end up assisting in part of the investigation—we head in that direction and we secure more footage, continuing to retrace your steps. It's like following a thread that leads backwards."

Following a thread. As I've thought of reconstructing those two days, it's seemed more like trying to Krazy Glue the shards of a broken vase together, but I like the thread image. I decide right then to hire Mulroney.

"What's the fee for this type of investigation?" I ask. "I want to be mindful of costs."

"I understand that," Mulroney says. "What we generally charge is seventy an hour, but I would cap the job for now at two thousand dollars, and when we reach that point, we'll reevaluate. I'll keep you constantly abreast of the progress, and if after the first day I have any reason to suspect we're going to hit a dead end, I'll let you know."

"And I'd receive the remainder of my retainer back if we decide to halt the investigation for some reason?"

"Absolutely."

"Okay, I'm on board."

We cover a few more details. Mulroney's going to email me a contract later today, and he explains he'll need a couple of photos of me, which I promise to shoot over to him. Then he slides a slim notebook from his inside jacket pocket along with a Bic pen and asks what I was wearing when I resurfaced on Thursday, my exact home address as well as the Greenbacks office address, and for any details that might be even slightly relevant. I fill him in on the fact that my purse is missing as well as my phone, and I also describe the charge at Eastside Eats.

"Okay, a piece of the thread to follow. That's the only charge?"

"Right. I've been wondering whether I might have been mugged and the person grabbed the purse along with my phone. But wouldn't a mugger have tried to use the card again after buying lunch? Or one of the other cards?"

"He might have been looking mainly for cash. You carry much on you?"

"I think I had a few hundred dollars on me at the start of the week. I like to use cash when I can't write something off for business."

He shrugs. "If a junkie grabbed your purse, it would have

been plenty for a few fixes. This place Eastside Eats. You ever been there before?"

"No, but I checked online and it's the type of place I might stop in."

"Anything of note on your calendar for last week? Places you might have gone—or people you might have seen?"

"I had an appointment at one o'clock on Wednesday with a Dr. Elaine Erling—at her New York City office, not the Larchmont one—but I didn't keep it. There's a chance that at some point over those two days I showed up at Work-Space on West Fifty-Fifth Street, where I rent a small office. I hadn't planned to go in those days—my intention was to work from home—but who knows?"

He stuffs the notebook back into his pocket and reaches across the table to shake my hand.

"We're going to figure this out for you, Ms. Linden," he says. "And we can start immediately."

"Thank you." His words have triggered a rush of relief, though there's still fear pulsing lightly beneath it. "What can I do to assist in this?"

"For the moment, the most important thing is to be available so I can check in with you regularly and ask you questions as they come up."

"You can count on it."

Mulroney raises a finger for the check, and the waiter nods with a smile.

"You do a lot of meetings here?" I ask.

"A fair amount. I also like to stop by at the end of the day and think through my cases."

I offer to pay for my own coffee, but Mulroney insists it's on him.

"Oh, wait," I exclaim as he lays down a few bills. "I almost forgot."

I fish through my purse and extract the gallon-size Ziploc bag I've stuffed with the bloodied tissues. Mulroney's right eyebrow, the one with the scar, shoots up.

"These were in my coat pocket, though I don't have any memory of putting them there."

He cups the bag in one hand and peers at the contents intently.

"Did you have any cuts or bruises last week?"

"No, but I've gotten nosebleeds in the past. Can we do a DNA test to find out whether the blood is mine or not?"

"DNA's going to take a few weeks. Plus, you'll need to buy one of those home paternity tests. Actually, I think we should start instead by checking the blood type on the tissues, which can be done quickly and might tell us all we need to know. What type are you?"

"O negative."

"That's rare. If the blood on these turns out to be O negative, it's probably safe to assume it's yours. If it's not, we'll decide from there how much more testing we want. Why don't you give them to me, and I'll drop them off at the lab we use."

I feel a tiny swell of reluctance about handing over the whole bag but decide I'm going to have to put my trust in this guy. He was a cop. That's no guarantee he's ethical but at least he's experienced. Mulroney accepts the bag and tucks it into the soft black leather briefcase resting next to him.

As we're sliding out of the booth a few minutes later, another man approaches us.

"Jay, hey," Mulroney says. "Ms. Linden, I asked my partner, Jay Williams, to stop by to say hello. Since he'll be involved, too, I thought you should meet him."

He appears to be slightly younger than Mulroney, maybe in his midforties, African American, and handsome. Unlike his partner, he bears an exact resemblance to his online photo.

"A pleasure," Williams says, firmly shaking my hand. "Did you two have a good meeting?"

"We did," Mulroney says, lowering his voice as we move toward the front of the diner. "I'm going to make Ms. Linden's case a top priority."

Out on the sidewalk, Mulroney briefly recaps the conversation for his partner. I realize the meeting has gone longer than I planned, so I say good-bye and step off the curb and hail a cab. Less than ten minutes later I'm sinking into the backseat of a cab hurtling toward the studio on Ninth Avenue and Forty-Fifth Street. This all seems so crazy—hiring a couple of gumshoes—and yet I feel bolstered by my decision.

Once I arrive at the studio, I take the elevator to the ninth floor and proceed to the small suite rented by the production company that does my program. The guy manning the desk in the reception area nods hello and announces, "They're all inside, Ally."

I pray he doesn't mean Sasha, too. I'd been hoping to beat her here and have a few minutes to chat alone with Casey about the final segment of the show. But as I step into the outer part of the studio, I spot Sasha in the sound booth, shuffling a stack of papers. Casey and Rex, the engineer, are busy at their computers, but they both glance up when I enter. Sasha either doesn't notice me or pretends not to.

"Morning," Rex and Casey say nearly in unison.

"How's everyone doing?" I ask, watching for their reaction. I've been wondering if I might have contacted either one of them—perhaps in some lunatic way—when I was MIA.

"All good," Rex says and swivels his dark eyes back to the screen. In the year and a half I've been doing the podcast, I've probably heard the guy say a couple hundred words.

Casey, however, smiles and affords me her full attention, setting down a green juice concoction in a plastic cup the size of a rocket ship.

"Got anything for me?" she asks, eyeing my tote bag. I've worked with Casey for two years now and she's not only fun and considerate, but a pro in every respect.

"No, I'm going to stick to the plan I sent you last night. Our guest is on her way?"

"Yeah, but she texted to say she's running ten minutes late. So much for taking your own advice, right? In her books she warns people to *never* be late for a meeting."

"Ha. For the powerful, rules are meant to be broken."

Both she and Rex seem totally normal, making me think that neither has witnessed any bizarre behavior on my part. And yet everything in the room seems slightly out of frame to me. I feel like if I reached out to touch Casey or Rex, my hand would miss by an inch or two.

Is it simply because I'm still a little wobbly from last

week? Or is this out-of-frame sensation an alert about my mental state, one I should be heeding? Were there warning signs before the first dissociative state that I didn't know how to interpret? *Please*, I silently beg, *don't let this be happening again*. Maybe Hugh was right when he urged me to postpone the recording a week.

I'm also a little jittery, I realize, about my meeting with Damien. It's only a few hours away.

I inhale slowly, hold, then release. *I can do this*, I tell myself.

"Want me to grab you a coffee?" Casey asks, as if sensing my unease.

"Actually, I'll get it," I say, dumping my jacket and bag on the saggy couch. "But walk me to the elevator, will you, Casey?"

Outside in the hall, I thank her again for allowing Sasha to take over the last spot of the show.

"Not a problem," she says. She rakes a hand across the crown of her long, strawberry-blond hair. "I know it's all about keeping the sponsor happy."

In the café on the ground floor of the building, I order chamomile tea at the counter and carry it to a small table, where I sip it slowly and take a few more deep breaths. I feel more present suddenly. Maybe the disconnected sensation was simply jitters from the extra cup of coffee I drank at the diner.

By the time I'm back upstairs, my guest, the former Wall Streeter/book author Jamie Parkin, is in the outer part of the studio, chatting with Casey and Sasha. I discover she's fairly aloof in person, not what I was expecting based on the engaging shot on her book cover. *Damn*, I think. *I'll need to charm her, make her seem more accessible, but I'm hardly at the top of my game today.*

This, however, isn't Parkin's first rodeo, and she turns out to be a polished interview subject, with plenty of hard-won wisdom to share. She offers a few excellent strategies for not only negotiating one's salary but also for scoring promotions, perks, and opportunities at work.

For the next segment—"Your Money Q and A"—Casey joins me in the sound booth, and I respond to queries readers have submitted online, which she reads to me from her laptop. I've previewed them, of course, and scribbled notes in advance, and I'm pleased with how my answers come out. Sasha, I notice, is studying a sheet of paper in the outer part of the studio and briskly rubbing her hands, as if in anticipation of her upcoming role.

And now it's time for the final segment, "Let's Chat Dollars and Sense," which is meant to be a light, casual close to the show. As Casey departs, Sasha strides into the sound booth, takes the seat across the desk from me, and adjusts her headset. I catch Casey rolling her eyes at Rex.

"You all set?" I ask Sasha.

"Absolutely."

We're given the signal to start, and after introducing Sasha as my intern, I tee up the segment by saying that as essential as it is to learn how to negotiate your salary—as today's guest so wisely counseled us—it's equally important to be smart from the get-go about managing the money you make. I ask Sasha to tell us about some of the mistakes she sees her friends making and what she wishes she could tell them.

Unfortunately, this *is* Sasha's first rodeo and it shows. Her comments are stilted, and she also fails to tamp down her natural arrogance.

"How are your friends doing on the IRA front?" I ask. "Particularly the freelancers. Have they started to save for retirement yet?"

"Not all of them. It takes such a big chunk out of their earnings at a time when there are other important costs."

"What do they consider more important than an IRA?"

"A good professional wardrobe. Networking dinners. Vacations."

"I hate to hear that. Because the sooner you start feeding an IRA, the better."

I notice Sasha twitch in her seat, as if she's gearing up to make a particularly salient point.

"Actually, I have a different point of view on that," she says.

Her comment catches me off guard. When I mentioned the importance of IRAs on Friday, she didn't utter a word in disagreement.

"I'd love to hear it," I say.

"Having the right clothes, meeting the right people, taking trips that energize you can actually be excellent investments. They help you grow your career and earn promotions, which in the long run can provide more benefits than investing in an IRA in your twenties."

There's a hint of smugness in her tone. I almost laugh out loud. Is she hoping to throw me off my game? Casey shoots me a *WTF* expression through the glass.

"That's an interesting point, Sasha," I say. "As with everything else, it all comes down to the math, figuring the rate of return. It is important to look the part, network, and take vacations. But historically, investing in the stock market has paid off far better than investing in something like Louboutin shoes."

We wrap up a minute later, and after Sasha has hurried off to "an appointment I can't be late for," Casey shakes her head in annoyance.

"When is her last day again?"

"She's finishing up Thanksgiving week."

"Great, now I really *will* have something to be thankful for."

I know I should be more annoyed by Sasha's comment during the segment, but frankly, I'm just grateful about my performance today. The podcast was hardly dazzling, but I'd give it a solid B.

I take a cab back to the apartment, cobble a lunch together, and then read through the contract Mulroney's sent me. There don't seem to be any obvious red flags, so I sign, scan, and forward it to him along with a couple of recent photos of myself. It would have made sense, of course, to let Hugh take a lawyerly look at the contract, but I don't want to wait or run the risk of him talking me out of it. Finally, I use PayPal to forward the retainer. Minutes later Mulroney emails back to thank me and to confirm that he's already dropped off the bag of tissues at the lab.

I switch out of the black pencil skirt and turquoise V-neck sweater I've been wearing and change into jeans, a crisp white collared shirt, and boots. I take more pains than I probably should with my makeup, but I can't shake the desire to replace Damien's last image of me—foul smelling, rain soaked, coming apart at the seams—with that of a sane and pulled-together woman.

A few minutes later I head north on Broadway to the café in the West Seventies that Damien ended up suggesting. I remind myself there's nothing to feel guilty about, that I haven't told Hugh about the meeting simply because I don't want to upset him unnecessarily.

The streets are crowded with West Siders doing their thing: culture lovers dashing up the steps of the Lincoln Center plaza; people returning from work (half of the guys with messenger bags over their shoulders); teenagers meandering home from school; mothers and nannies pushing strollers, often with a second child perched on a little platform at the back. Once I wanted the latter—or a variation of it—in my own life. Why did the desire seem to dissolve overnight? When Erling's question—"Do you not want children, or do you not want them with Hugh?"—tries to force its way to the front of my mind, I fight it off.

I pull my sweater coat tighter across my chest. It's cooler today than yesterday. The sky's overcast and the air is raw.

Finally, I reach Seventy-Fourth Street, ready to hang a right. I pause at the corner and wait for the Walk sign to tell me to cross.

And suddenly, I sense something. Not the pit in my stomach. That sensation's been there the whole walk over, in fact from the second I woke up this morning and knew I'd be seeing Damien.

It's something else entirely. I can't help but feel that there's a pair of eyes on my back. That someone nearby is staring hard at me.

swivel slowly, trying to make the movement appear casual. A woman is attempting to convince a sweet-looking girl of five or six to zip her coat. Behind them everyone seems to be going about their business—glued to their phones or walking their dogs or trudging home with plastic shopping bags. No one appears remotely interested in me.

Is *this* a warning sign? I wonder. A vague, irrational suspicion that's actually a prelude to my mind going haywire again? No, it must be nerves, I reassure myself. Nerves about the idea of seeing Damien, and about keeping it from Hugh. The only observer right now is my conscience.

Just to be on the safe side, I fumble in my purse for the tin of cinnamon Altoids, slip one in my mouth, and force myself to concentrate on the flavor.

The light changes, the Walk sign on the far side of Broadway flashes, and I hurry across. By the time I arrive at the café, my pulse is racing. *Don't turn this meeting into more than it is*, I tell myself. Yes, I'm curious about Damien, and I probably always will be, but my only real goal today is to glean any clue about why I showed up at Greenbacks.

It turns out I've beaten him there. I settle at a table in the back and slip out of my coat. The place is only half full, and the setting—brick walls, buffed wood floors, soft lighting—calms me a little. But I've barely had a chance to take in my surroundings when Damien enters the café. He spots me immediately and raises his chin in greeting. Though I saw him only recently, he's in sharper focus now, and it's a shock to my system.

"Thanks for coming," he says as he reaches the table.

"No problem," I say. "I appreciated the call."

After lowering himself into the chair opposite me, he peels off his overcoat. Underneath he's wearing a black-and-white plaid shirt and gray wool tie. He crosses his arms on the table and leans forward a little, leveling his gaze at me.

Could *he* have been watching me on the street? I wonder. Had he spotted me on Broadway and followed behind at a distance to guarantee I was the first to arrive? That's not his MO, though. At work he was always strategic—clever, a chess player at heart. But not in his private life.

"I was really worried about you, Ally."

His comment—and the softness in his voice—throw me. I figured that last Thursday must have been unsettling for him, but what could I mean to Damien Howe at this point in life? Maybe all I'm seeing is simply concern for a former colleague.

I smile wanly. "It was a pretty scary experience."

"You look a lot better now."

"Do I? That's good to know, though I bet most anything would be an improvement."

The waitress sidles up at this moment, and after I ask

for a macchiato, Damien turns to her and tells her to please make it two.

"You bet," she responds, taking him in appreciatively—his deep blue eyes, the hawkish nose, and that hair. He's almost forty now, and though his hair isn't as long as it once was, it's still that crazy honey-gold color.

"I tried the hospital that morning," he says, after the waitress moves off. "But they wouldn't even admit you were there. At least I knew you were getting medical help *some-where*. . . . Are you feeling as well as you seem?"

"Still a little wobbly, but much better overall. I'm sure I created quite a stir that day. Were people buzzing about it?"

"Don't worry about that. As far as anyone knows, you and I had a meeting in my office, and you fainted. Did the doctors figure out what the matter was?"

"It's something called . . . dissociating. I lost my bearings and didn't remember certain things. I was actually missing in action for two whole days, apparently roaming the city on my own."

"That's awful. Your husband must have been going nuts."

Husband. He knows, of course. But so weird to hear him utter that word.

"He thought I was out of town giving a speech," I lie. I'm certainly not going to reveal anything to Damien about my marital issues. "He didn't know until the hospital called that there was something wrong."

"Fortunately, Caryn's still the office manager and she'd heard through former staffers what your husband's name was and what he did. My assistant found the number for his office online."

"That ended up being a lifesaver. I appreciate all the effort."

I need to arrive at the business at hand, but I don't want to rush him. I watch as he takes a sip of his macchiato, his fingers encircling the cup rather than holding it by the handle.

"So had something happened to you, Ally?" he asks after a moment. "To cause this thing?"

"Probably. An incident—or some combination of factors—must have stressed me out pretty badly, and it seems that part of my mind shut down as a way to cope."

"But you're not sure what it was?"

"No. I'm working with a therapist, but I still haven't remembered."

For a moment I consider sharing that my fugue state might be related, directly or not, to Jaycee Long. I'd told Damien about her not all that long after we started sleeping together. He'd made pasta for us one night at his place, this dreamy spaghetti carbonara with a sauce I fantasized about for weeks, and later—after sex and before more sex—we put on the TV to find a movie to watch. There was one, whose title I can't remember now, about the disappearance of a young child, and as Damien read the description aloud, I felt myself freezing up. "What's the matter?" he'd asked me, stroking my hair. And I'd told him. It had been easy to tell him anything.

But what's the point of resurrecting it now for him? This conversation is a one-off.

"Is there anything I can do?" he asks.

"There is something, yes," I say, glad he's given me an

opening. "I'm trying to get a handle on why, in this midst of basically losing myself for two days, I went to Greenbacks. Because maybe figuring that out will help me understand the rest."

He leans back in his chair, and for a brief moment, his knees brush mine. Startled by the touch, I shift my position slightly.

"And you thought I might have an idea?"

"I was hoping so, yes."

"All I know is that you seemed to believe you still worked there. You said something about it being your first day back."

I summon an image from that morning, of me stepping off the elevator. Yes, I'd had the sense that I'd been away for a while, but certainly not for years. "Like I'd been on vacation?"

"Right."

"But . . . but why Greenbacks? There are so many other places I could have gone that day. Like my *own* workplace."

He narrows his eyes and crosses his arms against his chest.

"You tell *me*, Ally." All of a sudden, his tone has cooled.

"Tell you what?" I ask, flustered by the sea change.

"Why do you think you showed up there?"

"Damien, I haven't the foggiest—that's why I'm asking *you*."

"It wasn't because of the story you're doing?"

"Story?"

"The woman who handles our PR says that someone who works for you called her a week or so ago. She said she was doing research and wanted to speak to the person on staff who oversees the financial advisory end. Maybe *that's* why we were on your mind."

I frown, momentarily at a loss. "It must have been my researcher, who's helping me on my next book," I tell him. "But I can't imagine why she'd want to speak to someone in that role."

He doesn't respond, simply studies me. The silence unrolls like a ball of yarn.

"Damien, I never suggested she talk to anyone at Greenbacks," I continue, more insistence in my voice this time. "So that call doesn't explain why I showed up out of the blue. And you and I didn't have any contact prior to this, did we?"

Another few beats of silence.

"We haven't talked since you left," he says coolly. "Per your request."

"Per my request? What's that supposed to mean?"

"You made it clear after you broke things off that you didn't want any personal contact with me."

I nearly gulp in surprise. I have no clue where this is coming from.

"Damien, I wasn't the one who ended things."

"No?"

"All I did was suggest that we take a break since people seemed to be wise to us."

"Kind of a breather, then? And we'd pick up again after the gossip died down?"

"Until I found another job. Or went out on my own."

"Months later."

"Well, what we were *supposed* to do?"

"Keep seeing each other? It was hardly against the rules. I own the damn company, remember?"

I can't believe any of this—not only what he's saying but the edge in his voice. I'm almost relieved when the waitress lays the check on the table.

"Look," he says, his tone softening, "I'm sorry if what I said upset you. That's the last thing you need right now."

"It's okay." I'm trying not to sound as flustered as I feel. "I appreciate you reaching out—and sending my coat over, too. I guess your assistant found it in the conference room."

"Actually, I found it." He fishes a few bills from his wallet and lays them on top of the check. "I went back in there afterwards—to see if you'd left anything."

He stuffs both arms in his topcoat, readying to leave. I'm briefly tempted to tell him I'm going to stay for another coffee, so I can avoid an awkward good-bye on the sidewalk. But I realize that the awkward good-bye would only happen in here instead.

After I pull on my own coat and rise, Damien gestures for me to lead and I snake through the tables with him trailing me. Outside, the wind whips my hair into my face.

"Take care," he says. "I'm sorry I wasn't able to help." Leaning forward, he brushes his lips across my cheek. Even in the cold, raw air, I feel my face redden in surprise. He's gone before I can manage a good-bye.

I wait until he's far ahead and then hurry toward Broadway myself. As I walk, I check my phone and spot a text from Hugh from a few minutes before: Home in thirty or so, he says. Everything okay?

Yes, all good, I write back. See you soon. I pick up my

pace so he won't beat me there, leaving me to explain where I've been.

The urgency distracts me a bit but still, I'm rattled. About the exchange with Damien. About the cool breeze that suddenly blew through the conversation. About his announcement that *I* dumped *him*.

Does he really think that? Or has he been rewriting history to serve his own purposes?

There's also the fact that he has no more idea than I do why I surfaced at Greenbacks. At this point it seems Mulroney is my only hope.

Halfway home, I decide to make a pit stop at a gourmet grocery store, where I pick up chicken cutlets cooked in a mushroom sauce, fresh broccoli, a head of lettuce, and a wedge of triple crème cheese. Surely it's going to take more than one evening to get things back on track with Hugh, and so why not make dinner special again? Recalling Gabby's advice, I realize she hasn't contacted me today. Knowing her, I'm surprised she hasn't touched base. But at the same time I'm sure she's jet-lagged and bogged down with work.

I'm turning the key in the door to the apartment when my phone rings. *Maybe that's Gabby*, I think, but Sasha's name flashes on the screen. Calling to fish for compliments, I'm sure.

"Do you have a minute to talk?" she asks. I can tell from the background noise that she's on the move, probably in a cab or Uber.

"Sure, but give me a second, okay?" Lowering the phone, I drop the shopping bags on the counter and tug off my coat.

"Okay, I'm here," I say, using my free hand to begin un-packing the bags.

"So how do you feel the podcast went? I was hoping I'd hear from you afterwards."

"Sorry, I was really busy . . . I thought it went well. Good show. I appreciate all the preparation you did."

"But what about *my* segment? Did you like it?"

I've been so preoccupied this afternoon with the Mul-roney contract and the meeting with Damien that I haven't thought for a moment about what to tell her. I refuse to lie—that would be of zero value—but I can do my best not to ruffle her feathers.

"It was a good start. I have a few suggestions, though— some little ways to improve going forward."

"I'm all ears," she says. Maybe so, but I can sense from her tone that her back is already up.

"Why don't we wait and do this in person? I also find it more beneficial to have these conversations face-to-face."

"'These conversations'? Was there a problem?"

"No, not a problem. I simply wanted to offer a few guide-lines."

"If you don't mind, I'd really like to hear them now. I may not see you for a few days—unless you can meet tonight."

That's not going to happen. "Okay, like I said, a good start, but some of your comments sounded a little rehearsed. On a podcast, particularly the type of segment we did, you want to come across as natural as possible."

"Are you saying I shouldn't have contradicted you about IRAs?"

"Of course not. That kind of stuff makes a segment

compelling. But the back-and-forth should be easygoing, as if we're chatting over coffee. I noticed you reading notes before we started, and I probably should have advised you to look them over last night and then forget about them. I'm sorry I didn't mention that."

"Okay," she says, sounding less irritated now that she's manipulated me into accepting partial blame. "And yes, that would have been good to know."

"Well, there'll be a next time. Remember, Casey is on vacation in a couple of weeks."

"Right, thanks. I'll look forward to it."

Using one hand, I've also managed to slide the chicken onto a plate and extract the remaining half baguette from the freezer.

"Unfortunately, Sasha, I have to go. I'm having an early dinner with Hugh."

"Of course. Say hi for me, will you? And tell him I finally remembered where I met him."

I freeze in place, holding the head of lettuce.

"Sure." I wish I could deny her the pleasure of asking where, but I can't resist. "Why don't you tell me, and I'll pass it on."

"It was at the Yale Club a few weeks ago—at a lecture on money laundering. I'd gone with a friend of mine, Ashley Budd, and she introduced us."

I've been gripping the phone so tightly I'm surprised I haven't crushed it, but now I let my fingers relax. I remember the night. Hugh had told me he'd be going with a friend of his from law school.

"I'll let him know. Have a good weekend."

As I'm setting the phone down, I spot another text from Hugh.

> Sry! One of the partners grabbed me. In sub station now.
> 15 minutes tops.

I could actually use the time. Sasha's call has compounded how uneasy I feel, and I'm craving a few minutes of silence alone. After washing and spin-drying the lettuce, and chopping up the broccoli, I retreat to the bedroom. Without turning on the light, I lie facedown on the bed in the darkness with my phone next to me. Lately, I've been keeping it by my side.

I close my eyes, taking four deep breaths. The room smells vaguely of anise and orange, from the scented candle I burned while dressing this morning, and I force myself to focus on the scent and stay in the moment.

It's going to be okay, I assure myself. No one was watching me earlier, it was simply my imagination. Yes, I'm still troubled by what happened to me years ago, but once I speak with the police in Millerstown and apologize for my deception, I'm bound to feel more at ease. Things will get better with Hugh, too. Tonight will be nice. If I know my husband, he loves a good cheese course.

And Mulroney will help me find the threads that lead to the truth, even if Damien had nothing to offer.

For a brief moment, I allow my thoughts to be tugged back to Damien. It's true that I was the one who suggested the break, after a fall weekend in New Hampshire. We often went away together because there was less of a chance of being busted out of town than in the city, and we purposely picked spots we figured our colleagues weren't likely to surface in. It had been an amazing weekend. Hiking on beautiful trails, reading on the porch of our inn, a three-hour lunch at a restaurant along a rushing river.

On Sunday, however, Damien's car had broken down and we ended up spending the night in New England. I called my assistant the next morning, saying I'd decided to extend a weekend visit to my dad's since he wasn't feeling well. Damien had emailed *his* assistant on Monday morning to say he had a last-minute meeting with an investor—and then made a point of showing up at the office midafternoon.

But clever Greenbackers weren't so easily fooled. A few of them had probably already had an inkling, and the simultaneous unplanned absences clearly ratcheted up their suspicions. I sensed them watching us more closely after that. I hated it. I didn't want people to assume that I'd slept my way to my most recent promotion. "We should put things on hold for a while," I'd told Damien. But I never meant forever. And it was gutting when I realized several months later that he'd started dating someone else.

What does it matter now, though?

I swing my legs over the side of the bed so I'm sitting on the edge, grab my phone, and try Gabby, reaching her voice mail. I leave a message asking her to call me, and before I have a chance to set the phone down, it rings in my hand. Mulroney.

"Ms. Linden?"

"Yes, hi." From the main part of the apartment, I hear

the sound of Hugh's key turning in the lock. "Did you receive the retainer okay?"

"Yes, thanks. We're all set on that front. And I'll be starting the canvassing at eight tomorrow."

"Great."

"I'm actually calling to tell you about the results of the blood test."

My heart lurches. "This soon?"

"Yeah. And you were right to wonder. The blood on the tissues isn't yours."

17

Ally?" Hugh calls out. He's standing now in the doorway of the darkened bedroom. I can only see his backlit silhouette.

"I'm in here," I tell him.

"Ms. Linden?" Mulroney says. I direct my attention back to him as I try to process his news.

"Sorry, that was my husband coming home. You're sure about this?"

"Very. It's a lab we use regularly. The blood on the tissues is A positive, which, by the way, is the second-most-common type. About 34 percent of the population has it pumping through their veins."

"So someone was injured in my presence."

"Seems like it. I'll let you go, but I'll touch base tomorrow, midafternoon-ish, fill you in on what we turn up by then."

"Is everything okay?" Hugh asks after I've signed off. There's worry in his voice. Maybe because he's found me in the bedroom without the lights on.

"Yes, fine, I was resting in here when my phone rang. Are you ready for dinner? I picked up a few things."

"Great. I'll change and be right out."

We brush past each other in the dimness and I hurry to the living area. Mostly on automatic pilot, I set the broccoli on to steam and nuke the chicken dish.

So Gabby's theory might be right, I think as I dress the lettuce. Rather than being a victim myself, I might have witnessed something happen to someone else. Maybe the person fell, or was mugged, or hit by a car, and I tried to assist him or her. Maybe I grabbed a wad of tissues to stanch the flow of blood, and then lost my phone in the confusion.

But I don't carry tissues in my purse. Did another passerby thrust them into my hand? Or did the injury happen at an indoor location, where I had access to a restroom?

The biggest question of all: Was whatever happened traumatic enough that it made me dissociate?

While I finish prepping dinner, Hugh returns to the great room, and slides into a dining chair, the sleeves of his pale-blue sweater pushed to his elbows. It isn't until I bring the food to the table, though, that I get my first really good look at him today.

I'm startled. His face is drawn, and his eyes faintly bloodshot with fatigue. I realize that I actually haven't seen him since last night because I was in bed sleeping when he departed for work today.

"This smells great," he says, pouring us each a glass of sparkling water. "But please don't feel you have to make a fuss."

"It's not a problem. If it was stressing me out, I'd let you know. How about you? You look tired, Hugh."

"I admit I've been tossing and turning lately. It's tough reshuffling the deck on a case at this late stage. And if we lose—and we very well might—it's going to bite me in the ass."

Hugh's not the kind of guy who would ever, say, throw his tennis racket in a snit or even sulk after losing a bet, but he likes to win, and it's tough for him when a prize ends up out of reach.

"You'll figure it out, Hugh, I know you will."

"Let's talk about something else for now though, okay?" he says.

Something else. Sure, I've got a few things that could *really* cheer him up. Ha-ha.

"Of course. I'm just sorry you have all this to contend with."

He flashes me a rueful smile. "Nobody said this kind of job would be a picnic. So the podcast went well?"

"Yes. The show wasn't a home run, but at least I felt comfortable doing it." I tell him about the interesting comment that my author guest made regarding executive presence, and I also share Sasha's provocative remark—and how it bordered on a dig.

"Sounds like she's best ignored. . . . How about your book? Have you been able to catch up on that?"

"I'm behind where I want to be, but I'm going to go over notes with Nicole this week, and I'll gear up from there."

"Is that who you were talking to?"

"Talking to?"

"On the phone when I came in."

"No, Nicole's on vacation until tomorrow. . . . That was actually a private investigator. I hired him this afternoon."

Hugh opens his mouth and immediately closes it. I

sense he's biting his tongue. What part does he mind? That I closed the deal without running the terms by him? That I did it at all?

"I know you weren't exactly wild about the idea," I say, "but I really think it'll help. When I was at Dr. Erling's yesterday, she said that my memory might never come back, and this could be the only way for me to find out where I was those two days."

"Well, it's your call, Ally."

I'm about to add that Mulroney has already turned up something worthwhile—the blood type on the tissues—but decide to save it for later. I sense the topic is only adding to Hugh's stress. It also doesn't seem like the right moment to raise my recovered memory.

"Hey, I've got a surprise," I say, switching gears. "I picked up a delicious cheese when I was out. I figured we could both do with something decadent."

He leans back in his chair, twisting his mouth a little in protest. "That was nice, but I don't think I could enjoy it tonight, considering how much work I'm facing. Can you save some for me for tomorrow?"

"Sure," I say, but I feel vaguely defeated. I rise from the table, collecting both plates. "Why don't you pull out your work and I'll make you an espresso?"

"Thanks. This way I'll be ahead of the curve and I can take all the time I need tomorrow to go with you to the neurologist."

I'd almost forgotten.

"Hugh, there's absolutely no reason at all for you to go. I was out and about today and I'm sure I can handle it alone."

"But I've already—"

"Say no more. I'll call you as soon as I'm through and fill you in."

"Okay, but if you change your mind, just let me know."

Despite my insistence on handling cleanup, Hugh helps load the dishwasher. I make an espresso for him and carry it to the table as he's laying out his work.

"Oh, by the way. Sasha said to tell you she remembers where she met you. At the Yale Club a couple of weeks ago."

He sips the espresso, his back to me.

"That lecture I went to?" he says after a moment. "If she says so."

"She apparently went with a friend of hers. Ashley Budd."

He half turns, his face in profile, and wrinkles his smooth, high brow in thought.

"Yeah, I bumped into Ashley that night. She's someone I knew back in law school. Well, please offer Sasha my profuse apologies for not remembering her."

He grabs a stack of papers and begins thumbing through it.

Quietly, I make a cup of herbal tea and take it to the alcove off the master bedroom, where I answer current emails, including one from Casey. She's in the process of editing and rendering the podcast, which will be posted tomorrow.

"Want me to shorten the chat segment in editing?" she asks. "The author interview was so strong, we could even let it run a little long."

"No, better not," I reply. "I'm sure Sasha will count her on-air minutes and complain if we're ten seconds shy of what it should be."

I also email Nicole, asking her to call me tomorrow so we

can touch base about my book. In addition, I mention that I'm curious why she wanted to speak to someone at Greenbacks.

As I'm about to snap the laptop closed, I feel my phone vibrate on the desk. A text from Roger.

Hope u r good. Too late to talk tonight? If not, pls call me.

There's an urgency to the last line that makes me nervous, and I phone him back immediately.

"Hey, what's up?"

"First, tell me how you are."

"Okay, I guess. No reoccurrences at least."

"That's great, Button. So glad to hear it."

"Were you able to talk to your police chief friend?"

"Yeah, that's why I'm calling. I let him know first thing Monday and he dropped by the house a little while ago to discuss the matter. His name's Ted Nowak, and you should definitely start with him."

"Okay, if you give me his number, I'll call and fill him in."

"I've already provided the broad strokes, and he says the next step is actually for you to come in. Says he'd like to meet with you tomorrow if possible."

My stomach drops.

"*Tomorrow*? Why such a rush?"

"Nothing to worry about. It turns out that, coincidentally, they recently decided to do one of those cold case investigations of the girl's murder. I'm sure Nowak is simply eager for whatever he can get his hands on to finally nail the mother or boyfriend—or both."

This full-court press is not what I'd anticipated for a case that's twenty-five years old. I thought it might take days or weeks for the police to even call me back, and that I'd eventually be interviewed, and a few notes would be added to the file.

"Okay, but I'm not sure how I'm going to be able to get out there tomorrow," I say. "I don't feel comfortable driving yet, or even taking a bus by myself."

"Would Hugh be able to leave work a little early and drive you? I could see if the chief could meet late in the day."

"No, he's in the middle of a case. . . . I suppose I could take an Uber out there after my appointment with the neurologist. It shouldn't be too expensive."

"Sounds like a plan. Oh, and just so you're aware, Marion was here when the chief came by, and I had to fill her in, though only in the vaguest way."

"What does she know?" I can't blame Roger, but I hate the idea she's in the loop.

"Nothing about what you've been going through, or what you remembered. I simply told her that the case might be reopened and you were going to do a follow-up interview with the authorities."

"Okay, thanks. I think I can probably make it out there by one or two and could meet with the chief after that."

"I'll let him know and get back to you with details. And Button, like I said, there's nothing to worry about."

We say our good-byes, and a long sigh escapes from my lips as I disconnect. Though I tell myself that Roger's right, there's no reason for concern, my heart's racing. At least it will be better to have the interview behind me instead of hanging over my head. And maybe the reopening of the case means that the killer *will* finally be caught.

I wander into the bathroom, set my cup of lukewarm tea on the stool, and fill the tub with water. I sink in and relish the slight shock of the heat on my skin. The room is dark now, except for the candles I've lit, their flames dancing while their woodsy scent seeps through the air.

I do my best to hold all my troubled thoughts at bay, to make my mind a total blank, but it doesn't work. My fears spill over, as insistently as water gushing from a tear in a hose.

I was missing for two days and still have no clue where I was.

I came home with tissues coated with someone else's blood.

I lied to the police as a child and now they want to meet with me pronto.

My husband seems awkward around me and I can't manage to connect with him in our usual way, no matter how hard I try.

My husband wants a baby and I don't.

I met with my old lover today and my insides are still roiling.

And there's no guarantee that what happened to me last week won't happen again.

18

The appointment with the neurologist, at a medical office building in the East Sixties, turns out to be as anticlimactic as I anticipated. He's in his fifties, I guess, and while not a gold medal winner in the bedside manner category, he's cordial. He examines me, asks a slew of questions—when I tell him what I do professionally, he chuckles softly and says, "Where were you when I needed you?"—and finally says he doesn't suspect a physical cause of what he calls my "TGA," aka "transient global amnesia."

He does, however, prescribe an MRI to rule out any tissue abnormality or a vascular, strokelike event as the cause.

I leave his office as frustrated as ever, though grateful that at least there doesn't appear to be something seriously wrong on the physical front. Lucky me: the problem's all in my head, not in my brain.

Ten minutes later, the Uber I've scheduled pulls up in front of the building, and I hop in, bound for Millerstown, New Jersey.

Hugh had been taken aback this morning when I'd announced my plans for the day over breakfast.

"You're going to *Jersey?*"

"Uh-huh. Roger and I are having lunch at his house since we had so little time to talk the other day."

I was whitewashing the reason for the excursion, but, yet again, it didn't feel like the moment to tell him about the possible reopening of the investigation—and my past deception. Though I'd looked for opportunities later last night, Hugh had kept his nose close to the grindstone and crawled into bed hours after me, staying entirely on his side. I couldn't help but wonder if he was avoiding physical contact with me.

The driver encounters only a few snarls of traffic leaving the city, and before long we're barreling west on I-78. I text Hugh an update on the appointment, then call the facility recommended by the neurologist and schedule an MRI on Friday. With that out of the way, I open my laptop and begin drafting my next personal finance column. I'm now a full week behind schedule, but the topic—applying for a mortgage—is one I'm comfortable with, and passionate about. Despite the 2008 financial disaster, people still don't seem to grasp that the mortgage their bank approves for them isn't necessarily one they can afford, and I feel obligated to keep shouting that through a megaphone.

For an hour or so, the work does a decent job of distracting me, though my thoughts are eventually dragged back to the interview ahead. I glance out the window to see that the bleak, industrial stretches of New Jersey have now given way to farmland, with distant silver silos gleaming in the sun.

The plan, which Roger and I worked out this morning, is for me to stop by his house for lunch, and then he'll drive me to the police station and wait until I'm finished. He apparently lobbied to sit in but was told family members are never allowed unless the subject is underage. Though I wondered at moments whether I should have postponed the interview until I found an attorney to bring along, I've finally decided it's okay that I didn't. It might signal that I have a cause for concern.

By noon, we've reached Millerstown. We turn down a narrow, paved road near the river and bump along past modest houses nestled in trees until we reach my brother's gorgeous home, set high on an embankment. It's part stone, part clapboard, with a widow's walk perched on top.

"Welcome!" Roger calls out as I unfold myself from the Uber and step out onto the driveway at the rear of the house.

The trees, I notice, haven't changed colors here, either, though there's an autumnal scent to the air—a mix of woodsmoke, sour apples, and the sweet scent of decaying leaves.

We hug tightly.

"So happy see you, Button," he says.

"It's good to be here. Thanks for all your help on this."

He swings open the large wooden door and gestures for me to enter first. Though it's called a manor house, his home isn't ridiculously big—only five large rooms on the ground floor and four bedrooms and an office above. But it has what they call great bones, and Roger has exquisitely renovated and decorated every inch. As usual, the river beckons me to the front of the house. Because of the sunny sky, I'm expecting a serene vista, but the water looks high and vexed today, and it's moving fast.

"Where's Marion?" I ask as Roger comes up behind me.

"She ended up having to drive to Princeton to meet a friend whose husband just announced he wants a divorce. But she sends her apologies."

I can't help but wonder if she's manufactured a reason to be absent.

"No problem." I sweep my gaze across the pale blue living room with the red patterned sofa and armchairs, impressive antique wooden side tables, and gold-framed landscape paintings. "I love your place and everything you've done to it, but do you ever miss Boston—you know, the hustle and bustle?"

"At times I do miss the action a little, but I'm glad I'm closer to Dad. And Boston reminds me too much of those tough years with Kaitlin."

Perhaps my situation isn't so unique from the one my brother found himself in back then: a marriage struggling because of issues related to the idea of becoming parents.

"By the way, did I tell you Kaitlin and her new husband adopted a child?"

"No, but I saw that on Facebook," I tell him. I don't add that she and I correspond by email sometimes. Though it wouldn't bother him that we're in touch, I'm sure he senses I'm not a fan of Marion's and I don't want to add any fuel to the fire.

"Well, I'm happy for her. It's what she longed for."

"Do you still have that longing sometimes, Rog?"

"A twinge now and then, yes. And I have to admit, I was lonely that first year in this house. But Marion and I have a pretty full life. . . . You ready for lunch?"

As we step into the kitchen, I see that Roger has laid out a veritable picnic on the long wooden table: fresh bread, cheeses, olives, salami, hummus, a glazed bowl piled with clementines.

"Oh my god," I exclaim. "I thought you said *light* lunch."

"Marion was going to make us a salad—you know what a health nut she is. But when she ended up having to head to Princeton, I decided to go a little wild."

Though I don't have much appetite, I manage to eat a few olives, half a clementine, and a couple of wedges of cheese on bread. I bring Roger up to speed about hiring Mulroney, and the blood test results, before turning the conversation to our father.

"Do you sense he suspects that anything's going on with me?" I ask.

"Not from what I can tell. With his heart situation, he doesn't seem as sharp as he used to be—though I'm hoping that will change when his strength is back in full force."

"I'm relieved that he *hasn't* noticed anything, because it'd be so stressful for him, and he might even try to come back early. . . . I wanted to ask you something else: How do you think he would feel if he knew about me lying to everyone years ago?"

"He'd understand, of course."

"And do you, Roger?" I can't forget how subdued he sounded when I broke the news to him on Sunday.

"Of course. It caught me by surprise when you told me, but there's nothing for you to apologize about. You were only a kid."

I look off into the middle distance.

"I hope you're not ruminating too much about this, Ally," he says.

"It's hard not to. But I'll feel better once this interview is in the rearview mirror."

I notice that a slice of bread smeared with goat cheese is lying untouched on his plate. Maybe he's more concerned than he's letting on.

"Do you think I should have brought a lawyer?" I ask. "I was afraid it might imply I had reason to worry."

"The same thing crossed my mind. But I came to the conclusion you did. Let's see how they respond today and then we can reevaluate if necessary."

"*They*? Do you think there'll be other people besides Nowak there?"

"Oh god, did I forgot to tell you? Yes, one more person. A detective from the Hunterdon County prosecutor's office."

He *did* forget to tell me. I'd been steeling myself for a one-on-one meeting.

"Whoa, I wish I'd known."

"I'm really sorry, Button, it slipped my mind. But it's nothing to be alarmed about. I believe it's the detective who's been looking into the case again."

He rises, hoisting a platter with each hand. "Coffee?"

"Better not. Here, let me help."

"Let's leave most of this here. I'll just stick the cheese and meat in the fridge."

Five minutes later, we're on our way to the police station in Millerstown. During the short drive, I suck on yet another cinnamon Altoid and take so many deep breaths, Roger must think I'm hyperventilating.

My hometown is a small, fairly charming place along the banks of the Delaware River, founded in the mid-1880s.

Thanks to preservation efforts, the town center is pretty much unspoiled by chain stores and fast-food stands and instead boasts shops selling antiques, scented candles, and tchotchkes. Roger makes the turn off River Street and pulls up in front of the police station, an old four-story brick building. Though I often come back to visit my father, I can't recall the last time I was in this particular location.

After Roger parks against the curb, I step out of the car. The woods where I found Jaycee are about two miles away, along the outskirts of town, and yet I feel their psychic drag even from here.

We enter into a large foyer to find a young woman sitting at a gray metal desk, circa 1950s. She's pretty, with long brown hair styled in waves.

"Can I help you?" she asks, swiveling away from her computer screen. She manages to be polite without being friendly. Perhaps an acquired skill for the job.

Roger speaks before I can, announcing that I have an interview scheduled with the chief. The woman nods, rises, and asks me to wait. But she returns quickly and leads me through a warren of tiny offices, obviously reconfigured from the original space. It's a sea of bulging cabinets, climbing manila folders, and bulletin boards plastered with brochures and announcements. Finally, I'm ushered into a windowless faux-wood-paneled room containing nothing more than a table and chairs. A man and woman are sitting there. He's in uniform; she's in a beige blouse and dark-brown wool blazer.

"So you're Ally Linden," the man says, rising and pumping my hand a few times. He introduces himself as Chief Nowak, and I realize I've glimpsed him in town in the past.

He's probably in his fifties, clean-shaven, a big guy with massive forearms shooting from his short-sleeved shirt. "We appreciate you coming in today."

"Well, thank you for making time so quickly," I tell him.

Nowak, I decide, seems kind, sympathetic actually. And so does Detective Jane Corbet once she's introduced. She rises, too, shakes my hand, and offers a smile. She's probably in her late forties, with short, dark hair and brown, penny-shaped eyes. Her only makeup seems to be coral lipstick, half of which now appears to be on the rim of her coffee mug.

I relax a little. Neither one of them looks ready to bite.

"Please, Ms. Linden, have a seat," the chief tells me.

I settle across from them at the gray metal table. Corbet, I notice, has a folder to the right of her notebook. It's fresh-looking and fairly slim, obviously not the file from years ago, which would surely be thick and dog-eared.

"We look forward to hearing what you have to say," Corbet says. "Do you need any water before we start?"

"No, I'm fine, thanks."

"Why don't you go ahead, then. And please, take your time."

I start. I describe, haltingly at moments, my trip home alone through the woods that Wednesday, with me eventually stumbling over a pile of leaves, realizing there was something buried under it, and then investigating. I explain how I tried to convince myself at first that I'd seen an old, discarded doll, how I agonized over whether to tell my parents or keep my discovery a secret so I wouldn't end up in trouble; and how finally, on Friday, I confessed and my parents called the police.

I glance at both people when speaking, but it's clear to me from the sure-footed way Corbet takes notes and manages to hold my gaze that she's the key player here.

As I finish, it occurs to me that I've barely taken a breath for the past ten minutes. I exhale quietly, waiting. Corbet lays down the pen she's been using and looks at me intently.

"That must have been such a traumatic time for you, Ally," she says. "I'm sorry you had to go through all that."

I almost tear up. She's not passing any judgment, not looking at me as if I'm a naughty little liar.

"I appreciate that, Detective Corbet. I'm the one who's really sorry, though. I wish I'd told everyone the full story back then."

Her elbows are resting on the table and she flips over a hand. "Ally, you were only a kid. I've worked many cases involving young people, including sexual abuse cases, and children almost always hold back certain details, at least in the beginning. Some things are just too hard to say."

"Thank you for telling me that," I say. It's a relief to hear that another child might have done the same as me.

"And kids worry, too, about how adults will respond," she says. "It sounds like you were scared your parents would punish you for going home via the woods."

I instinctively jerk forward, like I'm trying to catch something that's about to spill.

"No, they wouldn't have *punished* me," I correct her. "My father's a very kind person, and so was my mom. But they'd told me not to go into the woods without an adult, and I didn't want to disappoint them. And once I decided to admit I'd dawdled at school and taken the shortcut, I was afraid to make things worse for myself by saying I'd waited two days to report what I found."

"Okay," she says, scribbling down a few words. "I hear you." She uses her thumb to flick back through a few pages. "This has been very helpful, but let me review a couple of details. I want to be sure I have the sequence of events down pat."

"Of course."

She scans the page, without her gaze seeming to light on anything, and finally glances up. "The day you actually found the body was on . . . ?"

"Wednesday."

"And you're pretty sure of that? Not, let's say, Tuesday?"

"I'm sure." On Tuesdays my mother and I always had what she called our "tea date" after school, and she would have picked me up.

"And you took the shortcut so you wouldn't be late?"

"Right."

"At about what time did you find the body?"

"Around three thirty, I guess, or maybe a few minutes before."

She drops her gaze slowly to her notes and then looks up again, her eyes leveled at me.

"What held you up at school that day, do you remember?"

"I don't remember very clearly, but I have this vague sense of watching some older kids on the soccer field. I didn't realize how long I'd stayed."

"Had you ever taken that shortcut before?"

"Only with my mom, and only a couple of times."

"You discovered the body along the shortcut?"

"Uh, not exactly. It was a little farther away. I guess I'd wandered off the path by mistake and I was trying to make my way back. That's how I ended up trampling through the pile of leaves."

"And the day you reported what you'd found was . . . ?"

Why isn't that in her notes? Was she not writing everything down? I'm suddenly remembering fragments of my sessions with the police years ago, when they repeated the same questions again and again.

"Friday. I told my parents before dinner and the police came to the house a short while later."

She flips back another page, squinting as she scans it.

"Is there any chance you actually found the body the day before and don't recall correctly?"

I shake my head. "Definitely not. I remember two nights of lying in bed and worrying and then finally getting up my nerve to talk to my mom and dad."

She nods and taps the open page of her notebook. "Great. I think I have the timeline down. Just a few more questions."

"Sure," I say, relieved she's almost done. "Any way I can help."

"Do you recall if the body was fully covered with leaves before you stumbled on it?"

"I think so. I only knew something was there when I hit the body with my foot. And then I kicked more leaves off so I could see what was underneath."

"And did you recognize her?"

Her question, which I hadn't anticipated, makes my heart skip.

"No. Like I said, at first I thought it was a doll, and even after that, I didn't realize it was her."

"You knew Jaycee, though?"

The police must have asked me the same thing years ago, but I don't have any recollection of it.

"I didn't actually know her, but I'd seen her in the yard of her house. She lived a couple of houses down from a friend of mine."

I remembered feeling so sorry for her as she played with a stick in the dirt, dressed in ratty clothes. She seemed to be totally ignored by her family. And one day I'd seen her mother plop her down so hard she cried.

Corbet leans forward, arms on the table. Her face is pinched in concern.

"What happened to Jaycee, do you think? Why do you suppose she was killed?"

This question startles me even more than the last one. How does she expect me to have an answer?

"I have no idea. When I was a little older, I heard that the mother and her boyfriend had been suspects at some point."

"Do you think someone might have simply lost their temper and hurt her without really meaning to?"

My heart's racing now, like it wants to burst out of my chest. Where is she going with this?

"God, I don't know—but to me it doesn't make any difference. It was a horrible, evil thing to do, no matter what."

Against my will, my eyes well with tears. and I have to brush them away.

"I'm sorry," Corbet says. "It must be upsetting to relive this. We're almost done now. I know it was a long time ago, but is there anything else you recall that may be relevant? Did you notice anyone in the woods that day?"

"No one," I say, trying to regain my composure. "I remember looking behind me. And then I ran. I was scared."

"What about the spot where the body was? A piece of evidence that could have blown away by the time the crime scene unit arrived two days later?"

"Nothing comes to mind, unfortunately." *Please*, I think. I'm dying to be released from this windowless room. "I only remember leaves. And then seeing her. She was so pale. And her leg . . ."

A memory wiggles through, not visual but *tactile*: the rigidity of her flesh as my foot made contact. "I'm just remembering this now," I say. "Her leg. It felt hard when I touched it with my shoe. Stiff."

And when I leaned down and felt it with the tips of my fingers. But I don't add that.

I sense Corbet go on high alert, and she and Nowak shoot each other a look. It takes me a second to realize the meaning of what's spilled from my mouth

The body was hard to the touch. I know next to nothing about forensics, but I'm aware of what rigor mortis is. The stiffening of the muscles that occurs for a short time after death, then dissipates.

All this time I've been holding a clue about Jaycee's murder, maybe a critical one. And I've kept it to myself.

s it significant?" I ask, hating how weak my voice sounds. Of *course* it's significant. But I need Corbet to tell me how much.

"Hard like what?" she asks, ignoring my question.

"Uh, like something frozen maybe."

"Are you sure you're remembering correctly after all this time?"

"Yes, I'm positive."

"Do you recall if you told the police this years ago?"

"No, not in those words. I'm pretty sure I related the same thing I said to you earlier—that at first I thought I'd come across a doll. But I probably didn't explain that was partly because her leg was so hard. . . . Is this something that could really matter?"

"We'll have to present this to the coroner and factor it in with other details from the case." Her face is a blank now, giving nothing away. "But I'm glad you shared this with us, Ms. Linden. Was there anything else you recall?"

"No, nothing," I tell her. I'm so mentally drained right now it's hard to imagine summoning another thought even if I had one.

She turns to Nowak. "Chief, do you have any additional questions?"

"No, I think we've covered everything. I want to thank Ms. Linden for coming in. It's much appreciated."

Corbet concurs, capping her pen and wearing her sympathetic face again.

Nowak shows me out, and when I reach the foyer, I'm dismayed to see that the only one there is the secretary, murmuring into the office phone. With a hand over the mouthpiece, she informs me that Roger has stepped outside. I find him leaning against the building, chin in hand.

"Hey, sorry, I needed some— What's the matter?" He's clearly reading the distress in my eyes. "Didn't it go well?"

"I fucked up big-time," I say.

"In the interview?"

"No, years ago—by not admitting when I found the body."

"Hold on," he says, glancing around, "let's jump in the car first."

As soon as we're seated, I tell him about Jaycee's leg, how her body must have been in rigor mortis when I stumbled upon it.

"Okay, I'm not quite following," Roger says. "I know the term rigor mortis, but not how it actually works."

"When you die, your body stiffens after a certain period of time, and then eventually—at least as I understand it— the stiffness goes away." I stuff my hand into my purse and produce my phone. "Why don't you drive—I need to get out of here—and I'll google it."

While Roger fires up the engine and pulls the car away

from the curb, I summon the info on my phone, twice misspelling the term in my haste.

"Okay, here it is: 'Rigor is a result of chemical changes in the muscles following death, which cause the limbs to stiffen. It starts in the small muscles right after a person dies, and within twelve to twenty-four hours the body is completely stiff. . . . And then at about twenty-four hours from death, the limbs gradually soften up again. . . .' Uh, it says if the air is cold, rigor can take longer to form. But I don't recall it being chilly out that day."

"We don't know what condition her body was in when the police retrieved it on Friday, but it sounds like when *you* found her, rigor mortis had fully set in."

"Right." My breathing's become shallow, and I force myself to inhale deeply. "And that means she'd probably been dead for a day when I came across her. Maybe longer. What I told the police today could help them pinpoint the time of death."

"But don't you think they were able to do that years ago? I mean, they rely on other data, too, right?"

"They must, but I'm sure they consider all the factors together—and I deprived them of a key piece of evidence. You said the other day that the mother didn't report the girl missing right away. Do you know anything more specific about her and the boyfriend's alibis?"

"I probably did at the time, but not any longer."

"God, by lying about when I found her, I may have totally fucked up the case. It could have prevented someone from being prosecuted."

"Ally, first of all, you have to stop saying it was a lie. You were simply too frightened to recall and reveal every detail. And don't get ahead of yourself. There's more than a good chance your revelation doesn't alter an iota of what was determined years ago. Why don't I try to talk to the chief again tomorrow? Maybe I can get him to clue me in on the original investigation."

"Okay, but I'm not sure if the other detective will let him breathe a word. She's pretty tough—and very much in charge."

"She wasn't hard on you, was she?"

"I don't know exactly what you'd call it." Summoning the encounter in my mind makes my stomach twist. "She seemed sympathetic at first—she even said it was really normal for kids to withhold information—but things started to shift."

"What do you mean?"

"She asked me a few questions more than once, like she hadn't been paying enough attention when she first asked them. But I think she wanted to see if my answers matched. And then she wondered if I thought Jaycee had been killed by someone who hadn't really meant to hurt her. How could my opinion on that possibly matter?"

A car horn blares, and Roger jerks the steering wheel to the right. I'm making it hard for him to concentrate.

"I wouldn't put much stock in that," he says. "As far as we know, she probably did some kind of detective training program where they teach you a certain style."

"I guess. . . . I'm going to have to tell Dad about this sooner or later, aren't I? Because if my statement makes a difference, it's all going to come out."

The idea only adds to my discomfort. This is the last thing my dad needs right now.

"Why don't you hold off thinking about that for now? I hate the idea of telling him over the phone. I may end up flying out there in a few weeks and I could bring him up to speed in person."

"Okay. Maybe I could even go with you."

"I'd love that, Button. . . . What time did you schedule your Uber for?"

I glance at my watch. "Fifteen minutes from now." I knew I'd been cutting it a little close, but I figured I could change it if the police kept us waiting.

Roger reaches out with his free hand and gives my fingers a squeeze. "Why don't you push it back? We could have a glass of wine at the house or I could make you a cappuccino. You know what a good barista I am."

I express my thanks but tell him no. Part of me is sorely tempted to stay, but I need to get home and finally fill Hugh in. Plus, hanging at Roger's will increase my chance of running into Marion, who's bound to be back from Princeton by now.

And sure enough, she strides from the kitchen as we enter the house, dressed smartly in beige slacks and a matching V-neck cashmere sweater. Even from across the room I can smell her fragrance, that cloying mix of roses and jasmine.

"So how did it go today?" she asks, advancing. Her eyes flick back and forth between Roger and me as if she's watching a tennis match.

"Very perfunctory," Roger says, covering. "Ally talked to them, they asked her a few questions, and that was it."

She allows her gaze to light on me. "Oh, but it must have been hard for you, dear."

"Thanks, but it wasn't so bad."

"Well, hopefully this is one of those cold cases they'll be able to finally close."

"Would you mind if I poured myself a glass of water?" I ask her. "I have to take off in a minute."

"I'd be glad to get it for you," she says and disappears.

Next to me, Roger scratches the back of his neck, looking distracted. He's asked Marion nothing about her friend, the ditched wife, so maybe it really *was* a story concocted to explain her absence.

As I check my phone and report to Roger that my Uber is two minutes away, Marion returns with a glass of ice water, a small wedge of lemon bobbing on top. Am I too hard on her?

She and I say good-bye with an awkward hug, and Roger sees me outside, where a gray Toyota soon pulls up.

"Button, promise me you won't let this eat at you," Roger advises. "The bottom line is that you did the right thing by going in today. You have no reason to feel anything but good about that."

"Thanks, Rog. If Nowak does share details about the case with you, will you let me know as soon as possible?"

"Will do. By the way, I forgot to mention earlier that I looked up Dr. Hadley, and she passed away a couple of years ago. No one seems to have taken over her practice and that means her records might be long gone."

I nod, resigned—I hadn't expected any luck on this front—and hug my brother tightly. When I open the car door, the driver confirms my identity, and a minute later we're off. I twist in my seat to see Roger moving quickly into the house.

We've barely left the driveway when I spot a text from Hugh.

> How was the visit with Roger?
> Good. Will fill u in later
> Great. Any problem if I work til 8 here? I need access to files.
> Sure, no prob. see u then.

Despite my response, I'm frustrated. I now have so much to update Hugh on, and I feel the need to do it *tonight*, before I'm rear-ended by another discovery or situation.

I suddenly notice I have a voice mail that must have come in while I had my phone off at the police station. It's from Mulroney.

"Call me," he says. "I've got news."

Grabbing a breath, I phone back immediately, but to my chagrin, he doesn't pick up. "I'm available all day from this point on," I say in my message, not disguising how desperate I am to speak to him.

I'm about to scroll through emails when Nicole finally returns my call from the morning.

"Sorry to miss you earlier," she says. "But remember, I mentioned I was only coming in for the afternoon today?"

"Oh, right, yes." Something she'd told me weeks ago about how she'd been unable to find an earlier flight back from Jamaica wiggles into my head. Another memory slip on my part.

"I'll make up the hours at—"

"Don't worry about it. How was the wedding?" I say, at least recalling *that*.

"Nice. Of course, my sister wanted to save money by holding it during hurricane season, and we're just incredibly lucky the weather was okay. . . . Um, listen, I saw your question about Greenbacks. There must be some kind of misunderstanding. I never called anyone there."

"But if it wasn't you, who was it?"

Nicole hesitates briefly.

"Uh, I hate to throw anyone under the bus . . ."

"Just tell me, Nicole. Please."

I hear a quick intake of breath on the other end. I've never been short with her before.

"It may have been Sasha."

Why would *Sasha* be calling over there?

"What makes you say that?"

"I overheard her on the phone when she dropped by our office a couple of weeks ago, and she mentioned Greenbacks. I don't think she was talking to anyone in the company then, just talking *about* the place, but it caught my attention because I know you used to work there."

"Can you imagine any reason she would contact them?"

"Not really. I never ask her to handle any research involving the book or the column, so maybe it had something to do with the podcast."

I'm very clear with Sasha about who she should be calling regarding the podcast and I've never mentioned the name Greenbacks.

"Thanks, I'll speak to her. And look, I know you and I

need to catch up about the book. I've been a bit under the weather lately, but I'll definitely be coming into WorkSpace tomorrow."

"Okay, I'll have everything ready to review."

With the conversation concluded, I'm about to call Sasha and get to the bottom of the situation, when my phone rings. Mulroney's name lights up my screen.

"What's up?" I say, gripping the phone.

"We're starting to put pieces of the puzzle together."

Okay, wow.

"I'm all ears."

"I should have more later, but let me tell you what I've turned up so far. I'll start with Tuesday morning. You left your apartment building at around nine wearing a dark trench coat—I determined this through video footage, by the way—and for the next hour and a half or so, you hung out in a café kind of place called—I've never been sure how to say it—Le Pain Quotidien, several blocks from your home."

"That would make sense," I say, not bothering to correct his pronunciation, which made the last word in the name sound like *quotient*. "If I need a change of scenery, I sometimes go over there with my laptop. Except—except I don't have a digital record of working on anything that day."

"According to a waitress I spoke to, you ordered tea or coffee—she doesn't remember which—and leafed through a couple of magazines. She's almost positive you had a purse and thinks she remembers you looking at your phone but isn't sure."

"The magazine part is the only thing that's odd. I usually don't do that sort of thing in the middle of a workday."

Of course, maybe I simply needed to decompress after fighting with Hugh the night before.

"She says the main reason she remembers is that when you were paying the bill, you asked if she wanted the magazines, and she took them. She said you seemed pretty distracted and told her you were in a rush and needed to get the train to Forty-Second Street. You paid in cash."

"Forty-Second Street?" I feel myself squinting in confusion.

"Can you think of any reason you would head there?"

"None. I usually do a podcast on Tuesdays at a studio on Ninth Avenue and Forty-Eighth, but we weren't recording that particular day. And there'd be no reason for me to go as far south as Forty-Second. I try to avoid Times Square as much as I can."

"Hmm."

"Do you think if something *did* happen to me that day, it might have been in that area?"

"Possibly, though we don't know how long you were there. Could you search your emails for any reference to Forty-Second Street, in case an appointment slipped your mind?"

Well, that's one way to put it.

"Will do."

"Now on to Wednesday, where I have an even bigger surprise. I dropped by Eastside Eats and it turns out there's a second location—on East *Seventh* Street—and that's where you actually bought food that day. A counter person there recalls you coming in around the lunch hour. The charge on your credit card bill would have indicated the name but not the address."

"That one makes even *less* sense," I exclaim. "I would have no reason whatsoever to be in the East Village."

"You ordered a sandwich, she thinks. Maybe coffee, too. She remembers you because—and you can't take this personally—she was worried at first that the credit card you were using might not be yours."

"*What?*"

"She thought you seemed a little disheveled and you hesitated before signing your name. *Plus*, you didn't have a purse. You pulled the card out of your coat pocket, which means that if you did still have your purse with you when you lost your phone on Tuesday, it was gone by this point."

"Weird," I say, baffled. "My purse was missing, but I still had a credit card."

"Yeah. Doesn't sound like you were mugged."

For a minute I'm silent, attempting to absorb everything he's shared so far. It's like one of those times when a friend tells you a story about something funny or crazy you did one night years ago when the two of you were out barhopping together, but you can't recall a single, solitary moment of the evening.

"I think I should go down to the East Village," I announce finally.

"That's a good idea. It might trigger a memory. Start at Eastside Eats and then walk around the area, too. I don't have a complete picture yet, but it seems like you spent quite a bit of time there."

"What do you mean?"

"You came to the sandwich shop from farther east and headed back in that direction when you left. And we also found footage of you walking near Tompkins Square Park, along the western end."

"I don't get it. I once took a night class at NYU and used to explore the area when I was down there, but that was years ago, right after I moved to the city after graduation."

"We'll figure it out. I need to jump on another call, but let's speak later."

After we sign off, I fling myself back against the seat. I have no reason to doubt Mulroney, but his revelations aren't computing for me. What was I doing in that part of the city?

And more importantly, what had caused me to run from myself and everything that mattered to me?

20

Due to bad traffic, I don't make it back to the city until close to seven. But that still means I have an hour to kill before Hugh arrives home. I peel off my dress, change into jeans and a sweater, and order dinner for the two of us from Pavone's. That's twice in seven days, but I lack the energy to devise a more original plan.

Next, I do as Mulroney suggested and search through my emails for any reference to Forty-Second Street. There's nothing. But when I sit down to flesh out and update my timeline, I realize that with Mulroney's help, I'm definitely making progress.

MONDAY
evening: dinner, TV, argument

TUESDAY
7:00: still in bed
9:00-ish: took call from Dr. Erling
9:00–9:17: sent emails
9:30: hung out at café

11:00-ish: left for 42nd Street
Before 3:00: *possibly witnessed someone get injured???;*
            lost phone
3:00 to 3:30-ish: called WorkSpace

WEDNESDAY
Noon-ish: bought food at Eastside Eats, East 7th St.
Afternoon: walked near Tompkins Square Park

THURSDAY
8:05: arrived at Greenbacks

Now I turn to my laptop and google *rigor mortis* again, doing a deeper dive than I'd been able to in the car with Roger. It turns out there are other variables besides air temperature that can stall its onset or hasten the process. Muscle mass or recent exercise, for instance. But the bottom line is that the stiffening of muscles begins a few hours after death, reaches its peak approximately twelve hours after death, remains that way for twelve more hours, and then subsides, completely dissipating by the thirty-six-hour mark.

Which makes one thing pretty clear: Since Jaycee's body already seemed frozen when I accidentally kicked it on Wednesday at three thirty, she must have been killed much earlier, possibly Tuesday. By Friday, her body would have passed out of rigor.

I keep reading. Rigor isn't the only factor a coroner relies on in determining time of death. There's also body temperature, stomach contents, and something called lividity, the settling of blood in the lowest surface of the body postmortem, causing purplish-red discoloration of the skin. All those years ago, the Millerstown area coroner obviously took those factors into consideration when making his or her determination. But still, if I'd been completely forthright, it would have certainly been of help.

I take a long, deep breath and type "Jaycee Long" into the search bar. I probably should have done that six or seven weeks ago when I first started discussing my past with Dr. Erling, but I wasn't able to summon the nerve.

To my surprise, there's next to nothing online. It seems like the area newspaper that serves my hometown didn't begin digitally archiving stories until about two years after the murder. I'm going to have to trek to the library out there and comb through microfilm to read news coverage of the crime.

Though maybe I won't have to. If I'm lucky, Chief Nowak will be amenable to sharing details with Roger about the original investigation, including how seriously the mother and her boyfriend were viewed as suspects.

Mercifully, the intercom jars me from my thoughts, signaling that dinner has arrived. I pay at the door, set the food out on the counter, and pour myself a glass of wine. My whole body is vibrating with tension.

By the time Hugh arrives home, it's after eight—8:25, actually. He gives me a quick hug and yanks off his tie.

"So sorry. The case is such a mess."

He returns from the bedroom a few minutes later wearing jeans but still in his blue-collared shirt, the sleeves rolled to his elbows. The sight of him dressed like that fills me with tenderness. He'd worn his shirt that way on our second date—our third encounter—and the night when I began to feel the first spark of desire.

Desire. I realize that the last time we had sex was the Sunday before I fell apart.

While I microwave the chicken piccata, Hugh grabs a barstool at the island and I end up serving the dinner there. "Do you want wine?" I ask, before sliding onto a stool next to him.

"No, I still have work and I'll need to focus." He drops his gaze to my half-full wineglass. "You think it's okay for you?"

"I've been having wine here and there, and it doesn't seem to be a problem. . . . Hugh, I know this isn't the ideal moment, but I have to talk to you. I put it off before because of all the pressure you're under at work, and I realize I shouldn't have."

"Is it about the neurologist?" He levels his gaze at me, his face tensing with concern.

"No, there's nothing beyond what I told you, unless the MRI turns up something on Friday. But there are a few things I need you to know."

"That sounds ominous."

"I wouldn't use that word. But there's stuff you should be aware of. First, the investigator I hired called with a couple of updates."

"Okay, shoot."

"Those tissues that were in my coat pocket? It turns out the blood on them isn't mine. Mulroney—that's his name—had an analysis done, and it's type A positive. I'm O negative."

"Wow. So whose blood is it?"

"I don't have a clue, but I keep coming back to something Gabby said—that maybe when I was missing, I tried to help a person who'd been injured." A stray thought crosses my mind as I'm talking. "Wait, what's your blood type? You aren't A positive, are you?"

"Gosh, I'm sure I knew at one point, but I can't recall at the moment." He smiles ruefully. "But if you're thinking you might have taken a swing at me and bloodied my nose, that didn't happen."

"Of course not, I'm just trying to put all the pieces together. . . . Mulroney also says that video footage he's secured shows me hanging around the East Village on Wednesday. That's where that food place actually was. And I apparently looked pretty disheveled."

He frowns. "Like you'd been injured?"

"No, I guess the same as on Thursday, as if I hadn't showered."

"But why the East Village?"

"I don't know—I can't remember the last time I was there. Can you?"

"Not really. I mean, we had dinner downtown a month or so ago, but that was the *West* Village." He spears a piece of chicken with a fork and chews it absentmindedly. "That all the guy has so far?"

"For now, yes, but more will come in time."

"Okay, I guess it's a start."

"There's still something else I need to tell you. Not about Mulroney."

I let it all spill out: my deception years ago, the way it came back to me the other night while sitting alone in our den, and my interview with the police today. Before my eyes, his expression morphs from perplexed to baffled to shocked. Not at all what I was banking on.

"Please, say something, Hugh," I insist after I've finished and he's sitting there, mouth agape. "You look horrified."

"Ally, that's ridiculous. I'm not horrified at all. But it's a lot to digest."

"I'm sorry, I didn't mean to snap. But I've been nervous about sharing all this with you. And like I said, I wanted to tell you earlier—but you've had so much on your plate."

"You can't hold things back from me, no matter how much pressure I'm under. I need to know this stuff."

"You're right," I say, feeling a fresh twinge of guilt. "I'll do better going forward."

"It didn't cross your mind that it might be smart to have a lawyer with you today?"

So he's doubly annoyed. Not only did I neglect to loop him in, but I didn't bother asking his legal advice.

"I considered it, but I was afraid doing that would make it look like I had a reason to be worried—and Roger agreed."

"Roger's a legal expert now?"

"I'm not saying that, but he has good instincts. And in hindsight, I realize that bringing a lawyer would have definitely rubbed this detective the wrong way."

"So how did she respond to this new piece of information?"

"She said they would share it with the coroner, but she didn't let on how significant she thought it might be."

"Was she critical of you?"

"Uh, she didn't seem to be. She said kids are often too

stressed to divulge everything in a situation like that, and they leave stuff out."

"That makes sense, I guess."

I start to tell him about the part of the interview that made me so uncomfortable, but I hold back. Despite just having promised to be more forthcoming, I don't want to dump anything more on Hugh tonight.

"Do . . . do you think my statement is enough, or that I'll be asked to testify if someone is arrested?"

"You'd definitely be required to testify," he says bluntly, as if he's thinking, *So* now *she wants my advice.*

He pushes around the last piece of chicken on his plate without bringing it to his mouth. Instinctively I glance at my own plate. I've barely touched a morsel, and now the lemon sauce has congealed into an unappetizing, glutinous glob.

"What you told me about finding the kid," Hugh says. "You only remembered it the other night? Out of the blue?"

"Not out of the *blue*," I insist. "It was after I'd come back from coffee with Roger. Something was nagging me, and I finally realized what it was."

Hugh sets his fork across his plate and swivels until he's facing me. "Is there any chance you only remembered this detail recently because you might have been in a fugue state back then, after you found the body?"

I shake my head.

"No way. I'm sure Roger would have told me if there'd been anything like that."

"Okay, I was just wondering . . . in light of everything that's happened."

"Trust me, I wasn't in a fugue state then. I lied—and then

I pushed away the memory, but I was all there." I change the subject abruptly. "Are you finished? I should let you work."

"Ally, I didn't mean to upset you."

"Don't worry about it," I say, turning so he can't see the disheartened expression on my face. "It's a relevant question."

We do a fast cleanup, and afterward I drift into the bedroom with a cup of herbal tea. There, I phone Gabby, realizing she never responded to my message from yesterday. I'd really love to talk to her, but the call once again goes straight to voice mail. It's so unlike her to be uncommunicative, especially since she's aware of the mess I'm in. Perhaps she's caught up in a work-related crisis.

I start to toss the phone on the bed, but instead do something I probably shouldn't and call my father. There's a decent chance, I realize, particularly considering how low my mood is, that he'll pick up on my anxiety, but I still long for the comfort of his voice.

"Hey, Button," he proclaims after I've announced myself. "What a lovely surprise."

There's an energy in his tone I haven't heard since before his heart attack.

"I thought I'd do a quick check-in before bed."

"All good on this end. I'm feeling stronger every day, and Quinn and the family have been spoiling me rotten."

"That's what Roger told me."

"He says you two have spent some time together lately. Glad to hear it."

"Yes, it's been fun. But I miss you, Dad."

Careful, I warn myself. *Don't go all weepy on him.*

"I miss you too, honey. By the way, I listened to your

podcast today. Excellent as usual. Your mom would be so proud of you."

He speaks that phrase often enough, but this time it makes me want to start bawling. I take a breath to guarantee my voice won't crack.

"Thanks. I like to think she would be."

After we hang up with a pair of "I love you's," I don't know whether to feel relieved or saddened. My dad clearly didn't detect any cues of distress from me, and I'm glad I haven't given him a reason to worry, but deep down a part of me *wants* him to know, wants him to notice the anguish in my voice so he can assuage my fears, especially after Hugh's deflating response tonight.

But in the end, how helpful could my dad really be? He's three thousand miles away. And he can't tell me where I was those two days—or why I felt an urgent, crazy need to leave myself behind.

I strip off my clothes, don a pair of pajamas, and slip into bed with my iPad. After a feeble attempt to engage with the book I'd been reading, I end up replaying my conversation with Hugh from earlier, hoping that if I can see his comments from another angle, they won't leave me so disquieted. I was praying for understanding and acceptance, and I came away with neither of those.

Maybe Hugh wasn't passing judgment. It could be instead that his annoyance over being left in the dark shaded his reaction. He might even be worried that I've put myself in legal jeopardy.

Or—and this scares me—maybe what I actually saw with him tonight was fear pooling to the surface. Fear that he married a woman who came unhinged not only last week, but at other times during her past. Where will that fear take him?

What if, as Hugh suggested, I *was* in a dissociative state years ago? One I don't even know about? And what if there's more that I don't remember from that day in the woods?

Clearly the interview with the cops in Millerstown is still weighing on me, especially the one weird question Corbet asked.

I throw off the covers, climb out of bed, and after plopping down at my desk in the alcove, I open my laptop. Then I google "Techniques detectives use in interviews and in interrogations."

A host of links pop up—to blog posts, descriptions of courses on the subject, even pages from textbooks. I start with the first link and begin scrolling, my eyes racing over the words. Cops, it turns out, use all sorts of cagey strategies to elicit the truth, sometimes pinning people to a psychological wall. Before long I find a reference to a common strategy that makes my skin crawl: offering a suspect an acceptable excuse for committing the crime. It allows—even encourages—the person to confess without losing face.

I realize, staring at the words, that Corbet had used that technique on me, when she mentioned the idea of someone losing their temper and not really meaning to cause any harm. My heart sinks.

Could she possibly believe I was the one who'd killed Jaycee Long?

21

SESSION WITH DR. ERLING

By the time I reach Dr. Erling's office the next day, I'm nearly jumping out of my skin.

She greets me warmly and ushers me into her inner sanctum. She's in slim black pants and a cobalt-blue silk blouse, perfectly polished as usual.

"How are you doing today, Ally?" she asks once I'm seated.

"Not good. I guess I don't feel as fragile as I did on Monday, but so many things seem to be unraveling at the same time. I haven't remembered anything else, by the way. Which makes it all worse."

"Why don't you start with what's worrying you the most?"

I tell her about going to see the police in New Jersey yesterday, my realization that the body was in rigor when I found it, and the possible ramifications of my deception.

"I feel really guilty," I say. "If I'd told the truth, it might have allowed the police to pinpoint the time of death—and figure out who the killer was."

"How did the police respond to the information you shared with them?"

"Oh, they pretended to understand why I wasn't forthcoming as a nine-year-old. But later, the lead detective asked these weird questions. It was almost like she was trying to trip me up."

"Trip you up how?"

"She wanted me to repeat certain details, even though she'd taken notes when I was talking. And then—she said this one thing that was really odd, like a trick question. . . . She wanted to know if I thought someone might have lost their temper with Jaycee and hurt her without really meaning to."

"Why did that feel like a trick question?"

I look away without meaning to.

"It was so out of the blue, and besides, how would I *know*? It was like this detective thought I might respond, 'Yes, that's exactly what happened. I took Jaycee from her yard to play with her in the woods and when she started to cry, I just wanted to get her to stop, and I ended up smashing her head with a rock.' I can see why innocent people confess to crimes they didn't commit. The police lay all these traps for you when you're already nervous and confused just from being there."

Erling steeples her hands and taps them lightly against her lips a few times. I'm familiar with most of her gestures, but I don't think I've ever seen this one before. Does it mean something?

"What was your response to her?" she asks.

"That there *wasn't* any excuse. And there isn't, not for hurting a child. It's been hard to even think about the whole thing again. That little girl being brutally attacked and dying and stuffed under a pile of leaves."

She leans forward and her expression shifts from neutral to sympathetic.

"It *does* sounds like the interview was very stressful," she says. "What if you looked at it another way? That the detective was probably just trying to do her job, covering her bases, and that it doesn't mean she really thinks you could have been the one who hurt Jaycee?"

"That's what Roger said. But what if the police want to see me again? And oh, you should have seen Hugh's reaction when I told him what I'd done back then. For a split second he looked totally wigged-out, like he'd just noticed I had one of those suicide belts strapped around my waist and was going to detonate it any second. Then he asked if I might have been in a fugue state at the time. Not with concern. More like—I don't know, like he was interrogating me. So much for the idea of Hugh and me talking more."

"What do you think was really going on in Hugh's mind when you shared your revelation with him?"

I gnaw on my thumb, considering. To me he came across as unsympathetic, judgmental even, but I know she's wondering if there was something below the surface.

"I guess part of him was *scared*," I say finally, "because what I was telling him didn't fit with how he views me as a person."

I realize as the words tumble from my mouth that this

is the first time I've formed this idea into a thought I can articulate.

"How so?"

"I think part of the reason Hugh was drawn to me—besides the physical attraction—was that he saw me as a together, responsible person, someone who'd been smart about her career and her life. He's always been pretty buttoned-up himself, and he knew he could count on me, that I was never going to drop the ball with what matters. And now I've become this kind of wild card. I came unglued, and he's wondering if it's not the first time—or even the last."

In some ways it's a relief to spell it out, but at the same time, I have no idea where I go from here.

"So what the hell does this mean for the future?" I ask before she can respond.

"Sometimes it simply takes people a while to process the turmoil a partner is going through and become more accepting. The more time you and Hugh spend talking, the better."

"But I *did* make time to talk to him, and look what happened. . . . I'm sure part of why he's so bothered is the mystery of it all."

"The mystery?"

"Me showing up at Greenbacks. Being gone for *two whole days*. Oh, that reminds me of something else I wanted to tell you. The detective told me yesterday that I was apparently roaming around the East Village on at least one of those days I was gone."

"The detective in Millerstown said that?" Erling's brow furrows in a rare expression of confusion. "How would she know?"

"Oh, sorry—no, not her. I'm talking about Kurt Mulroney, the private detective I'm using."

She still looks confused. "You hadn't mentioned you were hiring anyone," she says.

"Sorry, I guess I decided to hire him since I saw you last. It just seemed like the smart thing to do since my memory refuses to budge, and this way, I'll at least know where I was. He's obtaining as much video footage as he can, and so far, he's been able to determine that I was in the East Village on Wednesday."

"Why that neighborhood, do you think?"

I explain I have no idea, that the last time I spent any real time there was when I took that night class. I find myself telling her how I liked to have dinner after class in the garden of this little restaurant on East Ninth Street. I'd bring a notebook to scribble in and daydream about life, or sometimes just sit and people-watch.

Erling smiles. "It sounds like the time you spent down there was meaningful to you."

"Yes," I say, nodding. "But it was so long ago. And the restaurant I used to eat at closed down."

"Why don't you give some thought tonight to what it was like to eat there? Think about the experience of sitting at the table, enjoying your food, watching the other diners, and why you liked it so much."

"Okay."

"Have you learned anything else from the investigator?" she asks.

I glance at my watch. There are only a few minutes left to the session, but we still have so much ground to cover.

"Yes, there's something else that might be important. He figured out that the blood on the tissues—the ones that were in my coat pocket—was a different type than mine. So it's not from one of my nosebleeds or anything."

This time it's Erling who looks off, thinking.

"What do you suppose that means?" she asks, returning her gaze.

"I keep coming back to the idea that I might have witnessed something bad on Tuesday. That I saw someone get hurt or attacked, and I tried to help them, and that's what made me disassociate, not the fight with Hugh. And that would explain why I needed to borrow a phone."

"Borrow a phone?"

"Oh, gosh, sorry, I never got to that part the last time." The sessions are shorter than I wish they were and so much seems to be happening in between. "Remember how I told you I'd called the desk manager at WorkSpace, trying to find someone who knew when our appointment was? I apparently told him I was using someone else's phone. And so I think I lost mine somehow when this bad thing happened."

As I'm talking, I feel a trickle of sweat roll down the back of my neck and realize I've started to hyperventilate.

"I just wish I could figure it out," I add. "And that things were better with Hugh, and that I could share some of this with my dad. To make everything worse, my friend Gabby has gone MIA on me. It's like—"

"Ally," Erling interrupts, leaning forward. "I want you to take a couple of deep breaths right now. Would you like me to go through the process again?"

"No, I remember . . ."

I do as she says, inhaling, holding, letting each breath out slowly. It definitely calms me down a little.

"Good," Erling says, reading my expression. "I know it's important for you to figure out the truth, Ally, but I'd like you to consider taking the rest of the day to relax. You mentioned once how much you enjoy going to the café near your home. Take some time alone there before dinner, have a cup of tea, bring a book with you if you want."

"Right. I can do that." Of course, I'm behind on my *own* book and the column, too, but those will have to wait.

"I also want you to put a temporary halt on any data gathering. I know information seems extremely valuable right now, but it's clearly distressing you, and I'm afraid it might trigger another dissociative state. For the time being, I think you should stay offline."

"Okay," I say, silently swearing that this time I mean it. "I just wish it wasn't so long until my next appointment."

"Unfortunately, I'm fully booked tomorrow, but what if we plan to speak on Saturday? I don't have office hours on weekends, but I could do a session with you over the phone or via Skype? Do you use Skype?"

"Yes, of course," I tell her. "I'd really like to talk this weekend." It's a relief to know I won't have to wait until Monday.

"Let's say two P.M. Email me your Skype handle when you have a moment."

She rises, signaling the session is over.

"Thanks," I say, rising, too. "Then I only have to get through tomorrow."

"One last thing, Ally," she says as we walk toward the

door. "You asked what you should do if the police in Millers-town want to see you again. If that happens, I think it's important that you take an attorney with you."

My heart lunges forward. "You think I need an *attorney*?"

"Simply as a safeguard, Ally. You don't want to say any-thing you don't mean to. We can talk about that more on Saturday."

She walks me to the waiting room, says good-bye, and closes the door behind me. The next patient isn't here yet and I have the space to myself. I lean against one of the walls, trying to catch my breath.

It will be all right, I promise myself. *It's going to get better.* I'm *going to get better.*

But I don't know if I really believe that.

grab a cab home and as I'm turning my phone off silent, it rings in my hands. *Gabby.*

"I'd nearly given you up for dead," I say. I don't mean for it to come out bitchily, but I notice my frustration over not hearing from her leak into my voice.

"Well, I practically am," she says, her voice froggy.

"Hey, what's the matter?"

"I came down with the worst fucking cold. I think I must have picked it up from this guy who was in my row on the plane, hacking his brains out."

"Oh gosh, that's terrible, Gab." I now feel more than a twinge of guilt for being dismayed by her radio silence. "Can I do anything?"

"No, no, I'm just sorry to be out of touch. I wanted to call you, but I haven't been able to lift my head off the pillow."

"Have you checked in with your doctor?"

"Yeah, and she said it's probably viral so antibiotics won't help. What's happening with you? *Tell* me."

"Still trying to figure things out," I say, lowering my voice.

"I hired a private eye, like you suggested—an ex-cop named Mulroney—and he's turned up some interesting stuff."

I hear her cough into a tissue, a mean, dry cough that must really hurt.

"Wow, what kind of stuff?" she asks.

I want to tell her everything, but it doesn't seem fair when she's so sick.

"Why don't we talk in a day or two—once you're better. Can I at least bring you food? I'm planning to run out for a cup of tea later."

"Thanks, but I don't want you anywhere near this thing. And I'm okay in the food department. Right now, I'm living on DayQuil and can't bear the thought of anything else."

"Okay, I'll text you later to see how you are."

"Sounds good. And please, let me know if anything happens with you, okay?"

"Will do."

Poor Gabby. But I can't help but wallow for a moment. I need her right now, especially since I haven't been able to rely on Hugh as much as I hoped.

With my phone out, I notice I have two voice mails from when I was in session with Erling, one from Derek Kane, my point person at the company that sponsors the podcast. He asks simply that I give him a ring. The other's from Sasha, who's finally deigned to return my call from yesterday and a follow-up I made today. I'm sure she's been sulking about my less-than-glowing feedback.

I start with Derek, since the sponsorship is coming up for renewal at the end of the year, and I want to be certain I'm keeping everybody happy.

"Hey, thanks for calling back," he says. "You doin' okay?"

Is he making small talk, I wonder, or has Sasha mentioned that I was under the weather?

"Yes, great, thanks."

"Nice podcast this week. The company is planning to launch a new tagline any day now, and I'll get it over to you once I have the green light."

"How exciting."

"By the way, I thought Sasha hit it out of the park on the show this week."

How can he *possibly* think that?

"She worked really hard on the segment," I say, as diplomatic as I can be.

"Would you consider having her do it regularly until she finishes up the internship? She sounded a bit more—I don't know, a bit more of an expert than that gal you usually use."

I take a few seconds, then choose my words carefully.

"It's actually Casey's job as my producer to do the last segment with me, so I'm afraid it wouldn't be fair to bump her. And the chat at the end is meant to be a conversation with an ordinary person, not an expert."

"Well, you know best. It was simply a thought."

"I appreciate the input. And just so you know, Casey's going on vacation in a few weeks and Sasha will have another chance to handle the segment."

That seems to mollify him, at least temporarily, and he soon hustles me off the phone to take another call. Once again, I wonder why he's such a superfan of Sasha's.

I return her call next.

"Sorry to be out of touch yesterday," she says. "I've been

crazy busy. But I've done all the research for next week's podcast. Do you want me to drop by your place again so we can review it?"

"I don't think that's necessary, Sasha," I say. The last thing I need is her stopping by with more pops of color and sly-seeming comments about my husband. "Why don't you email me what you have, and I'll read through it. . . . And if I have any questions, I can give you a call."

"Okay, let me know."

"Before you go, there's something else I'd like to discuss. Do you have an extra minute?"

"Of course."

"Did you call the PR person at Greenbacks and ask if you could arrange an interview with someone there?"

She hesitates briefly before speaking.

"Yes, actually, I did."

"I never suggested you call anyone there for the podcast. I—"

"It actually wasn't for the podcast."

"Then what was it for?"

"I'm exploring an idea for a piece on Greenbacks, and if it pans out, I'll pitch it to a major website."

"But you used my name. That's not kosher, Sasha. Not when it doesn't involve me."

"Sorry, but I was hoping you'd understand because the piece is going to be important."

"Important how?"

"To be perfectly blunt, there may be something sketchy going on at Greenbacks—on the business side. I've gotten to know someone who works there and he tipped me off."

My stomach tightens.

"Something sketchy how?"

"Are we speaking confidentially? I know you used to work there."

"Yes, you have my word I'll keep it to myself."

"I hear they might have really inflated the number of accounts they have on the advisory side. Meaning they misled their investors."

I'm stunned by this. It can't be true. I was involved only on the content side, but I worked extensively with employees on the business team at Greenbacks, and I never heard so much as a hint of anything unethical.

But then again, that was five years ago.

"You're basing this on the word of one person?" I ask.

"Yes, but he's very reliable."

"Sasha, I know you want to do more writing, but it seems it would be smarter to focus on pitching solid personal finance pieces," I say, unable to resist giving her some unsolicited advice. "And save the muckraking until you have more experience as a reporter. But whatever you decide, please don't use my name again."

"Fine," she says curtly.

I sign off feeling flustered by her revelation. Damien's a rule bender, sometimes a rule breaker, but he's got scruples. Or at least I always thought he did.

I bite my lip, staring out the window. I'd toyed earlier with going down to the East Village later this afternoon, but I need to put that on hold for now. I have to do what Erling suggested—relax, pause my search for answers, and sit in a café with a hot cup of tea. This also means skipping a promised trip to WorkSpace to discuss book research with Nicole. I shoot her an email apologizing for not making it in today. I add that I spoke to Sasha about not tossing my name around in the future. Before I can change my mind, I ask her if she's heard any buzz about Greenbacks lately.

We reach my building and as I dash into the lobby, I notice it's begun to drizzle. It hasn't rained, I realized, since the day I resurfaced at Greenbacks. Autumn's rushing by and I've barely had a moment to savor it.

I can tell something's off the moment I step into the foyer of my apartment. There's a light coming from deep inside, seeping into the dimness of the great room. It means a lamp's on in the bedroom or den, but I'm positive I turned all the lights off before I left.

Then I hear movement, and the click of a closet door closing. Footsteps. Is a maintenance person here? We haven't put in a request, as far as I know.

I lurch backward and grab the front door handle, ready to bolt. But before I can spin around and flee, I see Hugh saunter into the great room, cell phone in one hand and a water glass in the other. He's headed toward the island but stops short in surprise when he sees me.

"Oh god, you scared me," he says, setting his stuff on the island top. "I didn't hear you come in."

"And I thought *you* were a burglar," I say, after exhaling in relief. "Why are you home so early?"

I slip out of my sweater coat, hang it in the closet, and stride into the great room.

"I'm not here yet for the evening," Hugh says. He's in a dress shirt, tie, and pinstriped suit pants. "Tonight's when we have that toast for the partner who's retiring. I ended up spilling an entire cup of coffee into my lap this afternoon, and there was no way I could show up in those damn pants."

"Oh, gosh, that must have hurt."

He grins, a Hugh grin that I haven't seen in a while. "It wasn't fun, but fortunately my manhood was spared."

"Good to know," I say.

"How was Dr. Erling?"

"I'll tell you about it later. I'm sure you need to go. Who is it that's retiring?"

"J. P. Ross. I mentioned it a few weeks ago, but maybe it's one of those things that, you know, slipped away."

"No, I remember now that you say the name." The words sound more defensive than I intended. "The only things I don't recall, Hugh, are those two days."

He nods, lips pressed together. "Okay, let me grab my jacket. I should be home no later than eight. I wish I could whisk you someplace nice for dinner tonight, but I'm going to have to work again."

"I'll figure something out for us. Do you want me to drop your pants at the cleaner?"

"No, don't bother. I'll take care of it tomorrow."

While he heads back to the bedroom, I move over to the kitchen island. I feel restless, still on edge from my appointment. My gaze wanders onto the countertop and is dragged by a gravitational-like pull to Hugh's phone. I almost never have occasion to touch it, but my fingers move in that direction, seemingly of their own volition.

Before I can think about it, I snatch his phone from the counter. I press the four keys for his password—for practical reasons we've shared ours with each other—and check the last number in the call log. It's an outgoing one to his office, eight minutes ago. Then I proceed to the address book, where I search for Sasha's name, and exhale in relief when it's not there.

"Speaking of the cleaner, your trench coat is back," he calls from the bedroom, making me jump. "I sent it out last week."

"Um, okay, thanks," I call back. "I'm going to run out for a while and it will be good to have it in the rain."

Next, with jerky fingers, I search for one more name. And with a jolt, I spot it there. *Ashley Budd.* Before I can determine if he's called the number lately, Hugh comes striding down the corridor. I'm still holding his phone in my hand.

"Here, don't forget this," I say, thrusting it in his direction.

"I won't," he responds, eyes curious. He leans forward and kisses me softly on the lips. "See you soon."

Okay, I tell myself as soon as he closes the door. *It might not mean anything.* She could have easily thrust her number on him when he bumped into her a few weeks ago at the Yale Club. Or he may have had it since law school.

Anyway, I can't think about it right now. I have to relax, *let go.* Instead of tea, I decide, I'll head to the bistro where I met with Roger and have a glass of wine.

My phone rings as I'm tearing off the dry-cleaning plastic on my trench coat. It's Roger. *Please*, I think, *don't let him be calling to tell me that Corbet wants to see me again.*

"Ally, hi," he says when I answer. "Everything okay?"

"Pretty much. I'm sorry I haven't called you yet. I so appreciate everything you did yesterday."

"Don't be silly, you've got a ton on your mind. I just wanted to check in, make sure you weren't fretting."

I sigh. "Unfortunately, it's been hard to keep the fretting at bay. Any luck with Nowak?"

"No, you were right. He told me he wasn't at liberty to discuss the case. Even managed to sound a little blunt with me, which isn't his usual style."

Is the bluntness a sign that he's suspicious of me?

"Seems like the best course of action is to leave well enough alone," Roger continues. "You did your part. And if they decide to open up the investigation again, you'll know soon enough. No need to worry."

"I appreciate the advice, Rog." I just wish I could follow it.

"Any more news from your private detective? What's his name—Mulroney?"

I take a minute to fill him in on the latest bread crumbs Mulroney's provided, and we sign off afterward, promising to check in with each other again soon.

I try not to let the news about Nowak's bluntness agitate me, but it does regardless. Plus, I'm still in the dark about the early days of the case. If I want details, I'm going to have to hightail it back to New Jersey and go through microfilm archives. I honestly don't feel up to it in my current state, however, and I consider my options.

Nicole doesn't have a car, and I wouldn't want her to wonder why I was looking into a decades-old murder, anyway. But there's another researcher I've used in the past, a married mom of two named Jennifer who lives in Madison, New Jersey, which is probably less than an hour from Millerstown. I shoot her a quick email asking if she's available to go to a nearby library and photocopy everything from the *Hunterdon County Gazette* on the murder of Jaycee Long.

I know this sounds a little off-brand for me, I add in a P.S. But I'm helping an author friend who writes true crime.

Just thinking about tracking down those articles is adding to my agitation. It's time to go. I grab my iPad and stuff it into my purse. Glimpsing through the windows, I see that the rain is coming down harder now. *That's okay*, I think. *It's a perfect night for sipping wine in a cozy bistro.*

But by the time I'm one block away from my building, I'm experiencing a flutter of foreboding and wishing I hadn't left. I feel as if I've heard my name whispered in a darkened hallway when I thought I was the only one present.

And then, once again, I have that strange sense that someone is watching me. I freeze, one foot arched in a half step.

Slowly I turn and scan my eyes over the people streaming around me, umbrellas bobbing and dripping with rain. No one seems out of place or even to notice me.

I resume walking, but I can't shake my unease. I turn again, glancing quickly behind me, and as I swing back around, my gaze falls on the sleeve of my trench coat, where beads of water have begun to gather on the outer edge.

Suddenly, a memory surfaces, unbidden. Me grabbing tissues. Wiping off fingers smeared with blood. *My own fingers.*

The thought makes me reel, but I try to grab hold of the image. Still, as quickly as it came, it slips from my grasp.

I'm at an intersection now, waiting for the light to change. I wonder if I should turn back.

But before I can decide, there's a jab between my shoulder blades, and then I feel something really hard being rammed into my back, knocking the air from my lungs and pitching me forward.

A second later, I fly into the street.

land hard and skid across the wet pavement, my palms burning as the asphalt tears my flesh. A horn blares, then another, and a car screeches to a halt only inches from my head, it seems. Terrified, I squeeze my eyes shut, as if that could protect me.

I sense people scrambling, and when I open my eyes, I see that several pedestrians have clustered around me.

"Are you okay?" a woman asks, squatting down.

"Better not touch her," a male voice says.

"No, I'm okay," I mutter, lifting my head. "I—" I'm having a hard time even catching a breath.

More horn blaring, insistent and irritated.

"Are you able to get up?" the woman says. She's in her twenties, I guess, and I feel instantly grateful for her kindness.

"Uh, I think so."

The man, who turns out to be middle-aged, and the woman help me struggle into a standing position and hobble to the other side of the street. The man has grabbed my umbrella and hands it back to me, still furled.

"Did you see who did it?" I ask.

"Did it?" the woman says.

"Pushed me."

She shoots the man a look. "I think you slipped," she says, glancing back at me. "The sidewalk's really wet."

"No, I felt it," I tell her. "A shove."

"A couple of people were trying to cross against the light," the man says. "And I think one of them must have jostled you. Are you sure you're okay? Can we call anyone?"

"No, that's all right. Thank you for your help."

They hurry off, but I remain there, still catching my breath, and trying to process what happened. Was I simply shoved aside by an asshole too impatient to wait for the light?

I glance down. My palms are raw, and even in the dark, I can see that one of my pants legs is shredded.

I sense someone else hovering near me and I turn to see an older woman with white hair tucked beneath a wide-brimmed vinyl rain hat. She seems to be standing preternaturally still, like an apparition only I can view.

We make eye contact, and she takes a step toward me.

"Are you sure you're all right?" she asks.

"I think so."

"You were pushed," she says.

"You *saw*? What did the person look like?"

"I didn't see it, but I *felt* it. An arm shooting out. You should call the police."

I survey the intersection. I can't imagine anyone who would do that sticking around to face the consequences.

"I think it's too late for them to do anything." There are

probably CCTV cameras trained onto the corner, like Mulroney indicated, but since people were so tightly bunched together, the video probably wouldn't reveal much.

"Still, you should call them. They need to know what's going on in this area. Good night."

Her concern seems to be more for the neighborhood than for me. As she turns away, water flicks off her rain hat. Moments later she melds into the pedestrian traffic, as if she was never here.

I'm still breathing hard and my coat's streaked with dirt, but I banish the urge to return to the apartment, wanting to get my bearings first. I hurry the remaining half block to the bistro, checking constantly over my shoulder. I collapse my umbrella and secure a table by the window so I can keep an eye on the street and whoever might be out there.

But for the moment, I glance down at the metal table and mentally play back the scene from five minutes ago. Reaching the corner, feeling the shove—almost more of a punch—and the fear grabbing hold of me as I was launched into traffic.

After the waiter takes my wine order, I inspect my palms. They're red and raw, with a few crisscrossed, razor-thin lines where the skin's been broken. And my forearms, which took the brunt of the fall, have started to throb like a headache. I gingerly peel off my coat and let it drape behind me.

Who would want to hurt me? New York has plenty of crazies, of course, people who think nothing of hurling total strangers onto subway tracks. Did I simply look the wrong way at someone who was unhinged?

Maybe that's all this was, and I need to mentally move on. Though I try to sandbag my swelling panic, it sloshes over the walls, threatening to spill. *I should call Hugh,* I think, *let him know what happened, but I don't want to pull him away from a work event. I could try Gabby, I guess. But she's in bed sick.*

My phone rings, and to my shock, Damien's name appears on the screen. My first instinct is to forward the call to voice mail, but I change my mind and answer.

"Hey," he says, "I wanted to apologize for leaving on such a weird note the other day. It wasn't fair of me."

"That's all right." What does he want? I wonder. "I appreciated you checking on me."

"Where are you, anyway?"

"At a bistro near Lincoln Center. Uh . . . I'm about to have a glass of wine."

"What's the matter?"

"What do you mean?"

"You don't sound very good."

It's true, I realize. My voice is quivering.

"I fell—well, someone pushed me—into the street. A couple of minutes ago. I'm not hurt, but it freaked me out."

"Where are you, exactly? I'm coming right now."

"Damien, no, it's not necessary."

"I'm not that far. I just left a client at Eighty-Fifth and Columbus."

The name and address spill from my lips. I can't believe I'm doing this. But I could use the company for sure.

While I wait for him to arrive, the scene from the intersection plays on a loop in my brain. Closing my eyes, I try to recapture the exact sensation I felt in between my shoulder blades. *Hard like a fist.* Is someone possibly after me?

It's only then that I recall the sense memory that was triggered seconds earlier, when I glanced at the sleeve of my coat in the rain: in my mind I could see myself dabbing at my blood-covered fingers. I can't be sure, though, if it's really a memory or simply an image I conjured up from thinking so much about those tissues. I glance back at my coat, bunched behind me on the banquette, but it stirs nothing now.

I'm halfway through my wine when I catch sight of Damien through the window, shaking out his small umbrella. A few seconds later he bursts through the door, and to my dismay, my heart skips at the sight of him.

He plops into a chair across from me, not bothering to take off his khaki raincoat. His face is dewy and his hair slightly darkened from rainwater.

"You sure you're okay?" he asks, his voice soft.

"Just rattled. Thanks so much for coming."

"Like I said, I wasn't far away. How scary."

I snicker. "This must seem like déjà vu to you. Me wet and disheveled again, looking like a total mess."

He flashes a smile. "Well, it's definitely not your usual look. Or, I should say, your usual look when I knew you. Did you see who pushed you?"

"No, and—maybe I'm wrong. There's a chance someone accidentally knocked me over. But it didn't feel that way."

"Could it have been a random crazy person?"

"Maybe."

"You don't have any enemies, do you?"

"I didn't think so. Though what do I know? Everything these days seems so jumbled."

"Because of what you went through last week?"

"Right—and . . ." Am I really going to go into it all with him? *Yes.* "Do you remember what happened to me when I was nine? Finding that little girl's body?"

"Of course."

I give him the entire update: what I remembered about the timeline, my meeting with the police yesterday.

He's quiet when I finish. God, is this going to be like Hugh's reaction all over again? But then he reaches for my hand. The rough calluses on his fingers make me realize he must still play the guitar.

"I'm sorry that you had to dig that all up again," he says. "I always sensed it bothered you more than you let on."

"I really appreciate that." And I'm not simply being polite. His words are comforting.

"Do you think what happened tonight is connected somehow?"

"I'm not sure. If what I told the police this week got out, it could be threatening to whoever killed Jaycee. Which might be her mother or the mother's boyfriend. And for the last twenty-four hours, I've had this weird sense that someone is watching me."

"I want you to be careful, Ally. Do you promise?"

"Yes, I intend to," I say, though I have no clue how I'm supposed to do that. "Look, I better go."

"You want me to walk you back to your building?"

"I can get back on my own, thanks." It wouldn't be good to have Hugh see me accompanied home by Damien.

I quickly pay the check, and as we emerge from the bistro, I notice the rain has eased into a light, misty drizzle.

"Oh, just so you know," I say, breaking the sudden, stilted silence, "that call to your PR person? It definitely had nothing to do with any of my projects. I found out the caller was actually this intern I'm using, but she's doing it for a story of her own."

His eyes widen almost imperceptibly. "Oh yeah? What's the topic?"

I'd promised confidentiality to Sasha, and I can't violate that now, but I still feel compelled to offer Damien a warning.

"You'd have to ask her. She's an amateur but she's trying to make a name for herself doing financial pieces. Looking for stuff that isn't on the up-and-up. Go figure."

That's the most I should say. If he's smart—and he is—he'll follow the lead.

He nods, that's all.

"But, Damien, just to reiterate, I wasn't involved."

"Take care," he says. No brush of lips on my cheek this time. "I'm going to watch as you cross the street."

I thank him and dart away, my panic mushrooming again as I hurry toward home. I'm careful at each intersection, always checking behind me. Less than ten minutes later, I'm unlocking my apartment door. And finally exhaling.

Hugh's not home, but then, it's not even eight o'clock yet. I ease through the apartment, flicking on lights, opening the door to the den. It's stupid to feel scared in my own home, but I can't shake the fear.

In the bedroom, I tear off my still-damp trench coat and

hang it on a hook in my closet, though I can't imagine wearing it ever again. My pants, I see, are beyond repair. I toss them on the floor, planning to trash them later.

I wash my hands and knees next, and as I'm spreading a dab of Neosporin on each palm, my phone rings from inside my purse. I do my best to dig it out without smearing the screen with the ointment. It's Mulroney calling.

"Now a good time?" he asks. He's in a car, I can tell, because his voice is echo-y from using Bluetooth.

"Yes, always," I say, tugging on a pair of sweats with my free hand. "Have you got news?"

"I do. But first, anything from your end?"

For a split second, I toy with telling him about what just happened but remind myself that it's probably irrelevant to what he's working on.

"No, nothing. I did have a moment tonight when I thought I was remembering something to do with the tissues, but it never quite materialized."

"Maybe in time. Tell me, have you been back yet to that communal office space you use?"

"No, but I'm hoping to go in tomorrow. Why?"

"I think that'd be a good idea. Because you put in time there on Tuesday."

"Are you *sure*? My intern was there Tuesday afternoon, and she said I wasn't around that day." Could I have come and gone before Sasha arrived?

"I'm not talking about the afternoon," Mulroney says. "Seems you spent the entire night at that location."

"I was there all night?" I say, stunned. Though WorkSpace

is filled with people doing startups and working weird hours, I'm usually out of there by six or so. "How do you know?"

"I was able to convince someone there to check your key card history for me. You were on the premises from around nine P.M. to six A.M."

I don't like the idea of someone being so indiscreet, even though it's of value to me in this case. But that's the least of what bothers me. The facility doesn't have anything like sleeping pods on the premises, so the revelation from Mulroney means that if I slept part of the time, I must have done it sprawled across my desk or even on the floor.

At least I was out of harm's way.

"But not Wednesday night?"

"No, your key card wasn't used again during the period we're looking into. But we have a bigger chunk of info to work with now. You're definitely going in there tomorrow?"

"I'll make a point to go. First thing in the morning."

"Can you take a good look around your office? See if you find any receipts, notes, anything that offers a clue."

"Okay. . . . But what about *Wednesday* night?" I ask again. I know my tone sounds almost peevish, but I'm desperate to know. "Is it possible I slept on the street that night—or on a park bench or something? My coat reeked."

"I'm still following the thread to Wednesday night. It's going to take a little more time, but we'll figure it out. By the way, I should have asked you earlier to download your credit card statement. Sometimes charges take a few days to post and I want to see if there are any charges besides that café on Seventh Street."

"Gosh, I never thought of that."

Mulroney chuckles. "That's why you're paying me the big bucks."

I find myself smiling, something I've barely done lately.

"Is there anything else I can do to help?" I ask.

"Just be patient. I hope to have more information for you tomorrow morning. One last thing: did you find any references to the Forty-Second Street area in your emails?"

"I looked, but there was nothing."

"Got it. Let's talk tomorrow once you've had a chance to check your office. I'll be on my cell all day."

"Okay . . . Thanks."

"Was there something else?" He's picked up the hesitancy in my tone.

"No. At least nothing to do with the case."

"Tell me. All I'm doing is driving to an appointment."

I find myself blurting out a choppy recap of tonight's incident.

"I'm glad you looped me in. Your gut says it was definitely a shove?"

"Yes. I'd had a sense, too, of someone watching me. And . . ."

Without having really planned to, I also tell him briefly about Jaycee Long, the case being reopened, and the fear I'd expressed to Damien: that someone might see me as a target.

I hear Mulroney sigh. "It's possible there's a connection. The girl's killer could have tracked you down. But there's something else I need you to be aware of. There's a small chance that the shove tonight could be related to an event that happened during the time you were missing. I'm thinking of those tissues."

I've been so busy thinking this had something to do with Audrey Long and Frank Wargo, I hadn't even gone there.

"You mean I was a witness to a crime?"

"Yeah. Maybe one big enough to traumatize you, and one someone doesn't want any witnesses to."

My heart freezes.

"So that would mean I'm definitely in danger."

"Let's not get ahead of ourselves. The person who pushed you is probably your basic New York City weirdo. But I don't like coincidences, so it's important to stay alert. Okay?"

"Okay."

For a few minutes after we sign off, I sit frozen on the edge of the bed. My heart's finally beating again, but fast and loud. Am I really in danger? Have I put *Hugh* in danger? I have to do what Mulroney advises. Be alert. But what exactly does that entail?

Finally, I propel myself off the bed and into the alcove, where I grab my laptop from my desk. I log into my credit card account and download the statement.

To my surprise, there *is* another charge. On Wednesday, at a place called Pairings. There's no way of telling from the statement what time I was there, though if I ate lunch at Eastside Eats, it probably would have been later. I type the name into a new browser window. It's a restaurant. On East Fifth Street. So I was still in the East Village.

I text Mulroney the update and hurry to the great room, where I grab the pad I've been using to write my timeline. Two more pieces to add to the puzzle.

MONDAY

evening: dinner, TV, argument

TUESDAY

7:00: still in bed

9:00-ish: took call from Dr. Erling

9:00–9:17: sent emails

9:30: hung out at café

11:00-ish: left for 42nd Street

Before 3:00: possibly witnessed someone get injured???; lost phone

3:00–3:30-ish: called WorkSpace

9:00–6:00 A.M.: spent night at WorkSpace

WEDNESDAY

Noon-ish: bought food at Eastside Eats, East 7th St.

Afternoon: walked near Tompkins Square Park

Maybe evening: ate at Pairings

THURSDAY

8:05: arrived at Greenbacks

Finished, I flop back onto the couch and think for a second. Was that charge really posted late or did Hugh decide not to share it with me for some reason? It can't be the latter. There'd be no reason for Hugh to lie.

Though he lied to me about Ashley Budd, didn't he? A revelation that in my panic tonight I've let slide out of view. He said she was simply a law school acquaintance whom he'd bumped into at a lecture, so why would he have her number in his phone?

Of course, as I'd tried to convince myself earlier, he could have taken it down that night, simply to be polite. Which means he hasn't deceived me. And why would he? Hugh's a straight arrow.

And then I'm on my feet again, practically flinging myself at his closet. I tear open the door and drop onto my haunches, peering at the area on the floor where he stacks his clothes for the dry cleaner. There's a neatly folded pile of about seven or eight items.

I lean closer and rifle through it, hurling each item of clothing behind me one by one until I've gone through everything.

There's no sign of the fucking suit pants. The ones that supposedly became unwearable because of the cup of coffee dumped in his lap.

24

A few minutes after nine the next morning, I'm barreling south in a taxi I had the doorman hail for me. Before darting into the cab's backseat, I'd quickly scanned the immediate vicinity. Everything looked perfectly normal.

It just doesn't *feel* normal.

As I promised Mulroney, I'm going to look for clues that might explain what I was doing at WorkSpace Tuesday night.

Surely if Dr. Erling knew about this, she wouldn't be pleased, but I'm not only going there to hunt for clues. It's my chance to finally catch up in person with Nicole—who must be wondering what in the world is going on with me—before heading to my MRI appointment on the East Side.

And if I were actually playing amateur sleuth, I justify to myself, I would have shown up at WorkSpace as soon as I was off the phone from Mulroney, but I was still too unsettled and anxious to leave the apartment last night, and besides, Hugh would have nailed the door shut if I'd tried to leave.

I still cringe when I think of the pathetic scene in our apartment. Hugh arrived home without my hearing him, and when he stepped into the bedroom, I was still squatting on the floor with his dirty clothes strewn behind me. I must have looked like a dog caught rooting through the trash bin.

"What in the world are you doing?" he'd demanded.

"I—I was looking for your pants." Inside, a little voice had warned me against accusing him of anything. Not without proof. "I was going to take them to the cleaners—before the stain set in."

"I told you I'd do it, Ally. Besides, I doubt they're open now."

I glanced at my watch, feigning surprise. "Oh wow. I hadn't realized how late it was."

"That was nice of you, though," he said, his voice gentler then. "If you really want to drop them off tomorrow morning, they're in the hall closet."

So there is *no bizarre Mystery of the Missing Pants*, I told myself. My husband hadn't deceived me, at least not about that. I rose, trying to make my movements seem casual, and began restacking his dirty clothes, setting them back in his closet.

"Sorry to seem so frazzled," I told him, "but something upsetting happened tonight."

I told him then about my fall, and the idea that it might be related to my missing days. To me as a possible witness.

"Ally, look," he'd said, putting an arm around me. "I know you trust this Mulroney guy, but his theory seems far-fetched. It was probably nothing more than a jerk who wanted to get across the intersection ahead of everyone else. Or a nutjob."

How could he be so sure? I wondered.

Later, after we'd picked at a pizza we'd had delivered, Hugh set to work again at the dining table, and I tried to read on the couch. From time to time, out of the corner of my eye, I caught him lifting his gaze and studying me, his pen poised in midair. Was he worried I was making things up, slowly losing my mind?

Shortly afterward I'd headed to the bedroom, but before crawling between the sheets, I checked my phone and saw a message from Jennifer, the New Jersey researcher I'd contacted. She had a pocket of time available the next morning, she said, and would photocopy the microfilm I requested.

Now I lean back against the taxi seat and try to focus on the people and buildings flying by, a blur of gray and black and silver punctuated by small smudges of color. My arms, I notice, still ache from the fall last night. *Stay in the present*, I command myself, but my thoughts keep getting tugged ahead, wondering what I'll find in my office. I root around in my purse for a cinnamon Altoid and shove it into my mouth. At the rate I'm going, I should invest in the company.

Once I arrive at the building where WorkSpace is located, I stop at the front desk and ask for my new key card. Hugh had submitted a support ticket for me last Thursday, deactivating the old card and requesting a new one. As I accept the card from the manager, I notice him glance briefly at my palm, which is still crisscrossed with scrape marks. I wonder briefly if he's the one who spilled to Mulroney, but I don't have time to dwell on that.

Stepping away, I scan the space around me—the boldly colored, mod-style community lounge, the rows of sleek wooden tables, and the offices behind them. The last time I remember being here was a week ago Monday, and yet it actually feels *longer. That's normal*, I tell myself. *So much has happened in between.*

After grabbing a water from the lounge, I make my way to the two-person office I rent, unlock the door, and—holding my breath—flick on the light.

My eyes go straight to the sleek wooden desk, where Nicole and I sit side by side. I pull back a little in surprise. Her area is neat as a pin, as usual; mine is messy, not at all the way I ever leave it.

I move closer. At the end of the day I like to line up my desk accessories—pen holder, stapler, tape dispenser, a tray of hot-pink Post-it pads—but they're haphazardly scattered around at the moment, as if I couldn't be bothered. There's also a used paper coffee cup on the desktop, along with a couple of grease-stained paper napkins, suggesting I ate a meal or a snack here.

Nowhere in sight, however, are any receipts or notes or Post-its scribbled with words, nothing that might offer a hint to what sent me on the lam from myself. I glance down at the trash can, hoping to find the bag the food came in, but it's empty, of course. The cleaning staff would have dumped out any contents the morning after I was here.

I text Mulroney to let him know that I've come up

empty, and with a sigh I straighten my desk accessories, toss the napkins and cup in the trash, and pull my laptop from my tote bag. Nicole won't be in until around ten, so I have a little while to prep. I open the most recent research file Nicole sent me for the chapter I'll be writing on credit cards and credit card debt and finally begin to peruse it. Research is the clay I craft my columns and books from, and usually I love diving in and having ideas sparked by what I read, but today it seems nothing short of tedious. My eyes keep bouncing off the computer screen, eager for anyplace else to alight.

Thinking caffeine might help, I traipse down the hall to the community lounge for a cup of coffee. A couple of familiar faces smile or nod at me from the couches. One guy, who's sitting farther away, at one of the desks in the open seating area, gazes at me. He's wearing a dark blue sport jacket over an orange hoodie. I've never seen him before, but his attention settles on me, his expression curious. Was he around when I spent the whole night here? Does he know something? When I return the stare, he quickly looks back to his screen.

Returning to my office with a coffee, I find that Nicole has arrived and is parked at her desk, laptop open, and staring intently at the screen. Hearing me enter, she glances up. She's twenty-six, pretty, and petite, with curly light brown hair just below her chin.

"Oh, hi, good morning," she says. "I hope you're feeling better."

"I am, thanks," I say, forcing myself to get out of my own head for a minute. "You look so refreshed. I take it the trip was fun for you."

"Fun enough, I guess. I wore SPF 50 every second, but I still ended up getting burned. . . . You want to go over what I sent you last week?"

Nicole is a terrific assistant and researcher and we get along well, but unlike Casey, she's fairly reserved and no-nonsense, never much of a gabber.

"Um, yeah," I say, sitting back at my desk. "And then I have a list of topics I'd like you to explore next."

She rolls her chair closer to mine, dragging her laptop across the polished wood. Though I absorbed little from reading her notes, I'm able to fake it by skimming a few sentences ahead as we talk. I manage to ask several questions and request that she flesh out a few of her notes. But I'm still having trouble concentrating.

"You want to take a break?" Nicole says after we've been at it for about forty minutes. "I know you said you'd been under the weather."

"I'm better now, but I didn't sleep very well last night. So yes, let's take a break."

"No problem, I'll get to work on these questions. And do you have any more stuff for me to proofread?"

"Uh, I'm actually a little behind cranking out new pages. Maybe next week, okay?"

She nods, not doing a good job of hiding her surprise. I *never* fall behind.

"You want anything from Starbucks?" she asks, rolling her chair back. "The micro roast here just doesn't do it for me."

"No, I'm good. But thanks."

She rises and grabs her coat from the peg on the wall.

"Oh, before I forget," she says, pausing. "I did a little digging on Greenbacks, per your request."

"Find anything?"

"There's a rumor floating around—wait, are you thinking of mentioning them in the book in some way? Because this is really gossip and it wouldn't be right to include it."

"No, not for the book." I hold my breath. Could Sasha be right about something unethical going down there? "Definitely not for publication of any kind."

"Okay, so it sounds like it's about to be sold to some big financial services company."

Ahh, the longed-for endgame. I take a few moments to reflect. I'd always known that a sale was Damien's goal—without ever hearing it from his own mouth. *Everyone* knew it. What you aim for with a startup is to sell it eventually, take home several boatloads of dough, and be the secret and not-so-secret envy of everyone you know. A term of the sale might require Damien to stay on and run the operation for a period of time, but then he would be free (and very rich), able to start some shiny new company or sail across the Pacific Ocean or do whatever he damn well pleased. If the deal went through, of course.

"Good for them," I say finally. "Did you hear any details?"

"About the sale? No, I'm not sure who the potential buyer is, though I could make a few guesses."

"You didn't hear anything negative about Greenbacks, did you? Irregularities or anything like that?"

"No, but there'd better not be if they're really hoping for a sale."

Exactly. If there's been inflation with the number of accounts, like Sasha alluded to, and the buyer finds out during the due diligence process, it could kill the deal. And Greenbacks would be tainted.

"Well, thanks for the intel," I say. "Since I worked there, I'm always a little curious."

"I don't blame you." As she turns to finally leave, her gaze falls to the surface of my desk. "I would have cleaned up your desk area when I came in yesterday. But I always want to be respectful of your space."

So the unaccustomed disarray caught her eye. I wonder if anything else did.

"Thank you, I was in a bit of hurry the last time I was here. . . . By the way, when you came back today, did anyone mention anything about me?"

"About *you*? I'm not following."

"I worked really late one night, and I wondered if anyone had noticed or commented. I don't usually hang out here after six."

She looks at me as if I'm asking her a trick question. "No, no one said anything. I doubt anyone here would find it weird you were working late."

Once she's gone, I rest my elbows on the desk and drop my face into my hands. I don't feel any real connection to Greenbacks anymore or to Damien, but it still bothers me to think that something bad might be happening there. Or that Sasha, in her foolhearted desire to transform herself from beauty blogger to muckraker, will cause people to think there's trouble when there isn't.

Regardless of what's going on—or not—at Greenbacks,

Damien would of course be pissed about the idea of Sasha nosing around. Or *me* nosing around if he thinks I really did put Sasha up to the call. I flash back on the bluntness of his first text to me the other day. Can we meet? I need to see you. And how the temperature dropped at the café when I mentioned the call to the company PR person. Maybe his interest in seeing me was never concern for my well-being but instead a fishing expedition. Even his coming to the bistro last night might have been nothing more than a ruse to learn more.

How stupid of me to allow myself to be touched by his texts and calls. I thought they were a sign that he'd cared more than I realized all those years ago.

I'm never going to be able to concentrate on work today, I realize. I scribble down a note for Nicole, saying something's come up but I'll email her later with her next assignment, and punch my arms into my jacket, desperate to get out of here.

But as I'm turning to leave, an unseen force tugs at me. I'd promised Mulroney a good look around and I need to be thorough. Bending slightly, I open the top drawer to the filing cabinet underneath my desk, which usually holds nothing more than a few empty hanging folders.

I almost recoil in shock. My purse is sitting there.

The soft black leather hobo bag that's been missing for days. It's crouched toward the very back of the drawer, like a little kid who's been hiding in a game of Sardines.

I spin around and stare through the glass wall of the office. Across the hall, three people are gathered around a drawing table in a slightly larger office, their backs to me.

Swiveling back, I grab the bag and tear it open. My wallet's inside, holding my license and the now-canceled bank card and credit cards, minus the one I used at Eastside Eats; my Metro card; and my WorkSpace key card. Rooting through the bag, I also find my apartment keys; rollerball pens; tiny Moleskine notebook; a comb; my makeup bag with blush, lipstick, and a Bobbi Brown foundation stick; a small Ziploc bag containing Claritin and Advil. There's no cash, I notice, other than twenty cents in the change purse.

No receipts either, or scraps of paper teasing me with hints.

And no phone, which seems to confirm that my purse and phone disappeared at separate times.

I peer farther into the drawer and pat my hand around in there. Nothing else. I yank out the bottom drawer next but it's entirely empty.

Nicole will be back any minute, I realize, and I don't want her to find me stupidly holding two full handbags. I stuff the hobo purse into my tote bag and quickly exit the premises. Once I'm on the street, I hurry down the block and duck into a Walgreens. I have no intention of buying anything but I drag one of the wheele plastic baskets up and down the aisles with me, trying to pull my frayed thoughts together.

It seems that I must have purposely left my bag at Work-Space when I left that Wednesday morning, taking only cash and one credit card, which I no longer seem to possess. It also means that my early theory that I was mugged is definitely dead in the water.

But why would I have left my bag behind—and my keys? It's as if I'd made a decision to travel light, unburdened, like someone on the run.

I tuck into a corner of the store and call Mulroney. I notice that he hasn't responded to my previous texts, but he may not have seen them yet.

"I ended up finding something at WorkSpace," I say when I reach his voice mail. "Can you call me as soon as possible?"

It's almost an hour and a half until my MRI appointment, but after exiting the drugstore and scouring the immediate area with my eyes, I hail a cab to the East Side. When the driver starts to turn onto the side street where the medical building's located, I ask him to drop me off at the corner of First Avenue instead, where I spot a small Italian restaurant.

Though it's breezy and crisp outside, there's a row of tables on the sidewalk, their blue-and-white-checked tablecloths snapping in the wind. I opt to sit inside, and a waiter in white shirt and black pants leads me to a table along the wall. The room is dimly lit but in a soothing rather than gloomy way, and music's playing in the background, a tenor singing an aria. Surprisingly there are already two other tables with diners, both groups of older women who have the look of regulars.

I take my phone from my purse and leave it on the table, so I won't miss Mulroney returning my call, and glance quickly at the menu. I order a bowl of spaghetti alle vongole, a dish I haven't had in ages, and a glass of Pellegrino.

There, that's better, I think. In the years before I met Hugh, when I was single and dating very little, I often went out to dinner alone at little restaurants in my Upper East Side neighborhood. New York is one of those cities where you can do that unself-consciously, and I loved those evenings. They were a chance to think and be a little dreamy and imagine all the good things the future might hold.

It *did* hold good things for me. *And it will again*, I tell myself. *It will, it will, it will.* I'm going to learn where I went those two days and *why*, and once I have all the pieces back, I'm going to address the situation with Hugh and find a way to sort through our issues as a team.

My phone rings, and I grab it quickly. Not Mulroney calling. It's Jennifer, the researcher.

"Hi, Ally," she says. "I got that material for you."

"Already?" I say.

"The library opened at nine, and there were only about twelve stories over a period of a month and a half."

"Great," I say, keeping my voice low.

"They had a scanner I could use, so I've already emailed you the file."

"That's fantastic, thanks. Just shoot me the invoice when you have a chance."

"Will do. . . . God, what a horrible case. Your friend's going to write about it?"

"My friend?"

"The author friend you're helping out."

"Oh, um, yeah, maybe. Thanks again, Jen."

We sign off and I quickly go to her email, opening the file. My fingers, I notice, are trembling slightly. Besides the fact that the microfilmed pages make me feel like I'm back in the twentieth century, they're tough to read this way. I squint, holding the phone closer to the window, and quickly scan the articles until finally I see the line I'm hunting for.

"According to Jaycee's mother, Audrey Long, her daughter was abducted sometime Wednesday morning, possibly around eight-thirty A.M."

Liar, I think. Because Jaycee had already been dead for hours.

scroll back to the first couple of articles, looking for what was said about the cause of death. According to the coroner's report, Jaycee died as a result of "blunt force trauma to the head," and she'd been dead several days by the time the body was found.

From there I slowly read through the dozen or so articles and put together a timeline.

Audrey was a cocktail waitress back then, working nights while her own mother babysat for Jaycee at the house. She told reporters—and obviously the police, as well—that when she left for work Tuesday night, Jaycee was in bed sleeping and was there when she returned. She checked in on her before going to sleep herself at around 2:00 A.M.

The next morning, Audrey claimed, she was roused from bed when a friend dropped by. She went to wake up Jaycee and discovered her daughter wasn't in bed. But she wasn't alarmed at the time, she said. Her boyfriend, Frank Wargo, sometimes stopped by and took the girl for a car ride in the morning while Audrey slept in, and she assumed that was the case. She even remembered, she said, hearing the front door open and close around eight-thirty and the sound of Jaycee's voice.

When Wargo didn't show up with Jaycee later that day, Audrey said she figured he was getting back at her for an argument they'd had but she didn't want to involve the police and thought Wargo would eventually surface with her daughter. By Friday she was worried enough—so she claimed—that she finally went to the police to report the girl missing.

Pretty pathetic.

Wargo, it turned out, had a solid alibi—at least for the second half of Tuesday and Wednesday morning. He was a professional truck driver, and on the day I found the body he was driving through the state of Georgia, having departed, he told the police, around 4:30 P.M. on Tuesday. They tracked him down in Delaware on his way home late Friday. He claimed to have been pissed at Audrey, and that's why he hadn't told her about the trip.

Audrey had people to back up her alibi, too. The grand-mother reported she'd checked on Jaycee several times on Tuesday evening before spending the night on her daughter's couch, and that Audrey was sleeping when she left just after eight on Wednesday morning. And the friend supported the story about showing up at nine to find Audrey in bed.

Which left Audrey practically no window of time to kill her daughter and dispose of the body between when her mother left and her friend arrived.

But none of that really mattered because Jaycee was ac-tually dead by then.

And that means the grandmother had also lied to the cops about checking on Jaycee. Hard to fathom a grandmother doing that, but perhaps she felt desperate to protect Audrey, or she was coerced by her.

I skim the articles, looking for any other references to Tuesday, the day Jaycee most likely was murdered, but there's just one. Several Millerstown residents reported seeing Jaycee with her mother at a supermarket late Tuesday morning, at around eleven.

My mind scrambles, trying to gather all the pieces of information into a coherent pattern before they're caught by the wind and lifted away. As the waiter sets down the pasta bowl in front of me, I fish out a pen and pad from my purse and start doing the math.

Knowing what I now know about rigor, Jaycee died twelve to twenty-four hours before I found her, which means between midday on Tuesday and 3:00 A.M. Wednesday morning. It seems highly possible that Jaycee was murdered in the hours before Audrey went to work and Wargo left town.

So, which one of them delivered the blow or blows to Jaycee's head? Audrey, in a rage over spilled apple juice or a bathroom accident or whining that wouldn't cease? Or the boyfriend, who had that long haul to Georgia ahead of him and might have already popped a handful of uppers, fueling his fury over a tiny infraction by a toddler? If it was Wargo, Audrey had covered for him. If it was Audrey, she probably convinced Wargo to help her dispose of the body.

It's clear the couple needed Jaycee's disappearance to coincide with times when they each had as good an alibi as possible. By choosing Wednesday, Wargo had a built-in one—his trip down south, easily documented. Audrey's situation was trickier, so she must have had to work on her mother.

And the friend's visit on Wednesday could have been concocted for Audrey's benefit. "Why don't you come by in the morning" . . . "Oh, hey sorry, I was still sleeping, worked late last night. Lemme get my kid up, okay?"

I turn my attention to the bowl in front of me, which brims with linguine and clams the size of tiny buttons. So sublime looking, but my appetite has turned, and the pasta smells like I've pressed my face against the pilings of a dock. I can't bear the thought of eating it.

I butter a piece of bread and take a bite, along with a few sips of sparkling water.

If my theory about the crime is right, I realize, Audrey and Wargo had been extremely lucky. The woods had been a stupid place to hide the body, perhaps chosen in a frenzied rush. If someone else had stumbled across Jaycee's body on Wednesday and reported it that day, the police would have noted the rigor. That would have stripped them of their alibis.

Despite how dispassionate Corbet seemed when I pressed her about the potential impact of my statement, she must have been agog on the inside. My admission could change everything. And it's clear to me now that there are two people in this world to whom I pose a terrible threat.

By this point the smell of clam brine is nearly making me gag, and I push the bowl even farther away. I signal for the check and apologize to the waiter for my hasty departure. Minutes later, I'm out on the street.

Dozens of cars and taxis shoot up First Avenue, but there's little pedestrian traffic in this area. I glance around, just to be sure. Also, waiting for the light to change, I try Mulroney again. I'm confused why I haven't heard from him. He'd acted so eager to hear what I might discover at WorkSpace.

When the Walk sign flashes, I dart across the avenue, heading farther east to the medical imaging facility, a good thirty minutes early.

"You're sure you have no metal anywhere on you?" the technician asks when it's finally time for the procedure and I'm sporting a medical gown. I sense I look checked-out to him.

"Yes, I'm certain," I inform him.

I've never had an MRI before, but I've seen pictures and basically know what to expect: a huge white machine shaped like a donut, people behind a window speaking to me over an intercom as my body slides into the donut on what looks like a long tray. The noise is worse than I'd expected, but I don't care. Somehow all the honking, thumping, knocking, blaring, buzzing, and foghorning force my brain to stop working.

Everything comes rushing back, though, once I'm on the street again later. I check my phone, which I'd had to store in a locker during the exam, and see there's still no call from Mulroney. I do my best to tamp down my growing irritation. Maybe an urgent issue arose with another case, or he could be chasing down a lead for me. Still, I leave him another voice mail.

My phone pings with a text. It's Hugh inquiring about the MRI. I almost sense he wishes there *was* something physically wrong with me, like he'd prefer "brain tumor" to "unbalanced" any day. I respond, saying thanks, the experience was uneventful and that I'll know the results once the neurologist has had time to review the images.

You headed home now? he replies.

Gonna run some errands. Back in a couple of hours.

I *do* have errands to run. It's been days since I bought toiletries or hit the gym or had my nails done. But there's something even more important on my list. I need to finally retrace my steps in the East Village, explore those streets in the hope that something I see will jog a memory, the way the rain on my trench coat did last night.

I shoot my hand up for a passing taxi and give the driver the address for Eastside Eats on Seventh Street.

After zigzagging east, the cabdriver hops on the FDR Drive at Seventy-First Street and zooms south. To my left the East River sparkles in the sun. On any other day, I'd stare out, mesmerized by the comings and goings of the tugs and barges, but I'm too wired to pay any attention.

When I exit the taxi outside Eastside Eats, I see through the glass window that the space inside is sparely decorated, but at the same time inviting. The tables have been constructed from planks of wood and are topped with glass jars full of herbs.

I step inside but don't bother going to the counter, where half a dozen people are milling around. Nothing about this place feels familiar, and sitting with a coffee at one of the tables probably isn't going to alter that.

Next, I wander farther east in the direction of Tompkins Square Park, which I apparently walked along last week. Years ago, the East Village was known for its counterculture, bohemian vibe, and it still gives off a hint of that, but less so now than when I roamed around here before or after my class at NYU. I pass a hip-looking shop selling clothes on consignment, a gallery, a patisserie, and several well-kept brownstone town houses. A group of art students saunters in front of me, carrying portfolios, the scent of their cigarettes wafting back toward me. Ahead of them is a cluster of Asian tourists snapping photos.

Why did I stop my sojourns down here? I can't seem to remember. Just because my course ended didn't mean I couldn't come back. Maybe once I met Hugh, there seemed no reason to visit here. Hugh's hardly a boho kind of guy.

When I reach the park, I make my way to the northern end at Tenth Street and flop onto a bench near two men playing chess. Did I come to this bench last week? Did I sit for a while as I'm doing now, with the warmth of the sun on my face? I have no clue.

Finally, I rise and retrace my steps south, but this time I go two blocks farther, turning on Fifth Street in search of Pairings, the other restaurant that showed up on my credit card statement.

It turns out to be a vegetarian place, rustic and charming, with brick walls painted white. There are about twenty wooden tables all nestled very close to one another and a bar/counter running across the back with a dozen stools. And like Eastside Eats, it's totally and completely unfamiliar to me.

Maybe it *would* make sense to spend a little time at one of these places and give my memory a chance to adjust. The restaurant is clearly open for dinner already—I spot a man sitting solo at a table—so I enter the hushed interior.

A waitress looks up and smiles. She's got short black hair, shaved along the sides, and a small silver hoop in her nose.

"I'm sorry, we don't serve dinner until five thirty," she says.

I glance over at the man sitting at the table and realize it's actually a member of the waitstaff, folding black napkins.

She must read distress on my face because she adds, "We're fully booked tonight, but there should be a seat at the bar if you want to come back right at five thirty. As you know, we serve a full menu there."

So she remembers me.

"Yes, that's right," I say, accepting the card. "I loved the food. It's . . . it's a nice place to come on your own."

"Isn't it?" she says. "Feel free to bring a friend next time."

I was alone, then, on Wednesday.

I exit and walk as fast as I can toward First Avenue, sweating in my coat, and flag down a cab headed uptown. I check my phone for the zillionth time, even though I've had the volume on max and would have heard a text or call from Mulroney come through. Nothing.

I place yet another call to him and this time the recording says, "The user's mailbox is full. Please try again later."

That makes no sense. An active private investigator would expect plenty of incoming calls and would keep his voice mail cleared to accept them. And even if he was crushed with work, he would at least respond to a paying client with a text.

What if this has all been a *scam*? And he provided a minimum amount of info simply to keep me happy? What if the blood-type results aren't even true? Maybe he never really had the tissues tested.

That'd be rich, wouldn't it? Personal finance "expert" falls prey to con artist.

But he *can't* be a fraud. He's a former New York City detective, and my gut told me that he was the real thing.

I rack my brain, turning up the few things I know about him. He mentioned that he lived on West Ninety-Seventh Street. And when we were at the diner, he admitted that he liked to drop by there in the early evenings and mull over his cases.

"Let me off at Ninety-Ninth and Broadway instead," I call to the driver through the plexiglass barrier.

By the time we finally pull up at Broadway Diner, it's growing dark outside and I'm ready to crawl out of my skin. I quickly pay the fare and charge across the sidewalk to the restaurant.

I pause once I'm inside, raking my gaze over the counter, as well as every table and booth. There's no sign of Mulroney. I turn and retreat outside.

Standing on the sidewalk, I feel the oddest urge to cry. Not because I've possibly lost a thousand bucks or fallen prey to a scam. But because my quest to know the truth seems hopelessly stunted, and some of what I've learned so far might not even be true.

But surely, I chide myself, *I'm overreacting.* It's only been eight hours since I first tried Mulroney and he might be doing a surveillance job that demands every ounce of his attention.

Except he said he would be on his cell.

I hurry the two blocks to Ninety-Seventh Street and wander between Broadway and Amsterdam Avenue. Hours ago, I was scared to be on the street alone, and now here I am casing an unfamiliar block at dusk. When I don't have any luck, I try the other side of Broadway next, swiveling my head as I walk to West End Avenue and then toward Riverside Drive. It's more deserted in this area, and a couple of times I turn to look behind me.

There's no sign of Mulroney here either. Did I honestly think I'd simply bump into him as he was headed home?

I try him one more time and hear the same message about the mailbox being full. If he's ridiculously tied up, why not have his partner cover for him?

His partner. He must have a phone as well. As I reverse course and hurry back toward Broadway, I pull up the company website and see that a second number is listed. Maybe it belongs to Williams. I pause just long enough to tap the hyperlink.

Two rings. And then a deep male voice.

"Jay Williams," he answers without enthusiasm.

"Thank god," I blurt out. "Jay, it's Ally Linden, your client. We met at the diner."

"Of course."

"I've been trying to reach Kurt all day, but he hasn't returned my calls. Do you have any idea why?"

"Where are you at the moment?" he asks. His voice sounds hoarse, constricted actually.

"I'm not far from Broadway Diner. I went there looking for him."

"Go back to the diner and I'll meet you there."

"What's going on?"

"Let's talk in person, okay?" he says.

I feel like I'm getting the runaround yet again.

"Jay, I need to know what's happening. Where's your partner?"

"I'm sorry to tell you this," he says. "But Kurt's been killed. He died yesterday evening."

The news nearly knocks me off my feet.

"No, it can't be," I say in stupid protest. "I *spoke* to him last night."

"What time?" Williams says.

"Uh, around seven or so. He was in his car. Driving."

"He died around eight or nine o'clock."

I can hear Mulroney's voice in my head, see his face as he sat across from me, scribbling notes with his big hands. How horribly sad.

"What happened to him?" I plead, the words catching in my throat. "Was it an accident?"

"No, that's not it. Kurt was shot to death."

26

A low, guttural sound escapes my mouth. I can't believe what I'm hearing.

"Please, it's better if we do this in person," Williams says. "I'm at Kurt's apartment, and if you head to the diner, I can be there in under fifteen minutes."

"Okay," I mutter.

I drop the phone in my purse and tear up the street, nearly at a jog. A few minutes later I burst, breathless, through the door of the diner, into a cacophony of clanking plates and chattering voices. It's nearly packed, but I find one free booth and slip into it. The smell is as overwhelming as the noise, a mix of sizzling ground chuck and burnt cheese.

In less time than I expect, Williams emerges through the doorway. Spotting me instantly, he hurries to the booth and slides in across from me. He's in jeans and a black leather jacket, his face pinched in grief.

"I'm really sorry I wasn't able to call all our clients with the news today," he says. "I had to give the cops access to Kurt's place today and then deal with the mess they left behind."

"Where was he killed?"

"In his car. At the edge of a park about thirty miles out of the city in Westchester County, not far from White Plains. He'd been shot twice in the head, at close range."

I try to prevent my mind from going there, but it does anyway. Mulroney's face blown off. Blood sprayed all over the interior of the car.

"Does it have something to do with one of his cases?" I asked, chilled by the thought.

"The cops think not."

A robbery, then? I wonder.

The waitress appears, ready to drop two plastic-coated menus on the table, but Williams holds up his hand.

"Coffee?" he asks me, his voice grim. "Or should we have an actual drink instead?"

"Yes, wine," I say. We order two glasses of red and as soon as the waitress moves off, I glance back at Williams.

"But what would he be doing in a park up there—at nine o'clock at night?" I ask. "When I spoke to him, he said he had an appointment."

Williams cups a hand over his mouth and then pulls it away. "Okay, I'm going to be perfectly blunt," he says. "His car was found in a spot known for anonymous gay sex. He might have been targeted by a predator. Or there's even a chance it was a hate crime."

"Kurt was gay?"

Williams shrugs. "Maybe bisexual. He certainly wasn't out, and I know he was married to a woman briefly in his thirties. He told me a few months ago that he was struggling with something and at the time I thought he was referring to depression. I tried to encourage him to open up, but I didn't have any luck. Now I'm wondering if he was trying to work out his sexuality."

It's not making any sense to me.

"But if he was gay and looking for casual sex, there are easier ways to do it. Why not go on an app like Grindr, instead of traveling to a deserted site miles out of town?"

"If he was feeling as conflicted as I think, the internet might not have felt anonymous enough for him," he says. "This is a spot for someone who is really on the down low. There are married guys who pull up there in their SUVs on their way back to the burbs at the end of the workday. And Jay would have been familiar with it from a job he did a year or two ago. The wife thought the husband was seeing a woman at work, but Kurt tailed him to several parking lots north of the city and discovered he was hooking up with other men."

"Why bother telling me he had an appointment? He didn't owe me an explanation."

"Maybe he was covering up for himself as much as for you."

I glance off, mulling over his words. For some reason my mind keeps resisting the story.

"Look, I'm having a hard time wrapping my mind around this, too," Williams says, as if reading my thoughts. "He did the same with me."

"What do you mean?"

"He left a message on my cell saying he had an appointment related to your case."

"*My* case? He didn't say that when we spoke."

"So maybe it wasn't true."

I feel a stab of fear, and instinctively I reach out and grasp Williams's forearm.

"Do you think there's any chance Kurt was murdered because of me? Because of something he discovered?"

"Ms. Linden, there's no reason to go there. Like I said earlier, maybe Kurt needed to tell himself he had a different plan than trolling for anonymous sex."

"But I was pushed into the street last night at an intersection. Kurt wondered if I might have witnessed something I shouldn't have."

"He ran that idea up the flagpole with me, too, but none of the video he obtained of you showed you in any kind of dangerous situation. Of course, there are still blocks of time unaccounted for."

The waitress returns with our drinks. I take a long sip of my wine and then a second. Williams has assured me there's no reason to panic and all I can do is take him at his word. Still . . .

"I'm sorry to make this all about me," I say, setting the glass down. "This is a big loss for you. I take it you guys were friends as well as partners."

"We were." He briefly presses a knuckle to his mouth. "This is tough, coming out of nowhere."

"Did Kurt have any family?"

"A brother he hadn't heard from in years, but he had a bunch of buddies, some still on the police force. I'm going to do my best to get ahold of people."

I nod.

"I don't want you to worry about this," he adds, picking up the distress I'm unable to tamp down. "And don't be concerned about the progress of your investigation, either. The cops took Kurt's computer, but we have a shared server and I'll start going through your file later tonight."

I feel grateful, which in turn triggers a flash of guilt. It pains me to think of Mulroney dead, but at the same time, I'm relieved not to lose any ground.

A couple in the booth behind us slide across the vinyl seats, preparing to leave. I glance at my watch and realize I've been gone longer than the couple of hours I promised Hugh. I explain the situation to Williams, and he says he has to hustle, too.

After paying the check, we step out onto Broadway, and Williams hands me his own business card, promising to check in tomorrow. Traffic is bumper-to-bumper so I say a rushed good-bye and hurry to the subway station three blocks south, where I can pick up the 1 train. I walk and text at the same time, telling Hugh I'm delayed but on my way.

I live only a few stops south, but this is my first time back on the subway since coming unglued, and as I descend the steps, my dread builds. Once I'm on the platform, I hug the wall, pressing my back tightly against the filthy tiles. The train roars into the station, and though there's an empty seat, I choose to stand instead, gripping the metal pole with both hands. I force myself to focus on the ads, repeating the words in my head.

Mercifully the entire trip takes barely ten minutes and in five minutes more I'm unlocking the door to the apartment and letting myself in. I'm halfway into the great room when Hugh pads toward me from the bedroom hallway, barefoot, hair wet, and a large white towel wrapped around his waist.

I'm surprised—he rarely showers in the evening, except on weekends, after a late tennis game or bike ride.

"What's going on, Ally?" he asks. I hear a tiny note of irritation entwined with his concern.

"Something awful happened."

His eyes widen.

"Sorry, I don't mean to me," I say. "The detective I was using—the private eye. He was murdered last night."

"My god."

I unload the details, catching my breath a few times as I race through the story.

"That's horrible," Hugh says.

"It *is*. He was a nice guy. He seemed to want to help me."

And in that moment, I can hear Mulroney again in my head. His husky voice, the way he chuckled about me paying him the big bucks.

"Ally, what is it?"

I press my hands hard against my eye sockets, still thinking it through.

"I can't stop worrying that his death has something to do with my case. He told his partner he was working on it last night."

"But what about your situation could make someone want to kill him?"

"What if I was witness to a crime during that time, and Mulroney was close to figuring it out?"

"That seems like an awful stretch."

"Remember the bloody tissues in my pocket?"

"You said those could have been from a nosebleed."

"But it wasn't my blood type."

"Right. But I just don't see how—"

"Why do you keep dismissing everything I say, Hugh?" I'm practically shouting now. "I feel like I'm sitting on the wrong side of one of your depositions."

"I'm not dismissing your ideas, Ally. I'm just playing devil's advocate, as I'm sure you'd do if our roles were reversed."

"Right, but I also need you to hear my concerns."

He steps closer, as if he's about to hug me, but as he does, his towel loosens. Using both hands, he rolls the top of the towel over a couple of times to keep it from sliding. "We can talk more about this after I'm dressed, okay?" he says. "I ordered Japanese takeout. It should be here any minute."

Is that the best my husband can do on the comforting front tonight? Call out for sushi?

"Sure," I say testily. "Why did you need to take a shower tonight anyway?"

"Just feeling grungy. I ended up working in the library at the office and it's dusty in there."

"The dust got in your hair, too?"

"Probably."

He turns, and I follow him down the corridor. As he slips into the bathroom, shutting the door behind him, I check my phone. There's a text from Sasha, sounding borderline annoyed and asking when we can review next week's material.

And another, oddly enough, from Damien. How are you? is all he writes. Is he really concerned—or trying to control the narrative about Greenbacks? I don't respond. Best to shut down contact with him going forward.

Before I can set my phone on my desk, it pings with yet another text, this one from Gabby.

I think I may live, she says.

r u really better? I respond.

Marginally. Soup eaten. Head now raised.

Can I do anything for u?

No, but thanks for all your texts. Sorry not to be there for u.

Now's not the time to fill her in. dn't worry about it. miss u! I reply.

I strip off my sweat-soaked blouse and swap it for a long-sleeved tee. As I'm wiggling into jeans, my eyes roam the bedroom. I've always loved all the white in here—walls, curtains, bedspread, the antique whitewashed dresser—and the space has always felt like a kind of sanctuary for me, and for us as a couple. But at this moment it seems stark and uninviting.

My gaze settles on Hugh's bedside table. His phone is lying there, nestled beside his keys, his money clip, and a crinkled receipt. I approach, nearly on tiptoe, and pluck the receipt from the pile. It's from a liquor store, for two bottles of wine, and my stomach clenches until I recall the plastic bag I spotted earlier on the top of the island.

I tuck the receipt back under the phone and listen. From the bathroom comes the sound of Hugh's electric toothbrush. With my eye trained on the bathroom door, I reach now for the phone and quickly type in the password. I go to recent calls and scroll down.

It takes a few seconds before I see a call to Ashley Budd. I nearly gasp at the sight of her name. The call was made two and a half weeks ago. And there are two more a week before that.

The whirring sound from the bathroom ceases. I set the phone back down and flip it over, so Hugh won't notice the screen's lit. I've barely withdrawn my hand when the door swings open. Dressed now, he quickly grabs his phone from the table and stuffs it in his back pocket.

"Food not here yet?"

"No." Although maybe the concierge rang and I didn't hear it because of the blood pulsing hard between my ears. Hugh lied to me. He's been in touch with this Ashley, Sasha's good buddy. He's called her more than once, meaning he might be meeting with her, or even hooking up. Was he with her tonight? For the very first time, I seriously consider the fact that my husband could be having an affair.

But then why no recent calls? Maybe he's put things on hold because of my problems. Or he's bought a burner phone solely for contact with her.

"Are you thinking about your detective? I'm sorry I didn't sound more sympathetic."

"Thanks."

"I picked up some wine. Would you like a glass?" The buzzer rings from the other side of the apartment. "I'll get that."

My stomach's roiling. I don't even know how I can eat tonight or carry on a normal conversation with him. Though honestly, when was the last time I had a conversation with Hugh that felt the least bit normal?

My phone rings, jarring me again. It's Jay Williams.

"Have you got a minute?" he asks when I answer.

"Of course." It takes all my mental energy to force my attention on the call.

"I looked through the notes on your case to see if there were any red flags."

"And were there?"

"None obvious to me. But can you get me up to speed on a few things? When you spoke to Kurt last night, I assume he filled you in on where he was in the investigation?"

I explain how Mulroney told me I spent all Tuesday night at my WorkSpace office, possibly sleeping, and even more time than previously noted in the East Village on Wednesday. I describe finding my purse and learning about my trip to the restaurant Pairings.

"It looks like Kurt also spoke to a waitress who saw you the first morning you went missing."

"Oh, right. And I apparently told her I needed to get down to Forty-Second Street, though I have no clue why. At this point in time, Tuesday afternoon is still a total blank. But that's when my phone went missing and when I think something must have happened to me."

"Okay, give me a minute while I skim the notes again."

In my mind's eye I see him leaning forward, squinting at his computer screen. Suddenly I'm aware of noises coming from the rest of apartment—the murmur of Hugh's voice as he pays the delivery guy, the crinkle of a paper bag. My stomach knots as I'm torn back to my ugly discovery from five minutes ago. What am I going to do about Hugh?

Williams has asked me another question.

"Sorry, can you repeat that?" I say.

"Did Kurt mention the letters G.C. to you? Do you know someone with these initials?"

"G.C.? No, why?"

"He added them with a question mark toward the end of his notes."

"Um, my best friend's name is Gabby Kane, but she spells it with a K, not a C."

"Okay, if anything comes to you, will you let me know right away?"

"Of course. Is that the last thing in his notes?"

"Yes, from yesterday afternoon. He apparently didn't have a chance to update the file any further before he went out."

There's a pause. I sense him hesitating.

"One more thing before I let you go." His tone seems ever more sober now. "I'd left messages for a few buddies of Kurt's, and one of them called me back a minute ago. He said he spoke to Kurt right around the same time you did, and they agreed to meet up later for beers."

"So . . . ?"

"He said Kurt told him he was on a job and couldn't meet him until after nine."

"Which is basically what he told us. That he was working."

"Yeah. Like I said earlier, maybe he just needed to hear himself say it, but there's a chance he really *was* working and went to that park for another reason besides sex. I'm sharing everything I know with the cops, and I'm going to go up there tomorrow and have a look around."

"You think he met with someone who ended up killing him?"

"It's possible."

"Something related to my investigation? I've never even *heard* of that park before."

"Look, we have a bunch of cases going at the moment, which means Kurt was sometimes dealing with more than one during a single time frame. He could have been meeting someone in regard to another case but making calls on the drive about yours. That said, I think it pays for you to be careful."

"*How?*" I ask, my panic ballooning. "How do I be careful?"

"I'd keep a low profile for now. If you do have to go out, travel by cab. Don't go anyplace unfamiliar. And get your husband to accompany you if you can."

My husband, the man I don't seem to know anymore.

I thank Williams for his advice, and after we hang up, I stand motionless in the middle of the bedroom. From a distance I hear a paper bag tear open and containers being plunked down on the counter. Then the pop of a cork from a wine bottle.

I'm not sure what terrifies me more: the idea that I'm possibly responsible for Mulroney's death and the killer is after me as well. Or that my husband might be involved with another woman.

But there's one thing I *do* know for sure. I have to get out of here. This apartment. And the city, too.

27

SESSION WITH DR. ERLING

"C an you see me okay, Ally?" Dr. Erling asks. We've just begun our Saturday Skype session and I'm looking at her from my laptop. She's sitting at a desk, and from the carved wood bookcase behind her, I can tell she's in her home office in Larchmont.

"Yup."

"This isn't an ideal way to meet, I know, but it's good we're able to connect this weekend."

I nod, agreeing. It's definitely not the best way—she seems almost two-dimensional—but I really needed the session. I notice that my heart's already starting to race a little. Maybe it's because of how much I have to unload—in less than an hour.

"Are you Skyping from your apartment?" she asks.

In a rush, I tell her no, I'm not there. That I took an Uber to New Jersey this morning, and I'm currently sitting in the den/library of my brother Roger's house.

"My sister-in-law is on some kind of girls' trip to Florida

this weekend," I explain, "but she comes back on Monday and then I don't know. I mean, I really don't have a clue where I'm going to be after that."

Erling's brow knits slightly in confusion. "Why don't you have a clue where you'll be?"

"I'm not sure what my options are. I don't want to be in my apartment right now—even in the city. God, I don't know where to start. . . . I'm pretty sure Hugh's cheating on me. I kept thinking that the reason he seemed so detached lately was because he was worried about me and also because of this colossal case he's in the middle of, but I started to hear these warning bells. So I checked his phone." Before she can react, I continue. "I've always been respectful of Hugh's privacy, I really have, but I had to know—and it turns out he's been in touch with this woman named Ashley from law school who he told me he barely knew."

"Did you ask Hugh to explain why he'd been in contact with her?"

"No, and I know that makes me seem like a total wuss. But I don't want to confront him yet, not until I have proof beyond something I found snooping. Right now, all I have to go on are the calls."

She does the pregnant pause thing, studying me but not speaking, as if encouraging me to fill the void.

"I know what you're thinking," I say. "That maybe she simply wanted to network or pick his brain about her career. But Hugh knows I'm not the superjealous type, and if he'd told me he'd run into her and they met for a drink so he could help with her job search, I'd be fine with that, I really would. But the fact that he said they weren't in contact *means* something, I'm sure."

"This must be very distressing for you, Ally."

It feels good to hear her say those words, to acknowledge what I'm experiencing. Roger's in the loop now, and I know he's in my corner, but I can't lay it *all* on him.

"I think it's even worse because I never saw it coming," I say. "I knew there was a strain in our relationship because of the baby discussions, but I thought we could work it out. And I certainly never imagined Hugh *cheating* on me."

Erling nods slightly. Does she relate on a personal level? Her house in Larchmont seems spacious, and though she appears to be single now, my guess is that she once shared the home with a partner. Was she married? Did the relationship end badly?

"How does staying at your brother's help you address the issue?"

I know what she's thinking now, too, that I'm running away from the problem rather than facing it head-on.

"It *doesn't* help, but I can't be around Hugh right now. It's impossible for me to act normal in front of him."

"What do you think the harm would be if you raised the issue with him?"

"He'll deny there's anything going on, just like he lied about really knowing her. He might even make the issue about me—claim it's related to my current mental state. And there's another reason I don't want to be in New York. Something really bad happened the other day."

"And what is that, Ally?"

I tell her about Mulroney's murder, and the chance that his death is connected to the investigation he was doing on my behalf.

"That was my cover story for leaving first thing this morning," I add. "I told Hugh I wanted to be someplace safer, and that part is true. I feel really scared in the city right now."

"Scared because . . . ?"

I look off for a second, twisting my hands. "What if when I was missing I saw something I shouldn't have? And the person who killed Mulroney wants to kill me, too."

"If this man had an active business as a private detective, I'm sure there were other cases he was working on that might have been inherently dangerous. It's possible that his death wasn't even related to his work. I can see why this may be worrying you, but it feels like a stretch to imagine that his death is connected to you or that your life could be in danger."

"But what about me being shoved into the street?"

"Shoved into the street? This is the first I'm hearing of this, Ally."

"Oh gee, that's right, it happened since I saw you last. Two nights ago, someone pushed me into the street at an intersection, and I'm almost positive it was deliberate. And I had this feeling before then that I was being watched. I just sense that there's someone after me and it has to be related to the missing days. If only I could remember where I was. . . . The other night, I had this tiny flash of a memory, but it was so elusive, and in a split second it was gone."

"Can you describe it to me?"

"My hands were wet with blood. And slippery. And I was dabbing at them with tissues. But that's all." And then I voice the fear I haven't been able to express to anyone besides myself. "God, what if I'm *complicit*? What if I hurt someone? I can't stand . . ."

"What triggered the memory, do you think, Ally?

"I think—I think it might be because it was raining, and I was wearing the same trench coat I wore when I was gone, and the sleeve was damp from the rain, like it was the day I showed up at Greenbacks. Remember how the same thing happened at the hospital, when I was looking at the white sheet . . . ? Maybe—maybe there are ways to spark more memories. Are there?"

I start gasping for air, like I did at the last session. It feels as if the oxygen is being squeezed from the room.

"Can you take a deep breath, Ally, and exhale through your mouth? Good. Two more. That's better. Now, can you describe your state of mind to me?"

"Frantic, I guess. I was doing so much better after I hired Kurt Mulroney—I felt in charge of my life again—but now everything feels out of control."

"Have you reported the incident in the street to the police?"

"No, there didn't seem to be any way they could figure out what happened. But this morning on my Uber ride to New Jersey, I received a call from a police detective in White Plains, near where Kurt was killed. I told *him* about the shove. He didn't say much, but I had the feeling he was interested, that maybe the murder *could* be connected to my case."

"Ally, it's good you were helpful to the police, and I know

you want answers, but I'm seriously concerned that if you keep pushing yourself, you'll dissociate again. What's the best way for me to help you understand that you need to focus on your health and well-being right now?"

Is she annoyed? I guess she has the right to be. She's repeatedly told me to allow my brain to rest, and I've repeatedly ignored her advice. She must wonder why I bother to show up and pay for her services.

"You don't have to help me understand. I know I need to take better care of myself. And going forward, I will. I promise."

She nods in approval, and smiles too.

"Excellent. Why don't you use the time away from the city to relax, read, watch TV, and enjoy time with your brother. No experimenting with ways to force memories back. Not right now at least. We can do that all in good time."

"All right."

"When I see you next, we can talk through possible next steps with Hugh. In the meantime, if you sense over this weekend that you're dissociating, I want you to call my cell immediately. And of course, you can call me if any memories, or what you call flashes, come back on their own."

"Yes, absolutely."

We say good-bye, and a second later she vanishes from the screen. The only sound now is the popping and crackling from the fire Roger made earlier.

And the hammering of my heart.

28

Shortly after I finish with Erling, Hugh calls my cell. It's as if his ears are burning.

"You make it to Roger's okay?" he asks. There's concern in his voice, but also a hint of irritation, like I detected after I announced I wanted to escape the city for a few days.

"Didn't you get my text?"

"Yeah, but I just wanted to check in. What are you and Roger going to do today?"

"Nothing special. Read. Maybe take a walk along the river at some point."

I don't inquire about *his* weekend plans. If I did, how would I know he was telling the truth?

"When do you see yourself coming back?" he says.

"I'm not sure, Hugh. I'm going to have to play it by ear."

"Listen, I can understand why you're shaken about this Mulroney business, but there's absolutely no proof it's related to you. I did a quick online search for that park, and it's definitely a gay pickup spot."

"His partner has doubts about that theory. It's possible he was there to meet someone connected to my case. The killer might have figured out Mulroney was close to discovering stuff that needed to be kept quiet and lured him to that location so that the police would read it wrong."

"So does this mean you're planning to stay with Roger until they arrest someone?"

"I said I don't know."

He sighs. "Ally, what's really going on?"

I'm not surprised he's guessed there's more at play here. A colleague of his once told me that Hugh's called "the duke of depositions" because he's masterful at reading a room, surmising what people are thinking and feeling, and then easing the truth out of them. But I'm not going to confront him about Ashley, at least not yet.

"I feel safer here for now. Besides, a little R and R isn't a bad thing, right?"

"If that's what you want, fine. Why don't we check in later in the day?"

"Okay."

"I love you, Ally."

"Same here."

Does Hugh mean that? If he does, how could he be seeing another woman? Gabby always says that smart women accept that all men cheat, that they cheat as predictably as the sun comes up in the morning, and that you're an idiot if you assume your guy is the one exception, and yet I'd thought that was Hugh. I knew there were no guarantees our marriage would last forever, but I never thought he would sneak around. He's always seemed so upright, a straight-shooting, play-by-the-rules-because-the-rules-keep-things-sane kind of guy. Have I once again been guilty of selective inattention?

Maybe he *is* a stand-up guy, and I'm reading this all wrong. But I can't talk to him about it until I know more.

I dig my laptop from the tote bag nestled by my feet. After lifting the screen, I pause briefly and then, almost with a mind of their own, my fingers creep around the keyboard until they've called up LinkedIn. I make certain my privacy feature is turned on and then slowly type in "Ashley Budd." With each tap of a key, I feel like I'm six years old and waiting, with my heart in my throat, to give one more crank of the handle to a jack-in-the-box.

The spelling complete, names materialize, and then additional ones do after I tap "see all results." One is for a woman who's a lawyer in Manhattan, so I figure that must be her, and with another click, her profile pops up and her photo enlarges.

I swallow hard. She's strikingly attractive, a brown-eyed brunette with thick, dark eyebrows. From the timeline in her profile, I see that unlike Hugh she attended law school immediately following college and is now in her late twenties. Like Sasha.

I feel a nasty surge of bile in my throat as I imagine Hugh kissing her. Making love to her. Was that the reason for his late-day shower? To wash off any trace of Ashley Budd?

Mulroney could have helped me answer this question, I'm sure. I could have hired him to investigate Hugh. And now suddenly I'm also imagining Mulroney—lying dead in his car, blood spattered everywhere.

I jump up from the couch, cross the room to the hearth, and throw a fresh log on the fire that Roger had lit for me earlier. I squeeze my eyes closed, and when I reopen them,

I try to simply absorb my surroundings. I've always loved this room, with its floor-to-ceiling bookshelves and shades of deep blue. The two windows, framed by silk curtains, offer a view of the side yard, ending with a row of majestic fir trees.

When I return to the couch, I finally compel myself to work, starting with a scan of the research notes that Sasha has forwarded me for the podcast. These prove to be about as scintillating as a recipe for boiling hot dogs. I shoot an email to thank her and say I have what I need, so there's no reason to review anything by phone.

"I'm currently at my brother's in New Jersey," I add, "dealing with a small emergency. There's a slim chance we'll have to post an old podcast this week and reschedule the upcoming show for the following week."

Next, I text Casey and pass along the same news, but flesh it out, asking her to alert the studio and also determine if the designated guest will be available at the same time a week later. I hate the idea of having to cancel the show—I don't want to take a single chance with this venture—but I can't imagine going back to the city as soon as Tuesday.

The door to the den swings all the way open and Roger, dressed in slim tan slacks and a cashmere cardigan, appears bearing a wooden tray.

"How was the therapy session?" he asks.

"I didn't love doing it by Skype, but I guess that's better than nothing. What's *really* helping is being here."

"So glad you could come out."

"I'm so grateful to you for having me," I tell him. What I don't say is that I know Marion wouldn't want me here for a weekend, and that the only reason I accepted his invitation was that he mentioned she was away.

"Just so you're aware," he says, as if he read my mind, "I've realized lately that Marion has been boxing you out in little ways, and I've had blinders on about it. I'm not sure why, but she seems slightly threatened by my other relationships. Not only with you. But with Quinn, too. Even Dad. I'm going to address that with her."

"I'd love to be back in your life more, Roger. Especially now." I smile ruefully. "Everything seems to have gone to hell."

"It will work out, Button. The cops will find this detective's killer. And you'll figure out what's going on with Hugh. Maybe it's not what you imagine."

He sets the tray on the coffee table, where I see he's loaded it with a lovely antique teapot, matching cups, starched white napkins, and a small plate of cookies, a superbuttery kind he knows I love.

"Oh, Rog, this is so sweet of you," I say, moved by the gesture. "And my, what a tray you set."

"My mother always seemed to enjoy laying out a tray of pretty things. I guess she passed the gene down."

"I wish I could have met her. She looks so beautiful in her pictures."

My own mother had been great about not only displaying photos of Quinn and Roger with their mom but also encouraging the boys to speak about her frequently.

"Well, that falls firmly into the realm of the impossible, doesn't it?" he says, pouring a cup of tea.

There's nothing about his tone that suggests bitterness,

but for the first time in my life, I wonder if Roger harbors any resentment—over his mother's death, his father's remarriage, my bursting onto the scene.

"Yes, unfortunately," I reply, for lack of anything better to say.

"You still take a smidgen of milk with your tea?"

"Please. You know, I've been so horribly preoccupied with my own troubles lately, I haven't asked a single question about you. Everything okay?"

"Uh, fine. Nothing much to report. And we need to stay focused on you right now."

"Fine?" I can't always read people as well as Hugh can, but I caught the brief hesitation before his response.

"Ha, have you noticed all my new gray hairs?"

"Yes, though I admit they give you a very distinguished air."

He sighs, passes over my cup of tea, and pours one for himself before settling near me on the couch.

"In all honesty, I had a bit of a financial concern earlier in the year. Not what you'd call a disaster but more than a hiccup, and it had me worried for a while."

"What happened?"

"Bad investment on my part. I was missing the game, I guess, and I took a risk that was ridiculously stupid—which I feel dumb admitting to you, of all people. The good news is that I contained the situation. There's no long-term fallout."

I'm stunned. Roger has always been the master of the smart, well-calculated risk.

"You promise?"

"Absolutely, it's all good. But it put a damper on my

relationship with Marion. I've always known she liked my money, but I didn't know how much until I revealed what was going on and saw the panic in her eyes. She looked like a horse trapped in its stall during a raging barn fire."

I'm stunned again, not simply by Marion's reaction, but by hearing my brother say this, especially after his remark about her boxing me out. I'm relieved she hasn't totally hoodwinked him, but I'd be sad to see him contend with a second failed marriage.

"Does this mean you're having doubts about Marion?"

"Some, yes. But like you with Hugh, I'm going to see how it plays out." He glances at his watch. "Why don't you enjoy your tea while I see to dinner. I thought we'd eat about seven, if that's fine with you."

I manage to flash him a smile. After he heads to the kitchen, I make an attempt to engage with a novel on my iPad, but my gaze slides off the screen and my thoughts are constantly towed back to Mulroney, and Hugh, and Ashley Budd. And what happened to me in this region years ago.

I'm spared further torture when I see a text from Gabby, saying she's fully returned to the land of the living and wants to meet tomorrow for coffee or drinks. I text back explaining I'm at Roger's but that I'll call her at some point this weekend. I can't help but wonder whether I'd feel less frantic if I'd been able to spend time with her over the past couple of weeks.

I notice through the window that the sun has sunk low in the sky. I grab a throw blanket from the back of the couch, drape it around my shoulders, and wander out to the flagstone patio on the river side of the house.

Some days, if the sun is bright, the river tints blue, but today it's somewhere between brown and pewter gray. When I was a girl, I used to go tubing on the river with my parents every summer, roping our tubes together and drifting lazily down it for hours. There's nothing inviting about the water I'm staring at now, though. It's flat and still, but it seems vaguely hostile, like there are dark things slithering beneath the surface.

I scan the area to the left and right of Roger's house. I know we're not as isolated as it feels, but you can't see the houses on either side of us because of the trees that line the property.

The wind picks up and I return indoors, where I gather my belongings from the den and lug them upstairs to the large, pale-yellow guest room. I've slept here only once before, shortly after Roger restored the house, because Hugh and I always stay with my father when we come out to New Jersey. With more than a twinge of wistfulness, I realize how much I'd love to be in my old bed there tonight, hearing my father puttering around downstairs.

As I'm changing for dinner, my phone rings, and with a jolt I see Damien's name on the screen. Ignoring his calls isn't working, so this time I hit accept.

"I wanted to follow up after the other night," he says, his voice disconcertingly soft. "I was really worried about you."

I pause, considering how much to share.

"I've recovered, thanks. But . . ."

And then I do launch in, telling him about Mulroney's death and my decision to come to Roger's.

"This is scary stuff," Damien says. "Can the cops do anything to help you right now?"

"Ha, you mean the ones from White Plains? I don't think they have jurisdiction here."

"Can *I* do anything, then?"

"I think the best thing you can do, Damien, is stop calling me. I appreciate your concern, but we shouldn't be in touch."

"Why?"

"You know why."

"You don't envision us being friends?"

I don't. I sort of tried it once before, in my last months at Greenbacks, and there was nothing rewarding about it. Besides, at the moment I can't envision anything except the next couple hours of my life.

"No, it's not possible. Sorry, I need to go. Thanks again for calling."

I tap the red button and hurry downstairs, trying not to dwell on the conversation. The living room is in total darkness, and the only illumination in the den comes from a small table lamp and the dying embers in the fireplace. What earlier seemed so comforting now feels gloomy, almost foreboding. It's as if the house has shape-shifted, like a woodland fairy morphing into a she-wolf.

"Rog?" I call. No answer.

I ease open the door to the dining room to discover that it's dark as well, but I see light seeping from beneath the kitchen door at the far end.

I cross the room and swing it open. And Roger's there, lifting a roasting pan from the oven.

"Were you calling me?" he asks. "Sorry, the exhaust fan makes such a racket."

"Want me to set the table?"

"Sure, I thought we'd eat in here since it's cheerier."

The meal turns out to be simple but delicious—chicken breasts that Roger's roasted with fennel and herbes de Provence, green beans, a Bibb lettuce salad, and fresh bread. We leave any talk of Hugh, Marion, murder, fugue states, and financial setbacks behind and speak about local politics, my upcoming book, and anecdotes from our dad's stay in San Diego that Quinn has been better at sharing with Roger than with me. Whether it's from the switch in topics or the crisp white wine, or both, my stomach unknots.

As we're loading the dishwasher, I start to tense up again and decide I have no choice but to spoil the mood. There's something I need to know.

"Rog, the other day Hugh asked me a question I couldn't answer, and I realized you might be the only person who could, besides Dad. Are you aware of any time in my childhood or past when I might have ended up in a dissociative state? Perhaps not as long as the one I experienced recently but some period when I lost track of myself?"

"What? No, certainly not. At least not that I witnessed or heard about."

"And not—back then . . . around the time I found Jaycee?"

"Um . . . no. No one ever mentioned anything like that to me."

"You hesitated."

"Only because the question caught me off guard. Why would Hugh suggest that?"

I smile ruefully. "Maybe he's trying to determine how much of a nutjob he married."

Later, I make an attempt to read in the den while Roger disappears upstairs to his office for a while. Hugh calls at about nine to say good night and I keep it brief, too exhausted to play at sounding normal. Shortly afterward, my brother returns and joins me on the couch with an art book, but he seems distracted now, flipping pages without lighting on them. When I glance up, I see that he's staring off into space, his head slightly cocked, and I half expect him to ask, *Did you hear that?* But he doesn't. A minute later he announces he's turning in, but I'm welcome to hold down the fort in the den.

"No, I should call it a night, too," I say. "Thanks for a lovely evening, Roger."

"My pleasure, Button."

I follow him upstairs and soon crawl into bed. Somehow, I manage to drift off to sleep pretty quickly. But when I awake with a start, I see that it's ten past eleven, and I've been asleep for only a few minutes. I lie on my back beneath the covers as my mind churns with now-familiar thoughts of Hugh in his towel, Hugh lying, Hugh and *Ashley*. And then Mulroney, dead perhaps because of me. The large dimensions of the guest room, with its soaring ceilings, don't help to put me at ease. But finally, perhaps from sheer mental exhaustion, I finally nod off again.

And then once more I jolt awake. The bedside clock now reads 3:12. At first, I assume my internal agitation has roused me, but as I shift onto my back, I see a faint light shimmering outside the two windows looking onto the side yard.

I scoot up in bed. Am I seeing car headlights from the road, the beams on high? But it doesn't diminish as quickly as those would.

I toss off the duvet, slip out of bed, and cross the room toward the window. Halfway there, I notice a fiery red bleeding into the yellow glow, and as I reach the sill, I gasp in shock. One side of the garden shed that sits near the edge of the property is engulfed in flames. Smoke is billowing up toward the treetops.

I stuff my feet into flats and race down the hallway toward Roger's room. Pounding on his door elicits no response, so I shove it open. From the dim light of the hall I can see that his bed is empty. God, where *is* he?

I notice there's light emanating from the base of the stairwell and rush down the wide steps into the center hall, pivot, and tear to the rear of the house. The chain's off the door. I swing it open and spill into the night.

"Roger?" I scream, staggering onto the gravel drive. I can hear the fire crackling from the side yard. "*Roger?*"

I'm about to round the building to find him when a force whacks me hard from behind. My knees buckle, the wind knocked out of me.

I try to right myself, but something comes out of nowhere and slams into my throat. It's an arm in a jacket, I realize. A man's arm. Panic explodes through my limbs. The grip tightens and he starts to yank me backward. Somehow I manage to struggle, clawing behind me. For a split second, I touch something scratchy on either his head or face.

I make an attempt to scream, but he reaches up, clamps a hand on my mouth. His feet keeping moving, though. When squirming doesn't free me, I kick at his shins. For a split second he freezes, still gripping me at a slant. Then, with his free hand, he punches the side of my face with the force of a battering ram.

The shock from the pain makes me crumble, but he hoists me up and keeps dragging. I dig my shoes into the dirt, trying to slow our momentum. One flies off, then the other. My feet are bare now, and stones and tree roots tear at the skin. We're descending, I realize. Down the front lawn of the house as it drops to the river.

Finally, he stops. I hear his arms fall by his side and I make an attempt to bolt. "Roger," I scream, but it comes out as a tiny squeak.

An arm shoots out and this time I'm yanked backward by the neck of my pajama top. The movement makes me spin a little in place and I finally see his figure. His face is obscured by a ski mask.

"Help," I scream, louder this time. "*Help!*"

Another punch to my face, and my cheek erupts in pain. He grabs me again with both arms and hauls me through the dirt and grass. Only a foot or so away I can hear the river water lapping against the banks.

And then I understand.

He's going to drown me.

try once more to fight him off, but it's useless. He drives me to my knees, then grabs a wad of my hair in his fist and plunges my head into the river. The feel of the ice-cold water is like an electric shock and my heart nearly stops.

I hold my breath, trying desperately not to inhale. Flailing behind me with my free arm, I make contact only with air.

I'm going to die, I realize. Right here, right now.

Then, even through the river water, I hear it—*thwack*. And a second later, the hold on me miraculously loosens. I tear my head from the river, retching. Propping myself on my elbows, I slide backward and gulp for as much air as I can.

Behind me there's the sound of footsteps, shoes scuffing in the dirt. Still on my knees, I turn to see the man in the ski mask a yard or so away. He's on the ground now, but trying to stagger to his feet.

In the glow from a security light I spot Roger a few feet beyond, legs wide and both hands grasping the oar of a canoe. He takes aim at the assailant and swings the oar, delivering a blow so powerful, I hear wood crack. Or maybe bone. It's the second blow, I realize. The man teeters for a few moments and finally collapses, faceup on the ground.

"Ally, are you okay?" Roger calls out, racing toward me.

"Uh, I think so," I say, though my cheek is throbbing and I'm shivering like crazy. I struggle to a standing position, noticing that the top of my pajamas is sopping wet.

Roger reaches my side and wraps his free arm around me.

"We need to get you inside, but first I have to tie him up."

He passes me the oar and hurries toward the nearby dock.

"Can I help?" I call out, my teeth chattering.

"Just stand guard, okay?"

I glance back at my attacker, making sure he's not moving. His chest rises and falls a little, so I know he's breathing. I can see he's six feet or more, on the stocky side. There was no way I could have fought him off on my own.

"What about the fire?" I call out, looking back toward Roger.

"I put it out already."

He unwinds a length of rope from a post on the dock and then returns to my side. Crouching down, he binds the man's ankles together, then yanks the rope a couple of times to make sure the knot is tight. I watch, weirdly detached, as if the experience is happening to someone else. Next, Roger tugs the guy's arms upward, overhead, and starts to secure his wrists together.

"Do you think . . . do you think he might have followed me from the city?" I ask, almost in a whisper. "Or knew I was going to be here?"

"What are you saying? That this might be the guy who killed the private eye?"

"Right. Can we take off the ski mask?"

He hesitates and then shakes his head. "Better to let the cops do that."

He finishes the knot with a jerk. After rising, he steps toward me, wrapping an arm around my shoulder again. I toss the oar to the ground and let him lead me up the embankment. The skin on the soles of my feet is raw from being dragged, and every step hurts.

"The river side door's locked, so we need to go in by the kitchen," Roger says.

We hurry along the perimeter of the house, and though we're on the opposite side from the garden shed, the air reeks with the smell of wet, smoldering wood. The kitchen door, I notice, is still open. Roger ushers me inside and double-locks the door behind us. It's chilly in the house from the door being ajar. Dark, too. Roger flicks on extra lights besides the one in the hall.

"You need warm clothes," he says. "Can you manage on your own while I call the cops from the kitchen?"

"Yes, I'll be fine . . ." Emotion overwhelms me and I choke back tears. "Roger, you saved my life. He was going to kill me."

"Oh, Button," he says, enveloping me into a hug. "It was terrifying to see him shoving your head down like that. I—" His voice breaks and I realize he's as shaken as I am. "I'll meet you in the den in a minute, okay?"

As Roger enters the kitchen, I head up the back stairs to

my room. I change into the sweater and jeans I'd worn that day and dig a pair of socks out of my roller bag. My feet hurt too much for shoes, so I don't bother. The shivering, I notice, has eased but not fully subsided.

It's only when I'm in the en suite bathroom, grabbing a towel for my hair, that I'm afforded a look at my face for the first time. The right side is bright red and starting to swell, as if it's being inflated with a tire pump. I gingerly rest a finger on my cheek. The skin feels incredibly sore, but my cheek-bone doesn't seem to be broken.

Before heading downstairs, I sit for a minute on the edge of the bed, trying to get a grip. Is the man tied up on the riverbank really the same person who killed Mulroney, who possibly shoved me into traffic? If so, what could I have seen or done that compelled him to hunt me down? And how did he know my whereabouts?

I return to the ground floor but stop in the kitchen first, grabbing a bag of pearl onions from the freezer and resting it carefully against my cheek. Roger's in the den as promised, now in corduroy slacks and a sweater, and standing by a freshly lit fire.

"Come here," he says, extending an arm. "I can tell you're still shivering."

"You called 911?"

"Yeah, and I assume they'll send an ambulance, too, since I said the assailant was injured. They— Oh my god, your face."

"I know. It's blooming like a flower in a time-lapse video."

"Should we call an ambulance for you as well?"

"I don't think it's necessary." I inch closer to the hearth

and savor the warmth of its flames. "From what I can tell, it's mostly swelling."

"What in the world happened? Did he grab you from your room?"

I shake my head and quickly rehash the series of events—seeing the flames from my window, racing outside, being attacked from behind and then dragged to the water.

"And what about you?" I ask when I finish. "You must have been putting the fire out when I came outside."

"Yup. I'd cracked my bedroom window, thank goodness, and so the smell woke me. I knew it wasn't in the house or else the smoke detectors would have gone off, so I ran outside and took the hose to the shed. I was mainly trying to contain the flames until I could grab a phone and call 911, but within a couple of minutes, I'd managed to put it out. When I started toward the house, I spotted one of your shoes in the side yard and I panicked and went looking for you. I was lucky the oar was on the dock because I'm not sure I would have been a match for him otherwise."

"Do you think he set the fire as a diversion?"

"Yeah, probably. Maybe to flush us out of the house so he didn't have to break in."

Our conversation is cut short by the faint sound of car tires crunching on gravel. It must be the police.

"I'll go to meet with them," Roger says, turning to leave. "You stay warm."

A minute later I hear the murmur of voices and the slam of a door. I slip out of the den and tiptoe on stinging feet to the living room, where I position myself by one of the tall windows facing the river. A minute later, I see the outlines of Roger and two uniformed cops, one male, one female, making their way across the lawn and down the embankment. Still shivering a little, I return to the hearth in the den. Before long I hear another vehicle approaching, accompanied by the whoop of an ambulance.

I try to stay in the present, to focus on the scent of woodsmoke and the crackle of the fire, but my thoughts keep being ripped back to the terror of having my head forced into the water, sure I was about to die.

The ambulance departs, with its siren wailing now. At least two more vehicles come up the driveway almost simultaneously, and shortly afterward, I spot the outlines of three people tramping along the side yard on their way to the riverbank. I'm still by the fire ten minutes later when footsteps approach the den and Roger bursts through the doorway, looking stricken.

"I've got news," he says. "But we need to talk quickly."

"Why, what's going on?"

"More cops have arrived," he says, taking two steps into the room. "And Nowak's on the way. They'll want to interview us separately."

"Do you know who it is?"

"Yes. Not someone from New York. It's Frank Wargo."

"Omigod."

"I didn't recognize him when they pulled the mask off, but they took out his wallet, and it's him."

"So he's been in the area after all." I press my hands to my head, my thoughts racing. "He wanted me dead—which means he must be the one who killed Jaycee. And he found out I'd gone to the police."

"It looks that way. Of course, he might also have been protecting the mother."

"Has he come to yet?"

"He stirred a bit when they were loading him into the ambulance. I suspect he has a concussion from the blow to his head."

"God, how did he know I'd talked to the cops? And that I was *here* tonight?"

His face darkens further. He shakes his head, but I sense there's something he's not saying.

"Do you *know*, Rog?" I ask, my voice almost hoarse.

"No, no. I'm just wondering if he saw you that day in town, going into the police station."

"Maybe." I bite my thumb, trying to think if I'd noticed anyone who might have recognized me, but the town had seemed pretty empty that day. "Or someone told him. And it definitely might have been Wargo who shoved me into the street in the city. . . . But he can't be the one who killed Mulroney. What would the motive be? And how would he have even known I'd hired him?"

Before we can hash it out anymore, a uniformed female officer appears in the doorway next to Roger.

"Ms. Linden?" she says. "I'm Officer Bruin and I'd like to take your statement now."

"Of course."

But she's barely gotten the words out when Chief Nowak, wearing a hip-length leather coat, comes up behind her and my brother. He greets both of us and then turns to the officer.

"Luanne, why don't I take Ms. Linden's statement. You

can handle Mr. Linden's. Roger, is there another room I can use?"

He suggests the dining room and the two of them trot off, my brother looking utterly weary.

"You've had a pretty harrowing evening," Nowak says, his voice warm. The sympathetic tone is wasted on me because I saw how little good it did me the other day.

"It was pretty scary, yes."

"Your brother said you don't want medical treatment, but I'll have to have my deputy photograph your injuries before we leave tonight. For now, can you take me through everything that happened, right from the beginning?"

I do my best. It was all so fast, it takes only a few minutes to recount. I also mention the incident in the city and pose the idea that it might be related to the attack here. As I wrap up, I allow myself a moment of perverse satisfaction, thinking that if tonight was clearly an attempt to silence me because of what I know about Jaycee's death, at least Corbet will stop eyeing me suspiciously.

"I'm so sorry you had to go through all this," Nowak says. "I take it you've heard that your assailant appears to be Frank Wargo."

I nod.

"Any idea how he might have found out you'd come to us with new information?"

"None whatsoever." I take a moment to choose both the words and tone I'm going to use next. "What about from your end? Any thoughts on how he gained access to what was in my statement?"

"Both Detective Corbet and I have been very discreet,

so no, I don't know. But I'm going to make it my business to find out."

As he's tucking his notebook back into his coat pocket, I briefly deliberate telling him about Mulroney's death but decide against it. As I'd pointed out to Roger, there doesn't seem to be a connection. Nowak summons the female officer from the other room and she takes shots of my face with her smartphone camera.

By the time all the police have departed, daylight is seeping through the trees beyond the house. My feet still sting, my head aches from having my hair yanked hard, and though I've been keeping my face iced, it's practically pulsing with pain now, as if it has its own heartbeat.

Roger and I take turns recapping our interviews, and I find that my anxiety has started to subside a little now that we finally have the house to ourselves.

"Are you going to call Marion and let her know what happened?" I ask.

"Yes, I don't want her to hear it first from someone else, but I thought I'd wait until at least eight. Are you thinking of going back to bed?"

I massage my temples, considering. "Yeah, if I'm lucky, maybe I'll sleep for an hour or two."

"Me, too. Feel free to knock on my door if you need anything."

"Yup. And thank you again, Roger. With all my heart."

I hobble upstairs, close the drapes in my room, and collapse onto the bed. Unanswerable questions drift across my mind and then, before I can give them any attention, they drift away. Finally, I feel sleep overtake me.

When I awake, sunlight is creeping into the room from the edges of the drapes. Almost instantly the events of last night stampede into my consciousness: the frigid river water rushing up my nose, my lungs ready to burst, the fear that I had only seconds more to live. Both my head and face are throbbing.

I close my eyes again. Erling's warnings about stress echo in my mind. I can't let last night overwhelm me. I force myself to breathe deeply and then roll out of bed.

The clock says ten thirty, I discover to my shock. I dress quickly, grabbing jeans and a fresh sweater, and then steel myself for a glimpse in the bathroom mirror. My face looks even worse. The swelling hasn't subsided, there's now purple bruising on my left cheek, and I'm sporting half a black eye.

After brushing my teeth and popping three ibuprofen tablets, I head downstairs, where welcoming scents waft from the kitchen. As I enter, I discover Roger setting a platter of french toast on the table.

"Morning, Button. I heard you moving around so I figured it was time for food. How are you feeling?"

"Achy, exhausted, but I'll live."

"Are you sure you don't want to see someone about your face?"

"Thanks, but I think it's all about icing it and trying not to laugh, which fortunately won't be hard this week."

"Help yourself to breakfast."

I plop into a chair and take in the spread on the table: slices of melon, a bowl of raspberries, a jug of orange juice. "How is it that even in a crisis, you can still cook up a storm? It's very reassuring."

"Some might call it fiddling while Rome burns."

Though I don't have much appetite, I help myself to a slice of the toast and a spoonful of berries. Roger takes a seat across from me and pours us each a cup of coffee from a French press.

"Did you reach Marion yet?" I ask.

"Yes, she managed to snag a reservation on a two o'clock flight to Newark."

As soon as the words are out of his mouth, he chokes back a sob.

"Roger, what is it?"

"I have more news. I think I know how Wargo got wind of you going to the cops."

I hold my breath.

"Remember when I told you I needed to offer Marion an explanation for your visit this past week, and I gave her a totally watered-down version—that you were simply being interviewed for the cold case investigation? Well, when I spoke to her this morning, she admitted that she mentioned it to her brother Adam when he stopped by—she's a world-class gossip, as I've come to learn."

I stare at him across the table, horrified. "Adam was in school with Wargo, right? You think he's the one who told him?"

"Not necessarily. She thinks he probably told some other people he knows from school, and it worked its way back to Wargo. He apparently doesn't live all that far from here, just over the river in Pennsylvania. I have no idea if he still has any contact with Audrey."

"But even if he'd heard I was being reinterviewed, why would he feel the need to kill me?"

Roger looks away. "I think Marion told her brother more than she's letting on right now. My guess is that she'd been eavesdropping on my calls to you—and the ones I made to the chief. And she probably told Adam that you had new information that could come out at a trial."

I shake my head, furious. "I can't fucking believe this."

"Also, Adam is probably aware of your address from Marion, and he might have shared that with someone as well."

"So that's how Wargo knew where to find me in the city."

"I'm so ashamed, Button. I want to strangle her."

So do I, I think.

"I can't believe she had the nerve to admit it to you."

"I'm sure it was purely strategic on her part. Better to lay her cards on the table now and manage the fallout, rather than having me learn about it later from a third party."

"Of course." Trying to protect her assets as best she can.

"Something else to consider," Roger says, grimacing. "You and I spoke about Mulroney last week on the phone, and like I said, I think Marion's been eavesdropping."

"Okay, but if Marion blabbed about that, too, and it got back to Wargo, it still doesn't give him a reason to kill Mulroney. I hired the guy solely to deal with my disappearance."

"What if Wargo didn't realize Mulroney's true purpose? What if he thought you'd hired a PI to investigate Jaycee's death?"

I nod dully. Maybe he's right.

"I should call the police here and in White Plains, then," I say. "Let them know the possible connection."

"Absolutely."

I have even less appetite than a few minutes before, but because of the effort Roger's mustered, I manage to finish my french toast and coffee. We use the time to strategize how to inform my father about the attack before the news makes its way to him and decide that Roger will call him as soon as it's a decent hour in California, and I'll follow up later.

When I return to the guest bedroom after breakfast, my phone's ringing from the top of the dresser. Hugh, probably. I need to loop him in, of course, no matter what our status is.

But to my surprise, it's Derek, my contact at the company sponsoring the podcast. Odd. He's never once called me on a weekend.

"Sorry to bother you on a Sunday," he announces. "Got a minute?"

"Of course. Is everything all right?"

"I was told you were dealing with an emergency—which, by the way, I'm sorry to hear—and that you might not be able to host the podcast this week."

I groan inwardly. This has Sasha written all over it.

"May I ask who told you that?"

"I don't recall exactly; I had a phone message from my assistant. But I'm thinking that rather than simply posting an old podcast, it would be great to give Sasha a crack at hosting the show. And that way we can introduce our new tagline rather than having to hold off another week."

My blood is boiling.

"There must be a bit of confusion, Derek," I say. "There was a slim chance I wasn't going to make it, but I've sorted it all out. I have every intention of being there on Tuesday. Should I call Bob and reassure him?"

Bob's one of the top dogs at the company, and the one I made the sponsorship deal with. The time has come to finally invoke his name.

"No, not necessary," Derek says, his upbeat tone fading. "Sorry if I misunderstood, and sorry, as well, for interrupting your Sunday. Have a good day."

"You, too."

Call ended and phone in hand, I collapse on the bed and study the ceiling, looking for answers that can't be found in endless feet of perfect dentil molding.

I need to go back to New York, I realize. For starters, I can't be in this house when Marion returns, especially after what she's done. And if Roger's theory is right—that Wargo killed Kurt Mulroney—I don't have any reason to be afraid in the city.

Plus, I need to host the podcast. Derek's aware that he's crossed a line, but I know he could find a way to outsmart me, paint a false picture of me to Bob as someone who's suddenly lost interest or is unwilling to be a team player.

And it's essential for me to talk to Hugh. Not only about the attack but also about us. Dr. Erling's right. I'm not going to find any answers sitting out here, trolling through LinkedIn.

I prop myself on one elbow and call him. When he answers on the second ring, we exchange awkward pleasantries and then I recount last night's events to him, the emotion drained from my voice.

"Ally, this is horrible. Do you want me to drive out and pick you up?"

"No, I'll take a car back. In the next hour. But . . . but I'm only coming if you'll be honest with me."

"Honest?"

"I think you have something to tell me, Hugh."

I hold my breath, praying he'll say, *Ally, what do you mean? There's nothing I haven't been truthful about.*

But he doesn't.

"Yes," he says. "I'll be honest with you."

30

While I wait for the car to take me back to the city, I sit in the kitchen with Roger, both of us quiet, lost in our thoughts. Once it finally arrives, Roger and I briefly cling to each other in the driveway.

"Thank you again, Rog. For everything."

"Just promise me you'll stay strong, Button."

I can't help but ache for him. Given what he's discovered about his wife, his marriage troubles have now intensified.

Minutes later I'm off, on my way to learn what's really going on in my *own* marriage. I want the truth from Hugh, and yet I'm scared it might break my heart. What if he's really sleeping with Ashley Budd?

I'm scared for another reason, too. If Roger's wrong and Wargo isn't the one who pushed me and killed Kurt, I might still be in danger. But there are no other easy places outside the city for me to hole up in.

The Uber driver's GPS thankfully takes us around Millerstown rather than through it. A couple of times I notice his eyes in the rearview mirror, and I assume he's wondering what collided with my face, but he doesn't ask. That's not Uber-driver style.

While we snake along rural roads, I place a call to Nowak and then another to the White Plains detective I spoke to yesterday morning. Neither answers so I leave voice mails saying I have information I want to pass along. By the time we reach I-78, I feel my eyes drooping from fatigue.

When I wake over an hour later, the road signs indicate we're approaching the George Washington Bridge. I check my phone and see a text from Jay Williams.

You doing OK? he asks.

Some stuff to share, I reply. Might be relevant. Or not. Can you talk?

Yes, but later today, OK? Any ideas about those initials, G.C.?

I realize that I've been so preoccupied and worried since I last spoke to him, I've completely forgotten the small task he assigned me. I tap on the contacts icon on my phone and search through the last names beginning with "C," but the only person with the initials I'm looking for is an old college friend named Ginger Colefax. Haven't talked to her in ages.

Sorry. Just checked. Nothing yet.

Okay, cul.

I drop the phone in my lap and stare out the window. We're traversing the upper deck of the bridge, and the silver-gray Hudson River blooms out to my right, bound for the sea at the tip of Manhattan. I've crossed this bridge on so many occasions. Not only after I moved to the city, on trips home to see my parents—and later just my dad—but also before that, when I was a girl and my mother and I would drive in to see a play or a museum exhibit. How I loved those afternoons.

And suddenly, as I gaze at the bridge beams, and the water, and the skyline of the city, I lose track of the moment. The day even. Of why I'm here right now, crossing a river. I jerk my neck to the front. I see the back of the driver's head, his shaggy black hair. Who *is* he? Where is he taking me?

And then just as quickly, I remember. I'm in an Uber. Coming from Roger's. Going to my apartment on the West Side. I almost weep in relief. After desperately fishing through my purse, I locate one of the Altoids and quickly place it on my tongue.

For the last few miles of the trip, as we barrel down the West Side Highway, I force myself to focus on every detail I see and feel. The warmth of the car, the bumps in the road, the brash messages on billboards, the river still on my right, sailboats bobbing on its surface.

"Yes, here," I announce to the driver as we finally approach my building. I scour the area with my eyes, not even sure what I'm looking for anymore. After mumbling a quick thank-you, I grab my roller bag, which I've kept next to me in the backseat for quick access, and swing open the car door.

To my total surprise, Gabby, red hair piled on top of her head, has just darted from the lobby of my building onto the sidewalk.

"Gabby," I call out. She freezes in her tracks, clearly startled, and spots me.

"Oh wow," she says, striding over. She's in a poncho, jeans, and short black boots. "I thought you were still away."

We embrace in a hug. As I pull back, I see that her eyes are strained from being ill, and she may have even lost a couple of pounds.

"I came home sooner than planned. What are you doing here?"

"I—my god, your *face*. Ally, what the fuck happened?"

"I was attacked last night—at Roger's. It's this crazy nightmare story. But I'm fine, and they caught the guy."

"This is horrible. Why didn't you *call* me?"

"I was going to, but I've got to get upstairs and talk to Hugh. Something's come up."

"Are things okay with you guys?"

I glance down. "I don't think so."

When I look up, she's shaking her head so that her earrings, long gold ones of her own design, swing back and forth. "I'm so sorry, Ally. I've been a terrible friend when you needed me the most."

"Gabby, don't worry about it, I know how sick you've been. Can we talk later today or tomorrow? I'll bring you up to speed on everything, I promise."

"Of course. In the meantime, is there anything I can do?"

"No, but I should really go. I— Wait, so why were you here?"

"Oh, I was dropping something off for you. Um, a little gift." She seems to read the confusion in my eyes. "I mean, I knew you wouldn't be able to get it for a few days, but I was in the neighborhood, so I left it with the concierge."

"That's really nice, Gabby, thank you." I hug her again. "Talk later."

After leaving her behind, I hurry into the lobby, my legs still aching from last night. The doorman, it turns out, is behind the front desk, filling in while the concierge's on break.

"Do you have a package for me?" I ask. "Something that my friend just dropped off?"

He smiles, steps through the open doorway to the storage area, and returns a minute later.

"I don't see it, Ally," he tells me. "So it must have been picked up already."

Which means Hugh is upstairs. At least he hasn't fled the premises, too nervous or ashamed to come clean as promised. As I head toward the elevator, I can feel the dread swelling in me.

I enter the apartment and find the foyer dark and the great room empty. After parking my roller bag in the great room, I grab a small bottle of sparkling water from the fridge and make my way down the corridor to the bedroom. It's empty, too, and the drapes have been pulled closed. I drop my purse on the bed and reach for a lamp, but before I have a chance to turn the switch, I hear a noise behind me and spin around. Hugh's in the doorway, standing motionless.

"You made good time," he says. His voice sounds joyless.

"Yup. Where were you just now?"

"In the den, working."

He fumbles along the wall for the overhead light switch and taps it on.

"Ally, your face!" he exclaims, as shocked as Gabby was. He steps closer. "Do the police know any more since we spoke?"

"Not that Roger or I have heard."

"You really should see a doctor, Ally."

"I don't want to see a doctor, Hugh. I want to talk to you."

His shoulders sag, an ominous sign. "Why don't we go to the other room?"

I follow him to the great room, where I perch on the edge of the armchair as he plops onto the sofa across from me. My breath feels trapped in my chest, unable to escape.

"I don't know where to start, exactly," he says.

Ah, so there are layers.

"Why don't you start with Ashley Budd," I manage to say. "Are you having an affair with her?"

I nearly cringe, waiting for the worst.

"No," he says. "I'm not having an affair with Ashley."

"With someone else, then?"

He shakes his head. "No, Ally. I'm not having an affair. I swear."

I exhale. Was Roger right, that it's not what I've been imagining? It's been hard for me to meet Hugh's eyes, but I force my attention there. His expression is bleak, at odds with his seemingly reassuring words. Is he in trouble at work? I wonder. Has he gambled away all our money? Been going to see hookers?

"Then what is it?" I ask.

"It *is* about Ashley, in a sense. After I ran into her at that event, I took her to lunch. And then for a drink a week later."

"Why?"

"I . . . I admit, I was attracted to her. I'd never felt that way in law school, but I did suddenly that night at the lecture. I tried to ignore it, but it was hard. I ended up seeing her a third time. For drinks again."

I wince and have to fight the instinct to shut my eyes, like I've just watched a hubcap fly off the car ahead of me on a highway and hurl itself toward my windshield. But another part of me muscles in and takes control. That part is clear-headed and dispassionate, processing the information as if I'm listening to a midday market report.

"Is that why you were so weird around Sasha? Because she knows?"

I'm thinking suddenly of the orange roses, how Hugh trashed them while they were still fresh. He didn't want any reminders of his deception blooming in front of him.

"Ashley didn't admit anything to Sasha, but it's clear she had suspicions. And she was playing some kind of nasty game by bringing Ashley up to both of us. Like she wanted to hurt you."

Pot, kettle, black.

"So are you going to see her again? Do you want to?" I say, hating the questions as they spill from my lips.

"I'm not sure what I want, Ally. Things have been so tense between us."

"And you're really not sleeping with her?"

"No, but . . . I kissed her. After we had drinks the last time. I swear to you, though. It never went any further than that."

Of course not, I think. *He was probably too busy—and guilt-stricken when I became unhinged shortly afterward.* That episode must have seemed to Hugh like the bad karma ambush from hell.

"I don't get it," I say, jumping from the chair and pacing behind it. "Why, if you're fantasizing about screwing another woman, pick a fight with me that Monday night about having—"

And then it hits me. Maybe he started the fight to illuminate our differences, drive a wedge further between us and lay the groundwork for a split—or at least help him feel less sorry about lusting for Ashley.

Or *maybe* the fight was never *about* babies after all.

"Hugh," I say. My heart aches like a hand that's just been burned. "What was our Monday argument really about?"

He lowers his head and rakes his hair with his fingers.

"Not about kids," he says finally, his voice breaking. "You . . . you saw a text from Ashley on my phone. You were upset and wanted to know what was going on. I told you exactly what I shared with you just now."

I stare at him, disbelieving for a moment. "Are you telling me you've been lying to me all this time, Hugh? About the fight?"

"You were in such a bad way when I met you at the hospital. I didn't want to make it worse for you."

The revelation is crushing. I think of the endless frustration and torment. The endless questions I've had.

"I've spent the past two weeks trying to figure out what made me spiral out of control, and all this time you've been keeping this from me. How could you?"

"I guess I felt that if you didn't remember, we had a chance to start fresh."

"Start *fresh*? Did you ever consider how much the fight over *her* might have factored into my fugue state?"

"I'm sorry, Ally. I—" He takes several steps closer and reaches out to touch my arm, but I yank it out of reach.

"Get the fuck away from me."

"Please, let's talk this out some more."

"There's nothing to talk out. I don't want you here to-night. I want you out of my sight."

"Ally, please—"

"You can come back tomorrow once I've figured things out for myself, but for now you need to go. To the Yale Club or a hotel or whatever. Just *go*."

He starts to speak again, then decides not to. He rises and leaves the great room. I grab a half-full bottle of pinot grigio from the fridge, pour a glass, take two gulps, and re-treat to the den, tightly shutting the door behind me. I try not to listen, but the sounds come faintly through the far wall: drawers opening, the thud of a suitcase onto the floor, Hugh speaking briskly into the phone, perhaps making a res-ervation. Then I hear his footsteps in the corridor along with the rumble of a roller bag.

There's a split second when the sounds cease, as if he's paused, deliberating whether to knock. And then he moves away. Finally, from a distance, I hear the click of the front door closing.

He's gone.

Instinctively my hands fly to my chest, pressing it, as if I'm trying to contain the surge of emotions. My husband's at-tracted to, flirting with, kissing, sort of seeing, another woman. That's bad enough, but his deceit about the fight registers as far worse. Because of his lie, I've been going down the wrong path in search of answers. Hugh, the person I love most in the world, fooled me in order to spare himself a shitstorm. This explains why he's seemed so remote since my day in the ER. And no wonder he wasn't more concerned when I disappeared. He knew I had every reason to take off without any word.

The bloodied tissues in my coat pocket had me more and more convinced that an incident outside the apartment had triggered my dissociative state rather than a rehashed fight about kids. But discovering his infidelity is a whole other story. Could that really have shaken me enough to make me come undone?

From far off, I detect the sound of a ringing phone. I swing open the door and hurry down the silent corridor. The ringing's ceased by the time I reach the bedroom, but I discover I've missed a call from Roger. I try him back immediately.

"So how bad is it?" he asks.

"Bad." I recap my conversation with Hugh, the words pouring out so fast they trip over one another. As I'm speaking, I glance around. There's not even a hint of Hugh's departure—no wire hangers strewn about or dresser drawers ajar—but still, the bedroom seems desolate, the loneliest spot in the universe.

"Ally, this must be gutting," Roger says. "But could you consider giving him another chance? He didn't *sleep* with her."

"I haven't had time to sort out my feelings yet. Besides, he seems smitten with this Ashley chick."

"Do you have anyone who can keep you company there tonight? What about your friend Gabby?"

"Uh, maybe . . ." Part of me just wants to be alone.

"I wish I could drive into the city tonight, but I need to be here when Marion gets home and find out exactly how much more she told her brother."

"Understood. Is there any news about Wargo?"

"No, nothing yet. Maybe he'll confess—or throw Audrey under the bus—but we'll hardly be the first to know."

"At least the cops are finally closer to the truth."

He makes me promise to touch base with him later and to also call Gabby. After we hang up, I end up shooting Gabby a brief text. Roger's right. It would be better to have some company right now.

Are you busy? I write. Can you come back over?

Sensing she might text back any second, I stare at the screen, but she doesn't respond.

For the first time since I've come up from the lobby, I wonder where her gift is. Maybe opening it will do me good. I trudge back down to the great room and scan the space for it without any luck.

I wander aimlessly for a bit, ending up in the den and praying for Gabby to respond. If she doesn't, what in the world do I do next? As I stand there, phone in hand, a smear of memory takes shape in my mind, fuzzy and vague. I'm here in the den. But not today. On another day, in the evening. I'm looking for something—I'm not sure what—and when I approach the desk, I see Hugh's phone lying on top of it. A text pops on the screen as I'm standing there, and mildly curious, I glance at it.

No apologies necessary. You can kiss me anytime.

I'm remembering the night of the fight, I realize. After we'd turned off the TV, he'd retreated to the bedroom, forgetting his phone on the desk. I close my eyes, trying to summon more, but that's all there is. I step back, shuddering. And then, strangely, I'm studying the phone screen but from farther away. I'm up near the ceiling, in fact. Watching myself on the ground below.

Out of my body.

No, no. *Don't let this be happening*, I think. I inhale to the count of four, hold it, exhale. And again. *Stay present*, I beg myself. *Stay* here.

The phone rings, startling me. Dr. Erling.

"Ally?" she says when I answer.

"It's me."

"I was calling to check on you. Is everything okay?"

"I think—I think it might be happening again. The fugue state. I came back to the city today, and I felt disconnected for a brief time during the car ride. I snapped back, but then a few seconds ago, it seemed as if I was out of my body, looking down from above."

"Is anyone with you?"

"No, no one. I made Hugh leave. He admitted he's been seeing that woman, the one I told you about."

"We can talk about that later. Have you tried the breathing exercises, Ally?"

"Uh, yes."

"And are you still having that sensation you described?"

"Not right this second. But I'm so afraid it will come back. I . . ."

"It's essential we meet in person, Ally. Right away. However, I don't want you taking the train. Can you arrange for a car, like you did when you visited your brother?"

"Yes, yes. I'll come right now."

"And you still have the address in Larchmont?"

"Yes, I remember it."

"If the sensation comes back, call me immediately from the car."

As she hangs up, a sob catches in my throat. *Please*, I pray. *Please let her help me.*

31

I order an Uber, but it's going to take twelve minutes to reach me. I'm afraid of staying in the apartment for even a second longer, worried that I'll be back on the ceiling again, staring down at myself. I quickly grab my purse and rush down to the lobby, where I perch on a leather bench, waiting.

When the car arrives, I nearly hurl myself into it. Once I've attached the seat belt, I grip the door handle as hard as I can, as if it's the only thing holding me to the present moment.

Jarring hip-hop is being piped in from both the front and back speakers. "Please," I nearly beg the driver after a minute, "can you turn off the music?"

"Yeah, sure," he says, and then there's only the sound of traffic outside the window and my ragged breathing.

The ride to Larchmont, even with unexpected delays, should take less than an hour, but right now, that seems unbearably, dangerously long. I can sense my mind itching to tear away from my body, making a sound like two pieces of Velcro pulling apart as it does so. I can't let it. I can't let it.

I'm beyond lucky that Erling can see me on such short notice, on a weekend no less. But I also need to make a plan for when I return to the city. I wouldn't dare be on my own tonight, especially back in the apartment. I send another text to Gabby, telling her that I'm heading to meet with Erling now but would love to see her tonight—and crash with her if that's okay. She answers immediately this time, apologizing for the delay and saying she'd love to have me stay.

And then, as if I'm being commanded by an alien force, I text Damien, too.

> Would you have time to meet later? Going to my doctor's
> in Larchmont but will be back around 7.

Rooting through my purse, I produce the tin of Altoids and realize I'm down to only two. I need to save them, I realize, for the car trip home, when I'll be leaving the safety of Dr. Erling's office.

I give myself a pep talk instead. I insist there's no real reason in the world for me to detach from who I am. I made a mistake as a child, but it's nothing to be ashamed of now. And no matter what happens with Hugh, I have good friends, a loving family, and work I'm crazy about. And even if I might have behaved stupidly during the two days I was gone—or done something I shouldn't have—that doesn't define who I really am.

Hugh. I know I shouldn't be thinking of him now, since it will only upset me more, but my mind keeps rushing there. If he does want to make a fresh start—his words—could I? What if Erling was right when she suggested the other day that maybe I *do* want kids, just not with Hugh?

I take deep breaths. Knead my scalp as hard as I can with the tips of my fingers, paying attention to the sensation. Finally, there's an exit sign for Larchmont, and minutes later we're turning onto Erling's street, with attractive clapboard and brick houses set graciously far apart from each other. It's quiet today, with no one in sight. Maybe people are tucked inside doing Sunday kinds of things.

We pull up to the house. I was hoping the mere sight of it would quell my anxiety, but my dread seems to mushroom. I need to get inside and talk to her as soon as possible.

I fling open the car door, blurt out a thank-you, and deposit myself onto the sidewalk in front of the house. There are a couple of majestic maple trees in the yard, their leaves already vibrant shades of orange. I stare beyond them at the lovely gray clapboard house. There's a light on in the office, as well as in what must be an upstairs bedroom.

Though I'm standing in front of the walkway to the front door, I know from my previous appointment here to turn right and head a few yards down the street to a second path, this one shooting to the separate entrance at the side of the house. A narrow conservatory serves as a waiting area for the office.

I hurry up the path, climb two steps, and enter the unlocked conservatory. The space has been winterized, so despite how brisk the day is, it's warm inside.

I press the buzzer by the inside door. It works the same way the system does in the New York office, triggering a tiny click inside so that Erling is alerted to a patient's presence with minimal disturbance to any ongoing session. But I'm sure I must be the only patient today. Praying it won't be long before I'm buzzed into the house, I position myself on the edge of one of the white wicker chairs. With my head lowered, I try to still my thoughts.

It's then, out of the corner of my eye, that I see a flash of something dark outside the conservatory.

I jerk my head up and run my gaze along the windows. There's nothing there now. Was it simply a tree branch jostled by the wind? Or was someone moving around outside, dashing toward the back of the house? I rise and make my way slowly down the length of the conservatory. When I reach the end, I peer out of the far window, but all I see is an empty bird feeder and a cluster of trees behind it.

A creaking sound startles me next. When I spin around, I realize it was Dr. Erling opening her office door.

"Ally, what's happening?" she asks, clearly registering the expression on my face. I see her eyes go to my bruise, too.

"I—I thought I saw something out there. Something black in the side yard."

She crosses to one of the bare windows and studies the surroundings.

"Do you think it was a person?" Her expression is wary, and I can tell I've alarmed her a little, especially since she knows about Mulroney's murder.

"I don't know."

"It might have been a crow," she says. "They tend to congregate at this time of day. But come inside, and I'll lock the door behind us."

I follow her into the large, comfortable office. Erling quickly locks the door, and I watch her push aside the cream-colored curtain above the door, taking a last look at the yard with a furrowed brow. My stomach is in knots now, as if someone is wringing it like a sponge.

"No need to worry now," she assures me.

She gestures for me to sit, and I choose the middle of the couch, the same spot I took during my first visit here. Erling relaxes into the armchair across from me. She's dressed more casually than usual—black pants and a knee-length gray cardigan buttoned over a paler gray blouse—but it's the weekend, after all. Her hair's pulled back into a loose French twist, instead of down around her shoulders.

"Your face," she says as I slip out of my coat.

"So much has happened since we spoke."

"How are you feeling right now?"

"Incredibly tense. Partly, I guess, from thinking I saw something. But at least I haven't had that out-of-body sensation again—not since I left the city for here."

"Good. You came by Uber?"

"Yes, it was easy enough."

"Since you'll need a car for the return, I suggest you schedule it now rather than trying to summon one when we're finished. They're sometimes hard to order here on short notice."

I feel a little frustrated by the delay—I need to tell her about Wargo trying to kill me and Hugh's deceit—but I fish out my phone first and program in the information for the trip home. My hand trembles as I tap in the details. I was so sure I'd be more at ease once I arrived here, but I'm still engulfed in a swirl of dread and anxiety.

"Sorry to make you take the time to do that," Erling says when I've completed the task. "But this way you're guaranteed a car, rather than having to take a train and then get home from Grand Central."

I nod dully. I take a deep breath to calm myself, which, for a second at least, seems to work. And then I find myself staring off in the middle distance, thinking. An answer slides into my brain, like a note on a slip of paper.

"Ally?"

"Sorry—I . . ."

"What is it?"

"Mulroney, the private detective who was murdered? His partner, Jay, went through the file on me and found notations Mulroney had made about the Tuesday I disappeared. There was a set of initials—G.C. Do you think it could mean Grand Central?"

"Hmmm."

"Jay assumed it was a person's initials, but maybe . . . maybe Mulroney thought I went to Grand Central that day. I could have gone by cab—or taken the number 1 train to Forty-Second Street and then the shuttle over."

"Does that make any sense to you?"

"Uh, not really. I don't often have reason to be in that area. And the only time I've been to Grand Central lately is to take the train here for the appointment I had with you. Unless . . ."

"Unless what?"

"Unless I was . . . confused." I touch my fingers to my temple. In my mind's eye I see myself walking up the side path to the conservatory in my trench coat, my heart thrumming in my ears.

"How do you mean?"

"Maybe . . . You said you wanted me to do my session here that week. Could I have misunderstood and come here on Tuesday instead? Or convinced myself it was Wednesday? Is that why I called Sasha—to try to figure out what I did wrong?"

"Is that what you think, Ally?"

"I—I don't know." I drop my hand and run my gaze around the room, hoping it will offer an answer. My eyes settle on the dark wood coffee table. There's a slim pewter tray with a glass and a pitcher of water, and next to the tray, a box of tissues.

As I stare at the tissues, my whole body begins to vibrate, as if someone is shaking me lightly from behind. An image begins to form in my mind—vague, blurred around the edges.

"I see myself," I blurt out. "I'm standing here. Here in this room. I . . . grabbed some of the tissues because . . . there was blood. And . . ."

I scrunch my face, trying to keep the memory from escaping.

"And what, Ally?"

"I *was* here. It was the wrong day. I—" A small wave of panic crests in my core and begins to ripple through my arms and legs. I struggle for air.

"Breathe, Ally," Erling says, but there's a weird edge to her voice. "*Breathe.*"

The image in my mind expands, amoeba-like. Now I see a woman lying faceup on the rug, eyes opened and glazed, blood pooled around her head. I'm dabbing at the wound with the tissues.

"There was a body on the floor!" I exclaim.

"That's right," Erling says, her voice eerily calm. "The body of a woman. I'd murdered her that day."

32

My heart slams again my chest, and I feel my mouth slacken in astonishment.

"I didn't plan to tell you, actually," Erling says, not letting go of my eyes. "Oh, I was going to have to deal with this awkward situation you and I have found ourselves in, but there was no reason for you to know the gory details. But now you've gone and remembered."

I stare, frozen in place.

"Who *was* she?"

"If you must know—and I suppose there's no harm in telling you at this point—she was a woman I knew years ago. Someone I'd . . . I'd had a fling with. Someone I was actually besotted with to be perfectly honest. Stupidly so."

"But wh—?"

"Why kill her? Our affair had been a dreadful mistake. She was a patient of mine, and after a while, I came to my senses. I met a man after that, married him, moved away. Got divorced. But she tracked me down. I teach a class on Tuesday mornings, and she was waiting outside the house when

I returned around eleven. I knew right away that this was going to be about me paying the piper. She wanted money, lots of it, or she was going to expose me—and she had the paper trail to prove things. I would have lost my license. My teaching job.

"As I hope you've seen, Ally, I love what I do and I'm good at it. I couldn't let her destroy it so I stepped out of the room to get us coffee and returned with a gun I keep. And then I shot her."

I'm speechless, words stuck in my head, but I sense the muscles of my face contorting.

"I can see you're horrified," Erling says. "But there's no reason to be. She was a dreadful human being—narcissistic, borderline personality. In lay terms, she'd be called a grifter."

"Did I *see* it?" I manage. My voice is barely a whisper.

"The murder? No, no. Unbeknownst to me, you must have arrived when I'd gone off to make certain arrangements. I'm sure it was as you guessed a moment ago. When I called Tuesday to ask if you'd mind coming the next day to Larchmont, you sounded very unsettled from the fight with Hugh; perhaps you'd already started to dissociate. You obviously took the train here that day rather than Wednesday. In my haste, I left the side door unlocked, and when I didn't answer the buzzer, you obviously let yourself in, wondering where I was.

"And even if you hadn't started to dissociate, Ally, that experience—finding a dead body for the second time in your life—must have triggered it."

"How did you figure it out—that I'd been here?"

"There were a couple of red flags that gave me pause. Your mention of the call you made trying to figure when our appointment was. The unknown person's blood on the tissues, of course. And then this."

She reaches into the deep pocket of her cardigan and extracts an iPhone. As my gaze settles on the blue rubber case, I realize it's mine.

"I found it peeking out from under the couch the day after Diane was here, the battery dead, and assumed it was an extra of hers that had fallen out of her pocket when she tried to get away." She curls her lips in a terrifying smile. "It made sense at the moment. A grifter carrying two phones. But as soon as you said you'd lost yours, I realized what had happened."

I'm frozen in place still, gripped by fear, but my gaze flicks to the outside door and back. Inside my shoes, I curl my toes, forcing a small part of me to move.

"So you killed Mulroney, too?"

"Yes, I'm afraid so. He called me. You must have mentioned my name to him, and he'd followed a trail of bread crumbs indicating that you'd taken the train from Grand Central on Tuesday. He hadn't pieced it all together yet, but he was getting closer, and I was concerned the information he *did* have might jog your memory. I told him I had something about you I felt obligated to share, something that might help him crack the case, and arranged to meet him in the parking lot. I knew what that spot was known for, of course. I've had patients who've cruised there."

My brain summons an image of Mulroney against my

will. So street-smart, but clearly with his guard down, a bullet going through his head.

"What about *me*?" I ask.

"About *you*, Ally? Are you wondering if I was the one who pushed you that night? Yes, that was me. I'm not much of a street fighter, am I?"

"But what about now? What are you going to do?"

It's such a stupid question. Because I can already see the answer, an abyss that's as deep and dense as a black hole.

"You must know that I don't *want* to hurt you. I've liked working with you. And I've liked helping you. But I'm not going to let you or anyone else take my life and my freedom from me."

"I wouldn't, though," I say, feebly. I lower my head a little, and let my eyes dart toward the door again, measuring the distance to it. To escape, I would need to rush past her, race to the door, unlock it, attempt to fight her off with my hands. It seems impossible, but I have to try.

"Of course you would," she says with a wry smile.

I take as deep a breath as possible, hoping she can't see my chest rise and fall. There's another door, I realize, one closer to me that leads to the rest of the house. I press my hands hard into the sofa, preparing to spring forward.

Another smile from her. I sense she's noticed my preparation. She sets my phone on the side table next to her and reaches into the space between the chair and the cushion. When she slides her hand out, I see she's holding a small black gun.

My stomach roils. "But they'll catch you," I say. "They'll trace the gun."

"It's from the black market, actually. Some of my patients are seriously troubled, and I felt I needed protection—but it's nearly impossible to obtain a firearm legally in New York State."

"The Uber," I say desperately. "It's evidence that I came here."

She chuckles. "When the Uber arrives to pick you up, I'll put on your coat and a hat of mine and be driven into the city. Later, I'll take the train back here to tidy up. That's basically how it worked with Diane, though she'd come by car. I wore her coat and her very fancy sunglasses and I stopped for gas and later abandoned the vehicle. Then I had all the time in the world to clean up. I took her body upstate, to a landfill near where I used to live. I haven't seen a word about her being missing. I assume no one cares she's gone."

As hard as it is, I force a smile.

"Ah, that's very clever," I say. "You outgrifted the grifter."

Erling raises an eyebrow. "I should appreciate the compliment, Ally, but I know you're simply trying to buy yourself time."

She's going to shoot me any second now. And dump my body in the landfill. I manage another breath and think of my father and brothers, of Hugh, too, still my husband. Would they ever be able to find out what had happened to me? Or would they think I'd disassociated again and fallen off the face of the earth?

As I picture Roger, an image fights its way into my head. My brother standing with the oar.

I open my mouth as if to speak again, as if there is

something I *must* say. But instead, I reach fast for the glass water pitcher. And once I grab hold of it, I fling it at her head.

She yelps and then screams, as the glass shatters against her skull and the water sprays everywhere.

I propel myself from the couch and rush to the closest door, flinging it open. I'm in the living room now. I can barely see because the curtains are drawn in here, too, but I tear through the room toward the front of the house, banging into pieces of furniture. Behind me I can hear Erling scrambling.

"Stop!" she screams.

I reach the front hallway, see the door to my left, but I can tell Erling's not far behind me.

Before I take another step, a noise shatters the air, a crack followed by the sound of splintering wood. She's fired the gun at me.

I can't reach the door in time. I lower my head and plunge straight ahead into the dining room and scan it desperately. I spot two hammered metal candlesticks on a sideboard, grab one fast in my fist, and shove open the door to the kitchen.

It's nearly dark in this room, too, the louvered blinds lowered. Holding my breath, I duck behind the door, leaving it open.

"Ally," Erling calls. She's in the dining room now, I can tell. "You're coming unglued again. Let me help you. Where—?"

She's only inches away now. I raise the candlestick.

As she charges into the room, I bring it down on her head with all the force I can muster. She drops to the floor facedown, the gun in her hand. Blood spreads from the right side of her head, like a flower blooming.

I turn and race back through the dining room, through the foyer, and out the front door.

And then I run, down the middle of the street. Miraculously a car turns the corner and heads this way. I wave my arms frantically, begging for the driver to stop.

33

A noise startles me and I jump a little in my seat. I realize after a beat that it's only Gabby, turning the key in the lock on her front door. She's home from work now. It's probably going to be a while before I stop being skittish.

A couple of seconds later, Gabby saunters into the living room, carrying a couple of Whole Food bags.

"Hey," she says in greeting. "You doing okay?"

"Much better," I say from the couch. "I actually worked on my book a little bit today."

"How was the new therapist?"

"I liked her—and she comes highly recommended by Dr. Agarwal, the shrink who treated me in the ER. Only time will tell if she wants to blow my brains out, too."

"Very funny."

"It's probably a good sign I can laugh about it."

"Totally. You like salmon, right? I picked up a couple of fillets for dinner. Let me pop them in the oven."

As she heads into the kitchen, I sink back into the couch in her lovely living room, an enchanting mix of modern and boho decor. I've been ensconced here for the past couple of days—since Sunday night. After I'd bolted from Erling's, I managed to flag down the car I saw turning onto her street and convince the driver to take me to the local police station. On the way, I'd called Jay Williams, who drove to Westchester immediately.

As I told my story in the police interview room that evening, shaken and exhausted, I wondered frantically about Erling. Had she taken off? Or would she try to completely spin the story, claiming that I was a deranged patient who had attacked her during a session, forcing her to try to shoot at me in self-defense?

But Williams apparently vouched for me, filling the cops in from his end and encouraging them to speak to the White Plains police about Kurt's murder. On our drive back into the city, Jay said that the gun Erling pulled was probably the same weapon she'd used to kill Mulroney, and the police would figure that out soon enough. Plus, when they searched her house, they would surely find traces of blood and DNA from the former patient and lover who became her victim.

It got better. While we were on the highway, Williams heard through a contact in the Westchester police force that Erling had been apprehended.

As shaken as the experience left me, I feel oddly okay now. Mentally stable. Fairly in control again. I haven't managed yet to dig up every answer I need, but I've gotten my hands on the one with the most value to me: what had sent my mind spiraling away from my body one October afternoon.

I've tried since I've been at Gabby's to stay on top of my work. No podcast this week—I ended up bumping it after all, calling Derek and informing him that Sasha wasn't ready to handle the show on her own. Next, I called Sasha and told her if she ever went behind my back again, it would be her final day as my intern. Let the chips fall where they may.

I've filled Roger in since I've been here. Hugh, too. And Damien. I still don't know if his "interest" in me was sincere, but he took the time and seemed to care. I figured I owed him an update.

Gabby reemerges a minute later, carrying a bottle of chardonnay and two wineglasses. She sets the glasses on the table, uncorks the wine, and pours.

"Are you going to keep working with the private eye?" she asks.

"Yeah, he's still trying to figure out where I was Wednesday night and very early Thursday, though of course I have the facts that matter most. You were right all along, Gabby. I *had* witnessed something terrible."

"Does that mean the fight with Hugh never played a role in your disassociation?"

"Not directly at least, though I was obviously pretty upset and discombobulated afterwards. It seems I must have turned my phone off when I was at Le Pain Tuesday, probably because I didn't want to see any more calls from him coming in."

"I assume you went by train to Erling's. But do you think you took the train back to the city after finding the body?"

"Williams is looking into it, but probably. When you dissociate, you can still function normally, and I probably wasn't totally unglued by then. I mean, I called WorkSpace, so I still knew who I was, plus I showed up there later. But I was probably in bad shape already. I left my purse in my drawer, almost as if I was leaving myself behind."

Gabby nods and takes a long sip of wine. "Erling must have been totally freaked when she started to piece the truth together."

"Absolutely. And in hindsight I realize that once she began having suspicions, she made sure she was in close contact with me. I think she even said little things to rattle me. She insisted I should have a lawyer with me if I spoke to the police again. That made me so tense at the time. And sometimes I just felt stressed being in her presence, but didn't understand why."

"Ugh, I'm so sorry for everything you went through. Will this affect how much you can trust the new therapist?"

"I don't think so. This one's very different, and she's a psychiatrist, too, so the approach won't be the same. She even wants me to try medication, something to help prevent a relapse. I feel *okay* right now, but I don't want to take any chances. If the case in New Jersey goes to trial, I'll certainly have to testify."

Gabby jumps up, ducks into the kitchen again, and returns shortly with a bowl of hummus and little squares of toasted pita bread.

"And what about Hugh?" she asks, plopping back into her chair.

"I told him I would meet him at the apartment for dinner tomorrow night. I can't put it off any longer."

I grab a pita square and scoop up hummus with it. This is the first time since Sunday that I've had even a hint of an appetite.

"Are you going to try to work things out with him?"

"I'm not sure. We'll talk tomorrow. And then, I guess, I'll take it from there."

I'm actually pretty sure what I'm going to do, but it doesn't feel fair to admit it to Gabby before I tell Hugh. He's still my husband.

"Well, just so you know, you're welcome here any time."

"Thanks, Gab. It's been so good to spend time with you again." A thought suddenly occurs to me. "Hey, by the way I never found the gift you dropped off for me on Sunday."

Gabby flops back onto the cushion, raking her hair with her hands. "Oh boy," she says with a sigh. "There never *was* a gift."

"What do you mean?"

"I'd gone to your apartment to talk to Hugh."

"Talk to Hugh about *what*?" I say, feeling a ripple of worry.

"The fact that I didn't believe he was telling you the whole story about the fight you guys had. Maybe it was from being in some kind of delirious state when I was sick, but it seemed strange to me that Hugh would think you'd taken off without any word simply because of a heated discussion over kids. That's not your style—so I suspected there was more to it than that. And I told him so."

It takes me a moment to process this.

"And what did he say?"

"He said that anything involving your marriage was between him and you. End of discussion. I had no idea you were coming home that day, and when I ran into you, I told you the first thing that came into my mind, which of course you'd figure out soon enough was a lie. . . . I hope you don't think I stepped out of line, Ally. It was only a theory at that point, and I didn't want to bring it up to you and upset you unnecessarily if it wasn't true."

"No, I appreciate what you did, Gab." And I do.

◆ ◆ ◆

THE NEXT DAY I arrive at my apartment shortly before three. It's strange to be back. All the white in the rooms—the walls and furniture and fabrics—which I always adored, seems stark after the seductive blue and gold and violet tones of Gabby's place. It's weirdly quiet, too. Usually, even this high up, I can hear the muted sound of rumbling trucks or sirens from the street or the wind coursing along the side of building, but today it feels as if the space has been hermetically sealed.

I use the next few hours to sort through my mail, run a couple of loads of laundry, and set out the items I purchased for dinner, everyday stuff that doesn't feel like everyday anymore. During this time, one lingering mystery ends up solved. As I'm trying to decide whether I'm ever going to wear my trench coat again, I notice an inside pocket I've forgotten about, and hidden in there is my missing credit card.

Hugh arrives home, as promised, exactly at six, and I let him hug me. I briefly welcome the comfort of having his arms around me and the softness of his shirt against my cheek.

"Jeez, Ally, I've been so worried about you," he mutters

into my hair. "I just wish you had let me see you before now."

"There's nothing you could have done, Hugh," I say, stepping back. "And the worst seems to be over."

"You've got to fill me in. There's still so much I don't know."

"I will. Are you ready to eat? The food's on the table."

"Terrific," he says, shrugging off his suit jacket. "I'll change later."

We talk as we eat, with me fleshing out the missing details for him.

He doesn't disguise how shocked he is and finally rests an elbow on the table, dropping his head into his hand.

"She would have killed you," he said, his voice cracking. "And she would have buried your body like that other woman."

"Hugh," I say, moved by his anguish. "Let's not think about that. Because it didn't play out that way."

"You saved yourself, Ally."

I chuckle ruefully. "I guess all those years of field hockey finally paid off for me."

He clears both our plates and returns to the table with a fresh bottle of sparkling water.

"Hugh, there's more we need to talk about," I say. "And that's the two of us."

He exhales, reaches over to grasp my hand.

"I want to make it work, Ally. I really do."

I sit silently for a minute or two, feeling him watching me intently. My lips are pursed, I realize. Perhaps on some level,

I'm scared of saying the wrong thing and later regretting it. But I'm pretty sure I know what I want.

"Look, on the one hand I'm relieved you didn't end up sleeping with that woman. But you were attracted to her. You took her out for drinks and flirted with her. You *kissed* her. I know we've been fighting lately, but that's hardly an excuse. And worst of all, you covered it up to protect yourself at a time when I desperately needed the truth."

"That's only because I wanted a second chance with you. I was afraid if I told you what had really happened, you wouldn't give me that."

"Or you didn't want me to know that you'd upset me so badly, I'd fallen apart."

He grimaces.

"It was terrible judgment on my part. But can you forgive me for this mistake? I know that marriages can survive this kind of thing, that it can even make them stronger."

"I'm aware of that, too. People drift apart or become preoccupied with work and they end up hurting or betraying each other. And on an intellectual level, I can see how it's possible to forgive and move on."

"So you *can* forgive me?"

"I *can* forgive you, Hugh, yes. But I would never be able to let go of it."

"Ally, please, it won't happen again."

For some crazy reason I flash on a piece of personal finance advice I've touted: *Never make financial decisions based on what you assume you'll be earning in the future.* Meaning don't buy a pricier car or house because you're due for a promotion or plan to inherit soon from a grandparent. There are no guarantees about how things will play out in the future. And I can't bank on the fact that Hugh's mistake is a one-off, despite what he's promising.

"I appreciate you saying that. And I have a feeling you'd try, at least for a while. But there's something I need to explain. As horrible as things have been for me lately, it's helped me realize a critical fact about myself. Ever since I found Jaycee Long in the woods that day, I've felt unsafe in the world. My parents tried to comfort me, and the therapist I saw when I was a kid did her best, but because I deceived them and couldn't show them how ashamed I was, I *couldn't* feel better. I think that finding the body in Erling's office made me come unglued because it reinforced that sense of being at risk."

"But—"

"Hugh, let me finish. I want to be safe again. I was attracted to you in part because you made me feel that way. But not anymore. If we stayed together, I would always be wondering and worrying—every time you got home late or needed to take a shower after work."

"Ally . . ."

"I've already made up my mind. We need to separate. One of us can take the bedroom and the other the den until we work out the specifics."

"Please, can't we see a counselor, and talk about this more?"

"If you want to work with a counselor to make the transition easier, I'll go with you, as long as you view it as nothing beyond that."

"All right," he says, finally, his head lowered. My sense

is that he knows it's pointless to keep talking, but that he might renew his efforts down the road. It won't matter. It's wrenching to think my marriage is over, but I can't see any hope.

Later, as I'm listlessly putting away laundry in the bedroom—Hugh volunteered to take the den—Roger calls.

"How are you, Button?"

"Hanging in there." The news about Hugh and me feels too damn fresh to share right this moment, so I save it.

"I've got an update on the situation out here," Roger says. "Is this an okay time?"

"Yes, I'm eager to hear."

"Nowak confided in me that Audrey's mother has apparently come forward. Says Audrey told her not to go into Jaycee's room the night she babysat, or the next morning, just peek through the doorway. She said it was because she didn't want Jaycee to wake up. There was a bulge in the bed, but the grandmother never saw the girl. She'd probably been dumped in the woods by then."

"Wow."

"Are you sure you're all right?"

"Yes, it's good to finally see the truth emerge."

We agree to talk tomorrow and finalize our plans to meet again this week, and he promises to fill me in then on the latest with Marion, though I sense his relationship is as doomed as mine. As for our father, we've given him a watered-down version of events and have been keeping him abreast.

After signing off, I deliberate what to do next. I feel an urge to go outside, to be in the world again now that I'm sure no one is trying to harm me. Before I can do anything, my phone pings with a text from Jay Williams.

> More info. After dinner at Pairings on Wednesday you walked south. Checked into the Element Hotel at about 9. You walked from there to Greenbacks the next A.M.

I stand motionless for a minute on the middle of the bedroom, staring at the screen. I'm thinking, trying to make sense of it. Using my phone I google the Element, find out it's a boutique hotel smack in the middle of Nolita, an area south of the East Village and north of Little Italy. I have no memory of staying there that night, needless to say. But that area once mattered to me.

It's been a while since I updated my timeline so I grab my purse and fish it out, adding the details I've become aware of since Monday.

MONDAY
    evening: dinner, TV, argument

TUESDAY
    7:00: still in bed
    9:00-ish: took call from Dr. Erling
    9:00–9:17: sent emails
    9:30: hung out at café
    11:00-ish: left for 42nd Street
    *11:30-ish: took train to Erling's; found body; lost phone;
        took train back to city*

3:00–3:30-ish: called WorkSpace
9:00–6:00 A.M.: spent night at WorkSpace

WEDNESDAY
Noon-ish: bought food at Eastside Eats, East 7th St.
Afternoon: walked near Tompkins Square Park
Maybe evening: ate at Pairings
Night: stayed at the Element Hotel

THURSDAY
8:05: arrived at Greenbacks

There are now many fewer blanks, but I still have questions. I return my attention to the phone and quickly text Damien.

Can you meet me at the bar of the Element Hotel tonight?

34

Damien is already at the bar when I arrive at around 9:30. He's wearing jeans and a checked shirt, and his blond hair looks damp on the sides, as if he's smoothed it back with wet hands. There's a beer bottle in front of him and a glass he doesn't seem to be bothering with.

"It's really good to see you, Ally," he says. This time I *do* get a kiss on the cheek, one that lingers a little. And then an embrace, which I return.

"I appreciate you coming on such short notice," I say. The bartender approaches and I order a beer, too.

"I've been so worried about you."

"I'm actually doing okay, all things considered."

He smiles. "It must feel good to know you handled the situation brilliantly. Ms. Linden in the kitchen with a candlestick."

I laugh out loud. "That's *one* way to put it."

"Are you getting the support you need right now?"

"Pretty much. Though as of this week, I'm separated from my husband, and that's going to be really tough. Still, it's the right decision for both of us."

His expression is inscrutable, so I have no idea what he's thinking. The waiter sets my beer down, and I take a sip from the bottle.

"That *is* tough," he says. "Sorry to hear it."

"Thank you . . . I feel like all we've done lately is talk about me. What about *you*, Damien? What's happening in your life?"

"I guess life is good overall. I'm single at the moment and still living down here. Playing the guitar, though I don't know if I've improved since you last heard me. Trying to squeeze in as much travel as possible. And still loving every day at Greenbacks."

"Has Sasha surfaced again?"

"The beauty guru? I haven't heard anything else. Maybe she went back to covering split ends and dry cuticles."

"It's none of my business, of course, but could she make trouble for you—for the company?"

He narrows his eyes again, studying me.

"I'm not perfect, Ally," he says finally. "You know that. But I'd never fuck up something that mattered so much to me. . . . Is that why you asked me to join you tonight? To find out if I was cooking the books?"

"No, though it's good to know you're the same person from five years ago. But there *is* something I wanted to ask you. The private investigator I'm working with found out I stayed in this hotel the night before I went to Greenbacks."

"And you have no recollection of it whatsoever?"

"None."

For half a minute neither of us speaks.

"You're looking at me as if I might have something to contribute," Damien says, raising an eyebrow.

"Do you? This is two blocks from your apartment. I mean, the one you lived in when I knew you."

"Are you asking if we spent the night together, Ally? No. When I saw you in the conference room, it was the first time I'd laid eyes on you in five years."

"Okay. I . . . I just wondered. Because it seemed more than coincidental. Me being in your neighborhood—and the fact that I showed up at Greenbacks the next day. I thought maybe I did something crazy and invited you to my hotel room."

He smiles. "If you had, I would have been happy to oblige. Sorry, I don't mean to make light of it. Not knowing about a chunk of your life must be frustrating."

"Most of the blanks have actually been filled in by this point, thanks to the two investigators I've worked with. But what's frustrating is not knowing *why* I did some of the things I did. It's pretty clear why I fell apart, but why dump my purse in my office and set off on this crazy journey through the East Village? And end up here? And then Greenbacks? What was I hoping to accomplish?"

Damien reaches for his beer bottle and runs a thumb up and down its side.

"Maybe it's not all that complicated. You could try looking at it literally and see how that sits with you."

"What do you mean?

"When we spent time together, you told me you used to wander around the East Village. And daydream in a little restaurant there. So maybe you were trying to be in a place that felt good to you and recapture someone you used to be. Or experimented with being."

I reflect on his words. Is that really what those two days were about? If so, it also would mean that I'd felt a yearning to connect with Damien again.

"It's funny," I say. "My father always called me Button because I was so buttoned-up—but there's a part of me that wants to be different than that. Not a wild child, but *freer*. I've only let that side of me out once in a while."

"Why do you think that is?"

"Not sure. Perhaps I sensed my parents loved the girl who worked extra hard and didn't cross the line. But more importantly, I think finding Jaycee Long's body put the fear of God into me. It felt as if I was being punished for breaking the rules."

"You mean because you'd taken the shortcut that day?"

"Right. I'd never done—"

A thought flits around the edges of my mind, vaguely familiar.

"What?" Damien asks.

"I just remembered something. Another lie I told back then—though, thank god, this isn't as consequential as the other."

"Tell me."

"I told my family and the police that I took the short-cut home because I dillydallied around school that day, but that's only party true. Believe it or not, I was also looking for arrowheads."

"*Arrowheads?*"

"I was fascinated by the whole idea of them, and I'd heard someone say they were all over New Jersey, in fields and woods. That's probably why I was off the path, kicking at piles of leaves."

He laughs a little. "Sorry, once again the wrong response, but it's funny to think of you heading out with that secret plan."

"Yeah, and unfortunately I paid a price for it. But I never lost my love for arrowheads."

We've finished our drinks and Damien asks if I want another. Part of me wants to linger. I feel at ease in his presence. But I don't want to complicate my life any more than necessary at the moment. So I tell him no thank you, that I'd better be heading out, and I slip back into my sweater coat.

As I reach into my purse for my wallet, Damien shakes his head.

"I've got this," he says.

"Well, I definitely owe you then, since you got the last one."

He brushes my cheek with his lips again.

"Want to go arrowhead hunting some time? Believe it or not, that was one of my obsessions as a kid."

I smile.

"I'd like that. But . . . maybe down the road a little. I've got too much to figure out right now."

I leave him sitting at the bar and head into the night. I walk for a while, north and west, block after block.

I think I do want to see Damien again, but it's true, I have so much to figure out first. I need to process the end of my marriage and work through the grief that's sure to slam me when I'm no longer in shock. To commit fully to working with the new doctor so I don't relapse. To be there for Roger as he weathers his own marital issues. To make certain my career doesn't take a back seat in the middle of this.

And something else. I liked Damien's theory about why I chose to wander around the East Village. Maybe I really do need to reconnect with the part of myself that wants to be less buttoned-up. That secretly craves not being so much of a rule follower.

It's a beautiful night, I realize. The air is nicely crisp, and there's a light wind on my face. I pass a small market selling pumpkins out front, both orange and white ones, and pot after pot of mums. I have a sudden recollection from years ago of me and my mother making a list of costume ideas for Halloween. I wanted to be Batman, I told her, and she smiled and said, *Perfect.*

A free cab shoots by and I almost try to grab it, but don't. I feel the urge to keep walking. To be a city girl again.

As I wait for a traffic light to change, I think of the financial mantra many businesses live by: "The bottom line is the only line that matters." In certain contexts, I don't buy that philosophy, but at this moment in time, it makes sense for me on a personal level. When all is said and done, who do I really want to be? That's what I need to know.

ACKNOWLEDGMENTS

The amazing suspense author Harlan Coben once told me with a smile that research is a form of procrastination, and though I think he's right in certain cases, for me doing research is really essential. I'm so grateful to those who help me attempt to get my facts right and also provide fascinating information that enables me to add texture or twisty little details to my plots.

I talked to some dynamite people for this book and I want to thank them from the bottom of my heart: Jean Chatsky, personal finance expert and CEO of hermoney.com; Farnoosh Torabi, journalist and personal finance expert; James White, financial expert; Lucy Howell, LCSW; Lisa Chrupcala, former director of psychiatric services; Ann Pleshette Murphy; Dr. Paul Paganelli; Ernest MacVane, paramedic; Barbara Butcher, consultant for forensic and medicolegal investigations; Will Valenza, Glens Falls police department, retired; Joyce Hanshaw, retired captain from the Hunterdon County Prosecutor's Office; Raymond Berke, private investigator; Bill Cunningham, IT consultant.

Thank you, too, to the amazing group I get to work with

at Harper Perennial: Amy Baker, VP and associate publisher; Robin Bilardello, art director; the relentless Theresa Dooley, senior publicist; Lisa Erickson, director of marketing; Stacey Fischkelta, the kickass production editorial manager; my fabulous, spectacular editor Emily Griffin, who I thank the gods for every day; and Emily's terrific assistant, Amber Oliver.

I'd like to also express my gratitude to my great agent, Sandy Dijkstra, and the lovely team I work with at the Sandra Dijkstra Literary Agency: Elise, Andrea, Thao, and Jessica.

And then there's my wonderful home team: Isabel DaSilva, social media director, and Laura Nicolassy, my web editor. I couldn't ask for two more talented people.

I want to give a huge shout-out to my kids, Hunter Holbrook and Hayley Holbrook. They read this book late in the game when it was in galley format and while we were celebrating the holidays in Uruguay. They stayed up so late reading and tore through the book in days, which made me feel awesome. I'm so lucky to have them as my kids. And thanks to Hayley, too, for being my incredible trailer creator. Xoxo

Lastly, I want to say thanks to my wonderful readers, who are kind enough to check in with me regularly on Facebook, Twitter, Instagram, and katewhite.com; share their thoughts about life and books and more; and also review my books on *Goodreads*, *BookBub*, Barnes and Noble, and Amazon. I love hearing from you!!

ABOUT THE AUTHOR

KATE WHITE, former editor in chief of *Cosmopolitan* magazine, is the *New York Times* bestselling author of the stand-alone psychological thrillers *The Secrets You Keep, The Wrong Man, Eyes on You, Hush,* and *The Sixes,* as well as eight Bailey Weggins mysteries, including *Such a Perfect Wife.* White is also the author of several popular career books for women, including *The Gutsy Girl Handbook: Your Manifesto for Success* and *I Shouldn't Be Telling You This: How to Ask for the Money, Snag the Promotion, and Create the Career You Deserve,* as well as the editor of *The Mystery Writers of America Cookbook.* She lives in New York City.

You can contact her at katewhite.com.

BOOKS BY KATE WHITE

SUCH A PERFECT WIFE
A BAILEY WEGGINS MYSTERY

"What's not to love in Kate White's latest? . . . . *Such A Perfect Wife* is deep and dark and twisty, and packed with a delicious array of questionable characters, each harboring their own secrets."
—*Entertainment Weekly*

True crime writer Bailey Weggins, on assignment for the website Crime Beat, heads north from New York City to report on the mysterious disappearance of a young wife and mother. An anonymous tip soon leads Bailey to a grisly, bone-chilling discovery. Every town has its secrets, Bailey reminds herself, and nothing is ever as perfect as it seems. She keeps digging for answers until—when it's almost too late—she unearths the terrifying truth.

EVEN IF IT KILLS HER
A BAILEY WEGGINS MYSTERY

"White builds suspense masterfully, and this seventh in the Bailey Weggins series has the makings of another hit. Bailey is a smart, sexy sleuth, and her exploits make for thoroughly entertaining reading."
—*Booklist*

In this exhilarating thriller, one young woman searches for clues to the murder of her family, only to discover a shocking secret about herself that holds the key to everything.

THE SECRETS YOU KEEP
A NOVEL

"This can't-put-it-down murder mystery from the former editor of *Cosmo* follows an author pushed to the brink by escalating chaos. Crazy dreams guaranteed." —*Cosmopolitan*

A harrowing new psychological thriller about a successful self-help author who suddenly finds her life spiraling dangerously out of control. With unexpected, riveting twists, *The Secrets You Keep* is an utterly compelling psychological thriller that once again showcases Kate White's extraordinary storytelling talent.

HarperCollins*Publishers* | **HARPER**

DISCOVER GREAT AUTHORS, EXCLUSIVE OFFERS, AND MORE AT HC.COM.

BOOKS BY KATE WHITE

EYES ON YOU
A NOVEL OF SUSPENSE

"Sharp as a stiletto! White captures the cut-throat world of entertainment TV where the latest star should trust no one if she's to build her show... or save her very life." —Lisa Gardner, *New York Times* bestselling author

An adversary with a dark agenda wants to hurt Robin, and the clues point to someone she works with every day. While she frantically tries to put the pieces together and unmask this hidden foe, it becomes terrifyingly clear that the person responsible isn't going to stop until Robin loses everything that matters to her . . . including her life.

SO PRETTY IT HURTS
A BAILEY WEGGINS MYSTERY

"[A] delicious tale." —*New York Post*

Bailey Weggins is back in an addictive story involving the mysterious death of a supermodel. When Bailey starts to nose around, she finds herself a moving target—running closer to the truth and straight into danger.

THE SIXES
A NOVEL

"This is the perfect book to take on a transatlantic flight to Europe. Trust me I just did it. . . . A fast-paced plot that wraps itself up in time for you to race to the bathroom before the plane starts its descent." —*Vanity Fair*

Phoebe Hall's Manhattan life is unexpectedly derailed when her boyfriend leaves her just as she is accused of plagiarizing her bestselling celebrity biography. She relocates to a college town where a student's death sends her on a search for the truth and into the clutches of a frightening secret society.

HUSH
A NOVEL

"Utterly compelling . . . A classic page turner."
—Karin Slaughter, *New York Times* bestselling author

An ordinary woman flees the scene of a murder—and realizes it's not just the law that may be coming after her.

Bear Library
101 Governor's Place
Bear, DE 19701